FRIENDLY FIRE

The bombing ran through the team and continued up the road, shredding the earth and trembling it in man-made earthquakes. Howling shrapnel ripped a cow into bloody pieces. Her torn body fortunately provided a shield against the blast for both Dog and Preacher, who hit the ground with the dead cow almost on top of them.

Seemingly on its own volition, the hay cart leaped high into the night, splintering and raining weapons into the middle of the road.Chief Adcock and Dr. Death threw themselves face-down into the bar ditch. Shrapnel whizzed overhead and *thunk*ed into the earth all around.

The bombing passed on up the road and ceased as quickly as it began. The night returned unblemished except for the moans, cries and screams of the wounded, both human and animal.

"Our own people bombed us!" Dog cried angrily.

"It was an accident. We don't bomb civilians," Preacher said.

"Then what's all that hollering you hear?"

SEALS
STRATEGIC WARFARE

OPERATION
NO MAN'S LAND

MIKE MARTELL

AVON BOOKS
An Imprint of HarperCollins*Publishers*

AVON BOOKS
An Imprint of HarperCollins*Publishers*
10 East 53rd Street
New York, New York 10022-5299

Copyright © 2000 by Bill Fawcett & Associates
ISBN: 0-380-80828-5
www.avonbooks.com

First Avon Books paperback printing: December 2000

Avon Trademark Reg. U.S. Pat. Off. and in Other Countries, Marca Registrada, Hecho en U.S.A.
HarperCollins® is a trademark of HarperCollins Publishers Inc.

Printed in the U.S.A.

10 9 8 7 6 5 4 3 2 1

To the veterans of old ODA 213,
U.S. Army Special Forces

AUTHOR'S NOTE

The involvement of the United States with NATO in the Balkan campaign, in Bosnia and more recently in Serbia, continues to be steeped in political controversy. This novel, based on secret SEAL operations in Serbia during the eleven-week NATO bombing campaign against President Slobodan Milosevic, does not attempt to avoid this controversy; in fact, this account is set as it must be against that political background.

While this novel is grounded in fact and contains actual incidents and historical persons, it is a work of fiction with no intended references to real people either dead or alive other than the obvious ones. However, what occurs in *Operation No Man's Land* may very well be the *real* story behind Operation Allied Force in Serbia.

Yugoslavia and area

PROLOGUE

For over two hours now, this morning after the second night of Operation Allied Force and the NATO bombings of Yugoslavia, the Senate Armed Services Committee had been meeting behind closed doors. CIA Director Louis Benefield, to whom questions were being directed, leaned back in the padded oak chair at his end of the long table and regarded the senators posturing, grandstanding, and pontificating. Politicians! Did the windbags never cease campaigning? Even behind closed doors, even when the wide revealing eye of the TV camera was not on them? Benefield was convinced that it could be the end of the world and politicians would be wrangling over how it weighed on their chances for reelection.

"I would very much like a legal memorandum from the CIA," said Senator Denise Ryan, Democrat from Nevada, a woman as barren-looking and sharp-faced as a desert gecko. "I would like it to state whether or not the legal prohibition of incursion against heads of state also applies to organized crime and/or terrorist units and to heads of state who pose a serious threat to world peace."

Benefield rocked forward with his elbows on the table and his hands tented just below the straight-looking hard-sad eyes. Eyes like those of a cop who had seen too damned much of human nature. He knew what Senator Ryan was fishing for, but he wasn't about to take the bait so easily. Let 'em squirm.

"Would 'organized crime units' include the Crips and the Bloods in Los Angeles as well as Don Gambino?" he asked, soto vocce.

"Director, you know quite well what I mean," Ryan scolded defensively. "What is present law in respect to their takedown?"

"I would suppose you mean politicians?"

"*Foreign* politicians," Ryan hurried to respond, looking embarrassed. "Rogue political heads of state and their minions."

"You want to know if it's legal to assassinate Serbian President Slobodan Milosevic?"

Both NATO and the United States had warned President Milosevic that his armed forces would be destroyed unless he backed down over Kosovo's attempts to gain independence from Serbia, pulled Serbian troops out of Kosovo, and ceased his "ethnic cleansing" campaign against the region's Muslim Albanian majority. Finally—after so many threats they were beginning to sound hollow—NATO, led by the U.S., had commenced bombing Serbia Wednesday night.

Last night was the second night of bombing. More than one hundred NATO planes, including U.S. stealth bombers and fighters, took off in waves from bases across Europe. Loud blasts reverberated near Belgrade, Yugoslavia's capital. There were at least fifteen explosions around Kosovo's capital, Pristina. Bombs dropped on the Golubovci airport in Montenegro. More explosions were heard near Danilovgrad, where munitions dumps were located. Four U.S. warships in the Adriatic Sea launched a barrage of Tomahawk cruise missiles. Targets included barracks in Urosevac, in southern Kosovo, an airport in the city of Nis, military supplies factories, communications and air defense centers. Television and radio stations in central Serbia were broadcasting appeals for blood donors and asking surgeons to report for duty immediately.

The U.S. president appeared on TV to announce that the bombings would continue until the "Butcher of the Balkans" capitulated, however long that took. Political support for his actions, however, were tenuous at best. The Senate approved a terse resolution backing the attack, having little choice but to publicly support American troops on the eve of combat, but it stood posed to adopt a resolution requiring Congressional approval for funding it. House Republicans accused the president of using a "wag the dog" to draw attention away from his scandal-ridden administration and his pending impeachment trial for perjury. Even Democrats were privately suspicious of his timing and motives.

Military experts thought bombing alone would not bring Milosevic to his knees. Sooner or later, ground troops would have to be introduced, leading to an escalation of the conflict. Russian President Boris Yeltsin was siding with his old ally, Milosevic, and rattling what few missiles remained after the end of the Cold War and the Soviet social and military meltdown. He warned that Russia might send troops to Belgrade to expel any ground invasions by NATO and the United States. This would not be the first time a world war began in the Balkans.

It was in this climate of doubt, suspicion, and uncertainty that the Senate Armed Services Committee summoned the CIA director to a secret meeting to explore alternative options for ending the conflict before it blew up. So far, the senators had burned over two hours of hemming and hawing before reaching the as of yet unspoken conclusion that, somehow, Milosevic had to go. Director Benefield was the one who had finally introduced the *A* word that was on everyone's mind. Even the thought of assassination was enough to make most politicians reach for their Maalox.

"I just want to know what the law is," said Senator Joe Blythe of Delaware. He immediately qualified his remarks in case they were construed as being too aggressive. "Of course, arresting war criminals like President Milosevic is the ideal option, but I think we must consider more robust options."

"Robust?" said Director Benefield.

Senator Blythe squirmed.

"We have to think in a different way than we thought before," put in Senator Mavis of Oregon. "It's a very dicey thing to get into a situation where you're going to have licensed hit squads. At the same time, we need to find ways to be proactive."

"Proactive?" repeated Director Benefield, determined in a perverse way not to make the discussion easy on any of them.

After some throat clearing and papers shuffling, the vice chairman of the Armed Services Committee declared himself against assassination. It was a bad idea.

"We are the most open society on earth," he said. "We are the most forward-deployed on earth. And as a result of these things, our leaders and our citizens are at risk of retaliation."

Director Benefield leaned back in his chair and let them go at it. He accepted philosophically that nothing would be accomplished, no decisions reached. In modern politics, little was ever achieved without first doing a redaq. Public opinion polls guided everything; and since polls so often split, politicians weren't about to stick their necks out too far to take any stand.

Once the subject of assassination was broached,

the discussion heated up quickly. "First of all, it's hard to do," shouted the good senator from New York. "The United States isn't good at assassinations. Look how many times the CIA bungled plots to kill Fidel Castro in the 1960s. It would also make it more likely that some country or another would come back with an assassination attempt aimed at our president."

So it went until the din settled of its own weight. Questioning faces once more turned toward the CIA director, who sat calmly taking it all in. Although the senators knew the law on assassination as well as he, they merely wanted someone to make the decision for them on whether or not the law could be circumvented. In Washington, D.C., it was called the blame game. Someone had to be held accountable, to blame, for anything that might possibly go wrong. Politicians' seats were always at stake in the next election.

Benefield let a wry smile twist the thin straight line of his mouth. He was as good at the blame game as they. In this city, being able to duck it was part of survival training.

He leaned forward again with his hands tented.

"The executive order approved by President Ford and affirmed by President Reagan in 1981," he said without affection or unusual tone to his voice, "states, and I quote, 'No person employed by or acting on behalf of the United

States shall engage in, or conspire to engage in, assassination.' "

Senator Blythe threw up his hands. "Well. That settles that."

No, Director Benefield thought. *That settles nothing.*

1: OPERATION NO MAN'S LAND

Sometimes the CIA spooks carried their happy horseshit too far. Navy Lieutenant Jeb Hamilton, wearing a sports shirt loose-tailed over faded jeans to conceal the HK USP .45-caliber pistol tucked into his waistband, got out of the taxi and looked around. He was a tall man who had to bend down to speak to the driver.

"Are you sure this is the right address, pard?"

The guy was Lebanese, Iranian, or something from that region. He looked blank.

"Christ," Hamilton murmured before employing the slow, extraloud speech people commonly used on the deaf, stupid, or non–English speaking. "This *is* 2011 F Street?"

"F Street? Sure, sure. F Street. Two-oh-one-one. See?" He pointed. "Give money."

That was the number all right on a rundown square building, two stories tall, with white paint scabbing off the front. Next door to it was a

8

walk-up entrance to either a crack house or a whorehouse, maybe a combination of both. Two black broads in miniskirts sprawled spread-legged on the steps. One of them, Hamilton noted, wore no panties. The other wore blue. They watched the tall white man curiously as a gang of youth wearing their colors, Boston Celtic warm-up jackets, snarled along the filthy sidewalk. The way the man at the curb stared back at the gang members, with cold, deadly blue eyes, they decided he must either be a cop or he must be crazy. They kept moving.

It was a disgrace, Hamilton thought, that slums like these existed within view of the White House in the nation's capital. He paid the cabbie and went inside the "office" building. The first room was vacant except for two almost-bare desks temporarily parked in the middle of it. Behind the desks slouched a pair of male bureaucrats looking as much alike as Tweedle Dee and Tweedle Dum.

"Pappy?" one of them challenged.

Pappy was his code word, a challenge requiring a response. He was almost certain someone with a cute sense of humor had pinned that code to him because of his age. He was only thirty-six, but the U.S. Navy SEALs and SpecOps, Special Operations, itself was a young man's game where anyone over thirty was considered a retread.

"Social Security," Hamilton responded wryly, the response as cute as the challenge.

"You're early, Pappy."

Hamilton glanced at his Rolex dive watch. "*One minute* is early?"

"Time can be crucial. You'll have to wait."

They waited exactly one minute. Then Tweedle Dum said, "Go back outside. Turn left and go to the corner. Another cab will be waiting. Don't get mugged."

The spooks. Sometimes they were too much like *Spy vs. Spy* in *MAD* Magazine.

In this roundabout manner, at fifteen-minute intervals on that Friday morning even as CIA Director Louis Benefield was testifying before the Senate Armed Services Committee nearby, six SEAL experts in special warfare arrived in Washington, D.C., where they eventually ended up together in a cheap motel near the Southwest Freeway. A man alone in a room crossed them off his list one at a time. He introduced himself as Martin Smith. He had signed in as a district representative for National Sales Inc. He was holding a "sales" meeting in an adjoining room.

"Smith?" sarcastically demanded Bos'n Mate George "Mad Dog" Gavlik when he arrived fourth in the series. "Can't you Caspers come up with anything more original? It sounds like you're screwing around on your wife with her best friend."

"Are you packing?" Smith asked.

"You expect any sane man to come to this

shitpot city without at least one gun and a lawyer on retainer?"

"Leave your hardware here, along with your wallet, any jewelry, dog tags and anything else personal. You'll get it all back."

He pointed to the bed where there were three large unopened cardboard boxes. "Your box has your name on it. The clothing is your size. It has been stripped of all labels and identifying marks. Change in here, then go next door with the others."

There were three other boxes, opened, scattered on the floor. They contained discarded clothing where others before him had already changed. Mad Dog noticed a .45 handgun lying on top of jeans in one of the boxes. He emitted a kind of bark that was hard to recognize as laughter.

"Is this gonna be another 'No shit, there I was' deal?"

Smith had no sense of humor. Mad Dog started stripping. He possessed astonishing grace and agility for so large a man. His arms hung extraordinarily long and his legs were contrarily short, so that he had the quick swinging gait of a chimpanzee or mountain gorilla. Primatologist Jane Goodall would have loved him. Hair as black as his brooding eyes and crewcut matted his chest and arms and legs and grew all the way down his back. Although the heavy brow gave him the look of a Neanderthal, his eyes were shrewd, challenging and sparked with intelligence and energy. Mad Dog Gavlik was a daring man who had twice led successful summit assaults on Mount Everest and was currently in the middle of a seven-year project to climb the tallest mountain on each continent. *National Geographic* called him the most experienced and gutsy mountaineer of the twentieth century, without knowing that he was also a U.S. Navy SEAL.

"What about our fingerprints?" Mad Dog asked Smith.

"Everything about you was erased before you came into this room. The magic of computers. You can't even use your MasterCard. When you leave here, you leave completely sterile. You don't even officially exist. You know the routine. You'll be checked again before we sky up . . . Hold it, Bos'n. Take off your Fruit O' Looms too."

"Gentlemen prefer Haines. You wanna check my pee-pee while you're at it?"

"I'm sure you can keep that."

Mad Dog went next door wearing tan slacks, white shirt, lace-up shoes, and a sports jacket to replace his Levis and T-shirt. He closed the door and looked around the room already occupied by three other SEALs he knew from SEAL Team Two at Little Creek, Virginia.

Lieutenant Jeb Hamilton, a stand-up Mustang officer who had come up through the enlisted ranks, which explained why he was still only a lieutenant, stood up from the bed and walked over to shake hands. Ordnanceman Second Class Al Hodges, a wiry black man with a long soulful face and a cream-and-chocolate complexion, nodded. Bos'n Third Class John Nighthorse, a full-blooded Kiowa Indian from the Oklahoma Panhandle, rocked his chair forward from where he was leaning it against the wall.

"Whatta we got here so far?" Dog rumbled. "A grampaw, a soul bro', faithful Indian companion Tonto, and a guy with only one nut . . ."

Ragheads had shot off one of Dog's testicles on a mission into Iraq during the Gulf War.

"What's up, Mr. Hamilton?"

Lieutenant Hamilton shrugged. "I would think it has something to do with the NATO bombing of Serbia. Other than that? I guess we wait for the briefing."

Last night, each of six SEALs had received a visit from Chief Miller of Team Two Ops with a secret verbal order: *Consider this an alert. Pack your ruck and special gear for an operation. Leave it by your locker. It'll be picked up and waiting for you when you need it. Change into civvies and be at this address in Washington, D.C. tomorrow. Use a cab to get there. Don't tell anyone you're leaving or where you're going. Not your girlfriend, your wife, or your dog. Keep the time schedule I'm giving you. Understood?*

Until now, none of the men who had received the alert knew if this were a solo or team mission. They had been selected from different platoons and squads using some as yet unknown criteria.

Nighthorse got up and went to the window, but the curtains and blinds were drawn. Mad Dog tapped the walls and stomped the carpet. His quarters in Beirut had once been electronically bugged.

"They call together a SpecOps team like this when the job is to kill people and blow up things," he predicted with sinister undertones.

The last two men to arrive were Signalman Chief Petty Officer Gene Adcock, a thirty-one-year-old communications expert as tall as Lieutenant Hamilton, with shoulders as broad as a door, followed fifteen minutes later by Petty Officer First Class Ram Keithline. Even the Dog, who regarded most of mankind with not always unspoken contempt, turned slowly to regard the last man's entrance.

"Dr. Death," he greeted, using Keithline's nickname.

The seepage of cold air from out of a deep cave or from around a leaky coffin seemed to accompany Dr. Death. Although he was exceptionally fit, a requirement to remain in the teams, he was not an especially big man. The eyes were what commanded attention. They were gray-green and pale and seemed lidless like those of a pit viper. Like a cobra, he looked at men without seeming to blink.

He advanced deliberately into the room, as though he gave everything—eating, going to bed, making love—his total and undivided attention. His crewcut was as white as that of a very old man, although he couldn't have been thirty years old. Rumor had it that his hair went white like that overnight after he made his forty-first sniper kill on a drug lord in Colombia.

Dr. Death was the best long-distance shooter in the teams. He trained under Marine Gunny Sergeant Carlos Hathcock, the most successful sniper to come out of Vietnam, at the U.S. Marine Sniper School at Quantico before the gunny retired and subsequently died of cerebral palsy.

"When they call Dr. Death," Mad Dog commented, "death and destruction are bound to follow."

The six men who mustered in that obscure motel room that Friday morning were not only the elite of the world's military; each also brought with him unique talents. They were of that special breed first selected by the legendary Lieutenant Commander Roy Boehm, the *first* SEAL, when he received the go-ahead from President John F. Kennedy in 1961 to form an unconventional warfare unit to counter the worldwide communist threat. Boehm chose men who were more than killers, all muscle and neck and attitude. He required his SEALs above all else to have brains. He wanted independent, *thinking* operators. Men who put team and mission first, but who at the same time were individuals. Near-rogues in fact. Rough men, tough men with brains, talent, and skills, who could kick ass and operate outside protocol. Who could and *would* do literally any damned thing required of them. The name of the UW (unconventional warfare) game was *win*. So far, the SEALs had managed to escape the kinder, gentler military of women in combat and touchy-feely classes in COOing, Consideration of Others.

Shortly after the last man, Dr. Death, entered the room, before speculation on the mission had time to really get started, the motel door opened and closed so quickly it seemed Martin Smith simply appeared, as though teleported into the room *Star Trek*-style. He locked the door behind him and stood there resembling a young Harvard professor about to deliver a lecture on theoretical physics or the latter plays of William Shakespeare.

"This room has been debugged," he assured the SEALs. "This entire motel section is secured. We have people stationed to make certain it remains secured."

He paused momentarily to regard the gathering, then began with a feeble attempt at humor.

"I suppose you're wondering why we called you here ..."

THE BRIEFING

"As you know if you read newspapers or have been watching CNN," the CIA spook said matter-of-factly, "NATO, and by that we mean primarily the U.S., began bombing the Serbs Wednesday night. Provocation for the air launches is purportedly Serbian President Milosevic's attacks to suppress ethnic Albanians in Kosovo from seceding to become an independent province. Milosevic is being portrayed to the American public as another Hitler engaged in ethnic cleansing in Kosovo. Whether that's true or not—"

Mad Dog Gavlik interrupted with a cynical snort. "A draft-dodging president starts a war to draw attention away from Congressional investigations that he lied about a blowjob in the Oval Office and leases out the Lincoln Bedroom like Motel Six to bigwig donors—"

"Gavlik!" Lieutenant Hamilton stood up from where he sat on the bed with Chief Adcock and John Nighthorse. "We all have our opinions about this administration, but it's not up to us to question civilian policy. Criticism in uniform of the commander-in-chief can get you court-martialed."

Mad Dog gave a bark of cynical laughter.

"What're they gonna do to me—send me to the Balkans?"

"Whatever the reasons for bombing Serbia," Smith, nonplussed, resumed, "our mission is to protect United States interests—to ensure that the bombing does not escalate into a ground war that sucks in the rest of eastern Europe, starting with Russia."

"Interesting," the black man, Al Hodges, said. At Little Creek he was known as "Preacher" because he always carried a Bible. Smith had taken it from him in the other room. "Exactly who are the righteous guys in all this? Last month we were being told the Kosovo Liberation Army were bad-guy terrorists. This month the Serbs are evil. Which is it?"

"Neither side can be said to have clean hands," Smith acknowledged. "Milosevic and his ministers and generals are determined to suppress the Albanian rebellion in Kosovo, even if it means burning every town from the Serbian-Kosovo border to Macedonia. On the other hand, KLA rebels are retaliating against Serbian civilians. Europol is investigating solid evidence that the rebels are funding themselves partly through the heroine and cocaine trade and that they receive military support from China and Iran and from Saudi terrorist financier Osama bin Laden. You'll recall that the president ordered cruise missile attacks on bin Laden targets in Sudan and Afghanistan last year after our embassies were bombed in Kenya and Tanzania."

Lieutenant Hamilton strolled thoughtfully around the small room. In the light way the big man walked could still be recognized the handsome running back who thrilled sports fans of the Fighting Irish of Notre Dame before he dropped out and enlisted in the Navy.

"I assume Serbia is the purpose of this briefing," he jumped ahead, "and that we're to be inserted into Yugoslavia? Once we're there, who do we trust?"

"Ourselves," Dr. Death interjected in his hollow voice.

"There will be others," Smith countered. "You'll be provided complete area studies of Yugoslavia to look over during the flight to the NATO air base in Aviano, northern Italy."

"When do we leave?" Nighthorse asked in his soft, expressionless voice.

Smith looked around the room at the six men, sizing them up in turn. Each had been selected because of his skills and past combat experience. From having worked with SEALs before, the agent knew they could be intractable, headstrong, often fractious men, but that they worked well with each other when the chips fell and that they *always* got the job done. He ticked off their qualifications mentally as his eyes moved from one to the other. He had studied their personnel files at length.

Lieutenant Jeb Hamilton, team leader. Former enlisted man. Mature, icy, and decisive under pressure. Respected by both officers and enlisted. A veteran of clandestine black ops in Bosnia, Somalia, Iraq, China, Korea, and Russia. Fluent in Hebrew, Farsi, and Russian.

Chief Gene Adcock, second in command. Wounded twice during black ops, once in Colombia, again in Israel. Talented when it came to all forms of communications and electronic warfare. Spoke Spanish.

Boatswain Mate First Class George "Mad Dog" Gavlik. Abrasive. Opinionated. A fighter wounded in Iraq. One of his nuts shot off. Spoke German and Russian. An experienced mountaineer, invaluable in Alpine Serbia.

Ordnanceman Second Class Al "Preacher" Hodges. Grew up in the black ghetto gangs of Los Angeles on his way to the penitentiary and hell until he was "saved by Jesus" when he was seventeen and joined the Navy. Quiet and efficient. An artist with explosives. He could take a box of Tide laundry soap and some horse piss and sink Alcatraz into the San Francisco Bay. He spoke French fluently.

Bos'n Third Class John Nighthorse. Expert tracker, a skill acquired from hunting big game. A natural linguist proficient in a dozen languages, including both Serbo-Croatian and Albanian, spoken in Kosovo and Serbia. In Brazil, he had learned the Quechua tongue and trained Indians to track down and kill jungle-hiding terrorists.

Bos'n First Class Ram "Dr. Death" Keithline. A cold, deliberate man who, if he had a soul, kept it hidden. A loner. A man with a special skill who could peer through the scope of a rifle directly into the eyes of another human being—and then kill him at 2,000 yards. He had fifty-three kills on his record, from conflicts in Africa and Haiti to Iraq and Bosnia. The CIA had sent him with a team into Iran to assassinate two active Tangos—terrorists. Mission accomplished. Operation No Man's Land might ultimately come down to this man and his rifle. One shot—one kill—to end the war.

Smith avoided the sniper's eyes. He was one cold bastard, but necessary in a fucked-up world.

"Each of you was chosen for his particular abilities," Smith said, "and assembled to complement each other for one of the most hazardous and thankless missions assigned to any military unit since the end of the Cold War."

There was no response from the SEALs. Smith continued in his Harvard lecturing voice.

"Milosevic's army is scattered throughout Serbia and Kosovo and is expected to escape most of the bombings as it continues its scorched-earth policy against the ethnic Albanians of Kosovo. Milosevic is resupplying his army and continuing to push south in spite of the bombings. Milosevic's minister of state, Yevgeny Krleza, has close ties with Russian President Boris Yeltsin. It's Krleza who's brokering some kind of deal with Yeltsin to dispatch Russian troops to aid the Serbs against the KLA and as a defense should NATO attempt to invade on the ground.

"Let's look at the KLA now. The KLA has its roots in the Sigurimi secret police of Albania's late Stalinist dictator, Enver Hoxha, whose goal was a Greater Albania carved from Greece and other countries that make up Yugoslavia. Founders and leading cadre of the KLA were associated with the Yugoslavian communist secret police. The Albanian KLA rebels are split into two factions. The one that elected Ibraheim Rugova as its leader is almost powerless, although that's the one the U.S. is attempting to deal with in reaching a solution. The KLA is really led by a guy named Radovan Kradznic. While Milosevic intends Kosovo to remain a part of a Greater Serbia, Kradznic has aims on building a Greater Albania which will include Kosovo and Serbia."

Smith paused to let all this soak in. He suspected the SEALs already knew most of it. SEALs kept abreast of world affairs, especially those likely to turn into hot spots requiring their unique attention.

"I don't have to tell you what a perilous situation this has created for the United States and the rest of the world," Smith said. "The KLA is weak and scattered right now, although Kradznic has managed to amass sizeable units along the Serbian-Kosovo border. The NATO bombing of Serbia is likely to create a power vacuum into which Kradznic will move. Milosevic in Serbia or Kradznic in Kosovo, the outcome is likely to be the same—an escalating war that will suck in other countries."

"And that's where we come in," Lieutenant Hamilton said.

"Your team, Lieutenant Hamilton, will be flying to Italy by chartered jet immediately after this briefing. Your personal equipment and team equipment is already loaded on the airplane, including weapons. You'll be introduced into Kosovo by parachute tomorrow night under cover of NATO bombing. I'll provide further details on the aircraft en route.

"Your general overall mission is to work in a no man's land between the KLA and Milosevic's Serbs. You'll be assigned specific missions intended to prevent escalation of the war and create a stalemate between the two sides. I'll be your commo and operational link in Aviano. You'll be given orders and instructions after the completion of each mission for your next mission.

"Gentlemen, this war must be ended. As you can appreciate, you will be inserted completely sterile. This is a black operation from start to finish. If you are killed or captured, the U.S. must officially disavow all knowledge of who you are, why you are there, or even of your existence."

"Expendable," interjected Dog in the hush that followed. "We're not expected to come back alive."

"The United States cannot admit to having ground troops in Serbia," Smith emphasized. "We simply must take precautions to protect the president and—"

"Screw the president!"

"—the interests of the United States of America."

Mad Dog gave his wry bark of not quite laughter. "I regret that I have but one nut to give for my country."

"It sounds like a big job," Lieutenant Hamilton remarked with a low whistle.

"Saving the world?" Dog mocked. "Not too big for the U.S. Navy SEALs— the biggest, baddest motherfuckers in the valley."

2: LONE DOVE

PRE-MISSION

The anonymous CIA-leased Boeing 747 lifted out of Bolling AFB in D.C. in time for the passengers to have an early lunch. Urban sprawl quickly fell behind as the airliner climbed out over the Atlantic. It leveled at flight altitude with ETA in Italy at near midnight local. Aboard other than the flight crew and an Air Force staff sergeant steward with a Top Secret security clearance were six navy SEALs and a CIA agent with the unlikely alias of Smith. Seats had been removed and replaced with comfortable beds, cushioned executive chairs, full-sized galley and bar, and a polished oak conference table.

Chief Adcock whistled a note of appreciation at the lush green carpet. Mad Dog Gavlik question-marked his dark eyebrows when the steward served thick steaks to order, baked Idaho potatoes, and a Caesar's salad, topping lunch off with pie and ice cream.

"And the condemned were fed their last meal," he said soto vocce.

Smith loaded down the conference table with Yugoslavian area studies, maps, weather data, news clippings, order of battle information, and other general materials. Knowledge, preparation, and training converted to success and survival.

"You'll need to digest and memorize code words, radio freqs, E&E plans," Smith said. An unnecessary reminder; the SEALs knew their jobs. "Get everything ready, then get some sleep. This may be your last easy sleep for a while."

As team leader, Lieutenant Hamilton left the conference table last. It was both his duty and his nature to be thorough. Success lay in the details.

Skimming through a brief history of the region, he learned that strife and ethnic conflict in the merging borders between east and west Europe was nothing new nor recent. Ethnic cleansing did not begin with Adolf Hitler; it would not end with Slobodan Milosevic. The Balkan Peninsula had been conquered and reconquered for at least the past two-thousand years. Warfare was a part of its etiology.

Geographically, Yugoslavia was not that much different from neighboring Bosnia, where Hamilton had led several operations previously. The country was divided into three main regions—the Central Region, a narrow rocky strip of land along the Adriatic Sea; the Pannonian Plains, a mostly flat region in north-central Yugoslavia; and the Interior Highlands, which consisted of the Julian Alps, the Dinaric Alps, and several other mountain ranges extending out of eastern and southeastern Yugoslavia into Romania, Bulgaria, and Greece. It would still be cold nights in the mountains, with heavy rains possible.

Hamilton got up to check out their team equipment for rain gear. Personal mission gear along with team equipment—weapons, ammunition, radios, MRE rations, grenades, explosives, night vision goggles, parachutes, jump helmets, bottled oxygen, compasses, wrist altimeters had all been crated and banded and loaded aboard ahead of the SEALs' arrival. Under Chief Adcock's supervision, the men were now opening the crates, distributing the contents and preparing their rucks for insertion into Serbia. Among the litter on the plane's deck, Hamilton discovered six sets of heavy-duty but lightweight storm suits, each a dull black and made of a pliable, silent material. Smith *had* thought of everything. The lieutenant nodded his approval at the agent, who slouched in one of the executive chairs.

Smith rose and came to sit at the table as Hamilton resumed his studies.

"I was a psych major at Yale," he said.

"You have the look and demeanor of a professor," Hamilton replied without interest.

"You're of a different mold than the others, Mr. Hamilton."

"Am I?"

"You're thirty-six years old. You're well educated. You like classical music, opera, and used to attend the ballet and the theater . . ."

Hamilton was going through one of the area studies. He glanced up quickly. "Gavlik's hobby is classical Russian literature. Preacher is an authority on Biblical history . . ."

Smith went on, undaunted. "You met your wife, Judith, when you were playing football at Notre Dame. She died . . . what? Four years ago?"

Hamilton winced. His jaw tightened. "Are you taking this somewhere, Smith?"

"Terrorists killed her, wasn't it, Mr. Hamilton? You've spent the last four years volunteering to track down Tangos all over the world. You requested the assignment of chasing Osama bin Laden after the bombings of our embassies in Africa last year. You were turned down because it seems so many of your Ts have a habit of turning up dead when you catch up to them. Does all this sound like a different mold?"

"I didn't ask for *this* assignment. If it's going to be a problem—"

"On the contrary, Mr. Hamilton. Your different mold is also your best asset. You're a good small-unit leader, especially under pressure and under, shall we say, unusual circumstances?"

Smith smiled tightly, got up, and returned to

his former chair away from the table. Hamilton frowned after him. What the hell was that all about? He returned to the materials on the table.

This Serbia thing was all nasty business. The U.S. president and his secretary of state, Madeleine Albright, a short, dumpy woman widely ridiculed in the male-centered Arab world, were talking tough and demonizing the Serbs, backing them into a corner from which the only way out was to fight. Russian President Boris Yeltsin weighed in just as tough-talking. He called NATO's aggression a "gross mistake." He said he would hold the U.S. personally accountable for the air strikes. Not only would he ignore the arms embargo imposed by NATO, he had also alerted Russian troops for airlift into Belgrade if he deemed it necessary.

Serbia was armed with more than 85,000 regular soldiers and up to 200,000 reservists. Milosevic commanded a small air force of Russian MiG fighters and a capable air defense composed of SAM's. An SA-6 surface-to-air missile (SAM) had brought down USAF Captain Scott O'Grady's F-16 over Bosnia in 1995.

Facing off against Milosevic in the Kosovo Alps were Radovan Kradznic and an estimated 60,000 KLA rebel guerrillas.

And between the two forces, a six-man SEAL team on an operation appropriately code-named No Man's Land. Their mission: To sabotage, raid, create diversion, raise havoc, and carry out whatever other assignments it received in order to neutralize and reduce the effectiveness of both sides, to force peace into Serbia before the bombing campaign escalated into a *real* war. All to be conducted under a cloak of Top Secrecy.

Who the hell had dreamed this one up?

The Boeing 747 droned on through the night. Darkness blacked out the aircraft's windows. Hamilton stretched and wearily rubbed his eyes. Looking up from the table, he saw stuffed rucks and weapons arranged in a row in the middle of the cabin, ready to go. Smith, drinking a cup of coffee, still watched the SEAL officer without expression.

Nighthorse and Chief Adcock had both gone to bed and were sleeping silently; snoring was never tolerated behind enemy lines. Preacher Hodges lay on his bunk reading from a new Bible Smith had provided, one without handwritten notations. Dr. Death sat on his rack cleaning his sniper's rifle while Mad Dog sat cross-legged on the floor at his feet, drinking coffee. Dr. Death seldom spoke more than a terse phrase or two at a time unless the subject matter had something to do with weapons, ammo, or the art and science of shooting. The strange skeletal-looking weapon he was fastidiously cleaning and lightly oiling resembled an

Olympic match rifle, except it had been especially designed for far more deadly purposes.

"The Haskins M500 50-caliber sniper's rifle,"
he explained to Dog, his snake eyes taking on a
slight glimmer of life, "is custom made in
Arkansas for Green Beret and SEAL snipers."

He flicked off an imaginary speck of dust and
gently handed the weapon to Dog as though it
were fragile.

"Heavy," Dog said.

"Twenty-three pounds, including the bipod."

He pointed out its features one by one.

"Single-shot bolt action for accuracy. The bolt
must be removed to load each round. Precision
is what counts, not speed."

"One shot–one kill."

"Precisely. The fluted barrel reduces weight
and helps cooling. The muzzle brake deflects
gases to the rear to diminish kick. The scope is a
4x16 Elite with a 50mm objective lens for maximum light-gathering and a four-times zoom
range. The parallax focus adjustment with a
nearly 360-degree range for pinpoint accuracy

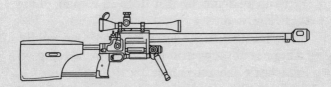

Haskins M500 50-caliber Sniper Rifle

makes this an ideal scope for long-range shooting. Semi-target windage and elevation settings are finger-adjustable. This is a scope designed by a rifleman for serious shooting. This is the most accurate individual weapon in the world. A good marksman can hit a target the size of a man at two thousand meters, a distance of a mile and a quarter."

Dr. Death was a good marksman. He showed Dog a box of twenty 50-caliber cartridges individually secured in a Styrofoam and heavy plastic box to prevent damage that could throw off the bullet's flight.

"This ounce-and-a-half bullet comes out the muzzle with five times the energy of a standard 7.62 NATO round," he said. "Several different bullets are available. The hardened tungsten-carbide penetrator inside this particular projectile can pierce four-inch armor, shatter a tank's gunsights, or cripple an aircraft engine. An incendiary inside the bullet's nose will touch off a fuel tank or detonate an explosive charge inside the bullet itself that shatters the bullet into shrapnel."

"I can imagine what it does to a man," Dog said, bemused.

Dr. Death's snake eyes regarded him coldly. "There's not enough left of him to sing in Preacher's heavenly choir."

Lieutenant Hamilton's attention was diverted to Smith when the Air Force sergeant came back and bent to whisper into the agent's ear.

Smith got up and went forward. He returned within minutes.

"I've just received the alert on your first mission assignment," he said. "It's not what we anticipated, but I expect we'll have to be adaptable. Part of the fog of war. You'd better get some sleep. Your team will be briefed as soon as we land in Aviano. You'll have less than an hour in country before we insert you into Serbia."

THE BRIEFING

The airfield at Aviano, Italy, like NATO military airfields at Brindisi in southern Italy and Tuzla in Bosnia, was a hive of fighters, bombers, and transports, coming and going. Lights blazed from everywhere in the middle of the night, casting strange shadows among war materiel crated up in piles to form streets among which buzzed uniformed workers. The SEALs of Operation No Man's Land, who for identification purposes were code-named Solitary Elk collectively in the weird jargon used by militaries, were hustled to a guarded room in one of the hangars. A one-star U.S. general and two other officers, both majors, briefed them among maps erected on stands.

"At nineteen forty-five hours tonight, our third night of air raids over Serbia," the general began in a crisp, all-business tone, "an American F-117A Nighthawk stealth fighter was shot down by missiles. It crashed near the town of Pozarevac south of the Danube River and about thirty miles from Belgrade. The pilot was Air Force Captain Ron McMasters. He parachuted from his cockpit and landed somewhere in this region."

He pointed to the map.

"It's mostly farmland. Our pilots are trained to move as far away from the crash site as possible before betraying location by activating their emergency communications. Voice contact was made after we received his emergency code. We now have a fix on him. Your target folder will provide you his grid coordinates and other

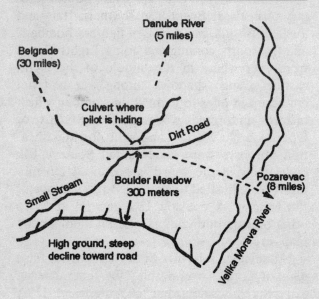

Rescue of Downed Stealth Pilot

vitals. There are Serb troops in the area looking for him. A search dog came within thirty feet of where he's hiding in a drainage culvert."

The general backed off and motioned to one of the majors who, filled with self-importance, said, "I'm Major Cantrell, S-1 shop. We're keeping Captain McMasters on the hook, but we're only communicating whenever necessary to prevent the bad guys from electronically triangulating him. So far, he's been in that culvert about three hours. Gentlemen, we understand that, whoever you are, you're the best we have at operating behind enemy lines."

"It's a job," Lieutenant Hamilton said when it seemed the major expected a response.

Major Cantrell looked at him with curiosity. "This is more than a job," he said. "Gentlemen, at oh-two hundred hours you will be parachuted into Serbia to rescue Captain McMasters. We have consulted with your handler, Mr. Smith, who advises us that you are engaged in other corresponding duties for which we have no need to know. Therefore, we have fed all the pertinent data to Mr. Smith during your flight over. He will provide the details of your mission."

The general looked around, seemingly put upon that he was not to be privy to what these mysterious men were *really* doing here. He led the two majors out and closed the door, leaving the SEAL team alone with Smith.

"Our *handler*?" Dog scoffed. "Nighthorse, ain't

that what they call chicken fighters in Oklahoma?"

"Stow the scuttlebutt," Lieutenant Hamilton
ordered. "There's not much time."

Smith handed a target folder to each man.
"This will give you grids, times, radio freqs, and
all the info you need for the mission. You have a
half hour to memorize everything and turn the
folders back to me. Briefly, this is how it's going
down: A C-141 Starlifter is on the tarmac now
warming up. It will fly a track over Romania as
described in your folders. You will HAHO—
high altitude, high opening—by parachute at
twenty thousand feet and fly a linear distance of
twelve miles to a DZ in a field near the downed
pilot. After recovering him, you will take him to
a safe house southeast of Pozarevac, where one
of our ground assets will provide details for his
extraction. This same asset will brief you on a
subsequent mission. It's all in the folders. Any
questions?"

"Why are we being used instead of regular
SAR forces?" Preacher asked. "Aren't we in
danger of being compromised?"

"Two reasons," Smith replied. "If we send in
helicopters and soldiers, we stand a good chance
of ending up in a firefight and losing more birds.
That would be reason enough for Milosevic to
claim we are invading with ground forces and
give Russia the excuse Yeltsin needs to send in
troops of his own. We can't risk that."

"And the second reason?" Chief Adcock pressed.

"The Serbs are claiming they shot down the fighter because they received advance information about the track it would fly. That enabled them to set up a SAMbush, a surface-to-air ambush."

"A spy?" Hamilton looked doubtful.

"It's damned hard to shoot down a stealth otherwise," Smith reasoned.

"Maybe they just got lucky," Nighthorse pointed out.

Smith threw out both hands. "We can't risk lives by counting on it being luck."

"If spies know our aircraft targets and tracks," Lieutenant Hamilton cut in, "isn't it possible they may have obtained intelligence about No Man's Land?"

"A remote likelihood," Smith said. "Not even NATO has been briefed about No Man's Land—only those with an absolute need to know. Which leads to the second reason why we're using you instead of SAR. If there *is* a spy in NATO and we activated Search and Rescue, it would be known and the pilot snatched by Serbs before we could get to him. As it is, we're officially pretending the pilot went down with his ship. The enemy doesn't know about you, and even if he did he would never expect you to rescue a downed pilot. This way you infiltrate the country undetected and you recover one of

our airmen as a bonus. It's the best of all
worlds."

"The best of all worlds," Dog countered, "is a
blonde and a Coors in a hot tub."

THE TARGET FOLDER

Military code names were stamped all over the
folders: Lone Dove. Inside the folders were grid
coordinates for all pertinent locations, including
the drop zone, the culvert where the pilot hid, and
the safe house. Photos of the pilot from his military ID provided his complete physical description, including the fact that he had a large mole
on his left shoulder blade and a half-moon scar
below his right knee. There were satellite photographs of the town of Pozarevac, the surrounding
countryside and the safe house. A close-up photo
showed it to be a whitewashed, two-story stone
farmhouse with a red-tile roof and a split-rail
fence enclosing a gaggle of African geese and a
spotted pig. The SEALs studied accompanying
topographical maps with interest in order to
acquire a feeling for the lay of the land.

"Steep hillsides, forests, and high mountain
plains and meadows," Chief Adcock commented.

"Memorize everything," Lieutenant Hamilton
said. "We can't carry the maps with us or call
Triple A. Here's the DZ clearing in the woods
north of this hill. SAT photos show there are no

houses in the near vicinity. It looks like we have
cover all the way to this road and the culvert
where he's hiding. We'll have to come out in the
open to reach the culvert, but once we're back
up the hill they'll have a tough time rooting us
out. We can skirt around the base of this mountain and stay in the woods all the way to the safe
house."

After studying things for awhile, Preacher
observed, "Looks like a stroll in the moonlight."

"Just us and God, Preach," Mad Dog chided,
"and a few thousand pissed-off Serbs."

THE PREPARATION

The SEALs had an hour aboard the Starlifter
to complete their preparation before jump time.
They had already changed out of their traveling
civvies and donned work clothes—camouflage
battle dress uniforms, BDUs, without patches,
tags, rank, or other markings. Dog and Dr.
Death wore Vietnam-era jungle slouch hats; the
rest preferred Marine patrol caps. Their nonreg-
ulation footgear included a selection of high-
topped mountaineering and hiking boots with
waterproof leather tops and ridged rubber soles
for traction and stealth.

Because they might not be coming out again
until the war and the operation ended, each man
carried all the weapons he might conceivably
need: a primary weapon, two sidearms, a Marine

K-bar fighting knife, grenades, C-4 plastic explosives with necessary fuses and cord, Claymore mines, plentiful supplies of ammunition. In addition, their rucks were stuffed with freeze-dried rations; rain gear; dry uniforms, socks, and underwear rolled in plastic as waterproofing: and other odds and ends like ponchos, heavy twine, binoculars, weapon-cleaning kits and spare parts. They were going in heavy, prepared to stay and fight.

Nighthorse hefted his ruck, checking its weight. "Damn!"

For convenience and uniformity in ammo requirements, they were armed with identical sidearms attached to their webgear and strapped down to their thighs. The Heckler & Koch MP5K submachine gun was only slightly longer than twelve inches and fired 9mm Parabellum NATO cartridges at a ripping 900 rounds per minute in full automatic mode. While Lieutenant Hamilton preferred the HK .45-cal as a second sidearm, he settled for the Glock 9mm semi-automatic pistol because of its lighter weight in frame and ammunition. Less punch per round, but more rounds.

Since the men had no knowledge of what missions they might be required to undertake, their main weapons were selected to perform a variety of specialized tasks, from clearing out a room to popping a target a half-mile away across a field.

Mad Dog and Chief Adcock each carried an HK11A1 light machine gun in 5.56 caliber. It weighed only eighteen pounds, five pounds less than similar MGs, making it the weapon of choice for long missions.

Lieutenant Hamilton and Nighthorse jammed their Russian-made AKMS 7.62-caliber assault rifles into their rucks for the jump. The AKMS packed a real wallop in the larger caliber while measuring a mere twenty-eight inches in length with the buttstock collapsed and folded—an ideal paratrooper's arm.

Preacher padded the workable parts of his M16A1 5.56 rifle with attached M-203 grenade launcher and secured it to his left shoulder, muzzle down. Dr. Death did the same thing with his Winchester Model 1200 pump shotgun, but disassembled and packed the Haskins into his ruck. The Haskins was an extremely specialized arm. For close-in combat he had the shotgun and a mixed bag of ammo to fire flechettes, slugs, or double-aught buck.

As the Starlifter droned through the night over Romania, the inside of the cabin glowing eerily red from lights designed to facilitate night vision, the SEALs made last-minute checks of their rucks, weapons, and parachutes. They applied black and dark-green camouflage makeup to their faces and looked out of the painted foliage with steady, white-rimmed eyes. Chief Adcock glanced up from attaching grenades to his webgear by taping the handles to prevent their accidentally being jerked loose.

"Skipper, maybe you'd better have the pilots take us up another couple of thousand feet," he suggested, not altogether in jest. "With all we're carrying, we're going to fall out of the sky like a ton of mud."

"Like a ton of *shit*," Dog corrected. "What are we gonna do about all the holes in the ground when we hit?"

"They can bury us in them if anything goes wrong," Preacher Hodges offered.

"You going to pray for us, Preacher?" Nighthorse asked.

"I already have."

The rough banter of men minimizing the effects of impending danger.

"Everybody have oxygen prepared?" the lieutenant asked. "Chief, check 'em out. Don't drop your masks in the air when we're coming in. We'll bury 'em once we land. We don't want to leave any calling cards announcing our arrival."

A little later, at thirty minutes before jump time, Hamilton ordered, " 'Chute up and ruck up. Put on your oxygen and night goggles when the green light goes on. Stay together in the air. Guide on me. I'll have glow tape around my ankles."

Parachutes went on using the buddy system. Rucks were snapped to D rings below reserve 'chutes in front. They would be dropped on fifteen-foot lowering lines a hundred feet up to minimize jumper impact. Weapons were either secured inside rucks or strapped to left shoulders.

"I'm not gonna *jump*," Mad Dog bitched. "If I can *get* to the door with all this, I'll be lucky to *fall* out."

Hamilton as jumpmaster gave final rigging checks, slapping each man on the butt as he finished. Ready to go. They sat side by side in the webbing with their backs to the outer skin, facing the center of the aircraft. Hamilton would be first man out the door, followed in order by Dr. Death, Preacher, Dog, and Nighthorse. Chief Adcock, a big no-nonsense man, would push the stick out into the black immense sky almost as a single element.

In those few minutes before action, even the bravest of men turned introspective. Mad Dog Gavlik sat bent over his reserve belly 'chute, legs spread around his ruck resting on the steel vibrating floor between his boots. He looked at the faces of the others to either side and studied their features without appearing to. Camouflage paint made fierce masks of their faces in the red cabin glow. He could tell nothing about their thoughts.

It unexpectedly occurred to him that he would have liked to call his mother before he left. He shook his head deprecatingly back and forth. Only a mother could love a "mad dog," right?

His brooding eyes switched to Hamilton when

the lieutenant stood up, wide-legged against the movement of the airplane. He motioned for the team to don black jump helmets, O2 masks and night vision goggles, all of which were cinched and taped to withstand the wind blast of door exit. They looked like a bunch of giant green-and-black insects.

Still standing, Hamilton dropped his hands in front and just as quickly brought his palms sharply upward. Behind him the jump lights next to the door turned from red to green.

"Stand up!"

THE MISSION

They took a walk out the deep end of the Star-lifter's door, diving into the black sky and punching an ice-cold hole through the darkness. Twenty thousand feet, nearly four miles, separated their plunging bodies from the dark curvature of the earth. Overhead, the blacked-out C-141 disappeared. Lieutenant Hamilton free-fell for eight seconds, stabilizing himself and "flying" while he bled off 2,000 feet. He checked his glow-faced wrist altimeter, then pulled the rip cord.

He sensed the 'chute slipping out the back pack, felt the canopy separating and filling with air. Then it yanked him skyward in that bungee-cord way. All of a sudden the rushing world quieted and slowed down. Floating, he looked around through his night vision goggles to check

the status of his men. The goggles lent everything a greenish, liquid cast as they gathered the
ambient light of the stars and low sliver of moon
to make night vision possible. Mushrooms
floated all around him. He counted them—five.
Good to go. The others would be guiding on the
identifying glow tape around his legs.

He checked the wind and found it with them,
checked the grid numbers for the DZ he had
previously punched into his GPS, Global Positioning System, taped with a compass to his left
forearm. He selected the correct flying track and
turned the 'chute onto it. After that, except for
making minor corrections to keep on course, all
he had to do for the next half-hour was hang
float-flying beneath the silk sky-blue square. He
left the steering toggles in the uppermost position for the best ground-to-glide ratio, to stretch
their range.

Unnoticed below, they flew across the border
that separated Romania from Serbia, falling out
of the night at more than twenty-five feet per
second, gliding toward a small clearing surrounded by forest less than three kilometers
from where a downed American fighter pilot
cowered in a ditch and prayed for rescue.

So far they were on the upside of the curve.

As he flew, Dog thought about the spy. If a spy
could have an F-117 SAMbushed, why not
SEALs? Somewhere in the mazes of the Pentagon where decisions were made, plans drawn,

units selected, and men assigned, someone *somewhere* knew about Operation No Man's Land and the team's insertion into Serbia. It could be that the spy had access to that information. Dog trusted no one outside the teams, especially not government. *Any* government.

He constantly scanned the terrain below between his feet as he sank toward it. He half-expected a "few thousand pissed-off Serbs" to be waiting for them on the DZ. His muscles tensed as he followed the lieutenant in. He was almost surprised when the team whispered out of the night and landed in a silence and peace that endured.

Quickly, using only hand signals to communicate, they rolled up the stick and piled their 'chutes, helmets, and extraneous air gear into a washout Chief Adcock located among the trees. Hastily covered with loose dirt and last fall's dead leaves, the cache would pass unnoticed anything except the closest inspection. Even if the gear were discovered, there were no markings to link it to the U.S. Lieutenant Hamilton had even taken the precaution of having Nighthorse make up Serbian names to tape to the insides of the helmets as a diversionary measure. *Josip Broz . . . Ivo Andric . . . Oskar Davico . . .*

The six men moved off the DZ, weapons now ready for use. Although this was their first time working together as a team, they were all veterans of numerous previous ops and knew the

game. In the SEAL lexicon, they were *operators,*
shooters, the highest praise one SEAL could pay
another. They settled automatically into their
previously assigned positions.

The Kiowa took the dangerous point position since he was most comfortable there. The
fact that he spoke the local lingo might also
give them the edge should they encounter
someone. Preacher Hodges took the right
flank, Chief Adcock the left. Mad Dog pulled
slack as tail gunner. Lieutenant Hamilton and
Dr. Death assumed the center command position of the diamond behind Nighthorse. Each
had his own area of responsibility, but that did
not mean he covered it exclusive of the rest of
the perimeter.

They moved in near-complete silence disturbed only by the occasional crunch of leaves
underfoot. Ahead of them in the distance, where
the lights of Belgrade should have been radiat-
ing off the sky, was nothing but more darkness.
The Serbian government had pulled down the
blackout curtains. Using his GPS, Hamilton
directed the route through the forest with a
downward gradient toward the Danube River.
Night-vision goggles allowed them to travel
swiftly, even in the timber. The night was cool,
almost cold, and damp with dewfall. Nonetheless, they were soon sweating.

They broke out of thick timber along a low ridge
line of tumbled boulders strewn downward

toward a rocky meadow dissected by a chuck-ling brook. A narrow winding gravel-dirt road crossed the brook. Dog and Nighthorse scouted both immediate flanks for a threat, finding only a darkened farmhouse less than 500 meters to the right. Dogs had barked, but everyone in the house seemed either asleep or gone.

"That's our culvert," Hamilton whispered, pointing.

It appeared to be a drainage or a pipe to allow the stream to run underneath the road.

"A tight fit," Adcock remarked.

"That's probably why search parties haven't found our boy." Hamilton turned to the team. "Everything seems to be clear. Dog, you and Preacher snatch the pilot. Those boulders will cover you most of the way. The Chief and I will cover you from here. Dr. Death? Take the right flank. The rally point is those twin oaks up on the hill behind us."

"Aye, aye, Skipper."

The Dog, trailed by Preacher, trundled off on his powerful short legs, the machine gun hang-ing at the end of one long arm looking almost like a toy in contrast to his size. If the length of his legs had conformed to the rest of his body, he would have been six-four instead of less than six feet.

Hamilton watched the two SEALs scurrying like crabs across the boulder field toward the road 300 meters away. Apparently the stealth fighter's wreckage lay not far from here, but there was no activity to indicate where. The Serbs had already searched this area; they shouldn't be back. Piece of cake. Too easy.

Dog and Preacher were halfway to their objective. Suddenly, a tremendous ball of fire shot up from the horizon in the direction of Belgrade, followed by a second and third explosion. Brilliant and roiling with angry flames. NATO air raids. Bombs delivered by aircraft flying so high they could neither be seen nor heard from the ground. Belgrade immediately opened up with ineffectual antiaircraft fire, filling the night with dancing Roman candle fireworks. Little or no sound carried across the distance to the SEALs, but the earth trembled from the shock wave and patterns of light flickered over the meadow.

Hamilton ducked his head to shield his eyes and prevent being blinded. Too late. Night-vision goggles, intended to take very small amounts of light and magnify them, seared the explosions into his retinas. He ripped off the goggles and flung them aside. All he could see were repeat explosions inside his eyes and brain.

Only Mad Dog, who happened to have glanced back toward Preacher at the very instant the action started, escaped temporary blindness. He peeled off his goggles. Preacher stood in a half-crouch, sightless. Up above him on the ridge line, the other SEALs were in a similar state of transitory helplessness. Dog was the first to spot the deuce-and-a-half Russian military truck that seemed to arrive on cue, as though directed into a B movie. It came roaring along the road out of the woods using only its slitted blackout lights. They resembled the gleaming eyes of a giant predator.

"Get down!" Dog hissed and dived for Preacher, bringing him low behind a boulder.

Preacher heard it. So did the other SEALs.

To the right of the rescuers gurgled the brook, full from recent rains. Ahead, the culvert was a black hole underneath the berm of the road. The distant sky full of antiaircraft fire silhouetted the moving truck. Dog expected it to continue on down the road. Instead, to his dismay, the gears down-scraped, grinding, as the vehicle slid in the gravel, coming to a halt almost directly above the culvert. Shadows of men began piling out of it.

It was obvious to the watching SEALs that these soldiers knew exactly what they were doing. They were men with a purpose. Somehow the location of the pilot, who had now been on the ground some seven hours, had been relayed to Milosevic's army. The NATO spy had struck again. What other explanation could there be?

It was a case of bad timing. Had the truck arrived a quarter-hour earlier, Captain McMasters would already be en route to Belgrade as a

POW and possible hostage. A quarter-hour later and he would have been with the SEALs on his way through the underground pipeline to safety.

As it was, there was no time for vacillation. The SEALs had been dispatched to recover the pilot—no matter who got in the way. SEALs were known for their decisiveness under pressure.

Dog bobbled up behind his boulder with the light HK machine gun at waist level. He went into rock 'n' roll with it, the muzzle blossoming, red tracers stabbing across the darkness into the truck and its astonished human cargo, creating havoc and confusion and death. High-velocity 5.56 bullets spanged and sparked against the vehicle, whining and ricocheting, red-streaking into the sky. Dog noted with perverse satisfaction the *thunking* the hot steel made when it slashed into flesh and bone.

Men were screaming in pain and fear and dropping on the road bed.

He sprayed the truck and its disembarking passengers with a full thirty-round mag. He dropped back down behind the boulder, released the empty magazine, and slapped in a fresh one from his pouches.

By now, his teammates were recovering enough vision to at least open fire in the desired direction. A steady stream of lead poured from the ridgeline, eating and chewing at the truck in a hellish din. Preacher leaned over the boulder with his M16, hammering away with it.

"Our Father who art in Heaven," he recited in a husky voice, *"hallowed be Thy name . . ."*

No one, nothing, could have survived so deadly a beating. Over 200 rounds expended in a condensed ten-second period. From the ridgeline boomed Lieutenant Hamilton's deep voice: *"Cease fire! Cease fire!"*

The silence that replaced the mad minute was near as deafening as the racket that had preceded it. It had been a massacre. *Better them poor bastards than us,* Dog thought.

They waited for return fire. None came. Instead, there was the pounding of boots on ground as a survivor jumped up to run. Preacher picked up the shadowy movement with his clearing vision. He quick-aimed and fired. The shadow dropped with a low moan.

"Thy will be done on earth as it is in Heaven . . ." Preacher said.

To which Dog gave a hearty, "Amen, bro'!"

Someone from near the truck groaned in pain, but that was all.

"Dog!" Lieutenant Hamilton called out.

Dog understood. Time was essential. Other bad guys may have heard the firing.

He darted forward, crabbing low. Preacher automatically followed as backup. They used the bend of the stream to guide them to the culvert opening. As they drew near, they heard the truck engine still racing but banging loudly in its guts from a stray round. The air was ripe with escaping steam from the truck and burned cordite and the peculiar copperish odor of freshly spilled blood.

With only perfunctory glances at the pools of shadow in the road that marked where dead men lay, the two SEALs went into crouches next to the culvert entrance. Water burbled into the pipe. Dog knew enough not to stick his head in front of the opening. Pilots carried those little .38s as survival pistols. The guy was probably scared shitless too.

"Americans! Americans!" Dog called out softly. "Lone Dove! Lone Dove!"—the jet jockey's code name.

At first there was no response. Dog touched Preacher's shoulder and, with a flick of his head, indicated Preacher was to make sure the Serbs were really dead Serbs. He called out again to the pilot as Hamilton and John Nighthorse trotted up to him using the stream bed to cut their outlines.

"Is he in there?" Hamilton demanded.

Dog got a little closer to the pipe's opening. "I don't know," he said.

"Fucking goggles," Nighthorse grumbled. "I still can't see anything."

"Don't stick your head in front of the pipe," Hamilton cautioned.

Dog tried it again. "Cap'n McMasters? Can you hear me, dude? Are you wounded? We're here to take you out. Lone Dove!"

He didn't blame the poor bastard for being cautious.

Preacher appeared. "Skipper, we got two of them stalling in meeting their Maker. I disarmed them. They're not going anywhere."

"John," the lieutenant said. The Kiowa got up and went with Preacher.

A rustling noise came from the culvert. "Americans?" asked a disbelieving voice.

"You got it, dude," Dog exclaimed. "You didn't think we were going to leave you out here, did you?"

A face pale in the wan moonlight blinked in the pipe's opening. It almost withdrew again at sight of the fierce-looking men outside with their painted faces, like a startled turtle sucking in its head.

"It's okay, Captain," Lieutenant Hamilton reassured him.

In the distance antiaircraft fire still lit up the skies over Belgrade, although the bombing sortie had ended.

The pilot relaxed with a long sigh. "I thought I was a goner," he whispered, although there was no need for it now. "I didn't think SAR would come this deep into Serbian territory."

Dog laughed. "We do it deep and often."

The pilot bellied out of the pipe like a soaked puppy coming in out of the rain. It was indeed a tight fit. Dog and the lieutenant helped him to his feet. It took a minute to get his circulation going. He still wore his black flight suit and a holstered pistol, but his helmet had been discarded or lost. He carried in one hand a satellite transceiver, a SATCOM unit about the size of a cellular phone. That was what he had used for communication with the bomber base at Aviano. It was the same radio the SEALs carried.

He glanced anxiously around, noticing for the first time the fireworks over Belgrade. He nodded approval. He shivered from the cool night breeze against his wet clothing.

"There have been soldiers and dogs by several times looking for me," he warned, his teeth chattering. "They're bound to be back now after this. In force."

He caught himself with a harsh intake of breath at the strange Asiatic litany of the Serbian language coming from the road.

"It's okay," Hamilton said quickly. "He's one of ours questioning the wounded. Are you all right?"

"I can't believe it, but yes."

"Good. Mission accomplished—almost. Let's pack our ditty bags and blow this joint."

"Ditty bag is packed, boss," Dog said.

POST-MISSION

The eastern sky became noticeably paler. Dawn was coming. The team kept moving, checking its backtrail frequently for trackers. The SEALs employed a bagful of tricks to throw pursuers off their trail. From the culvert, Nighthorse laid a false trail going the opposite direction from their actual withdrawal route. They took to the rushing stream then and waded it up-current for more than a mile to cover their tracks. After exiting the stream and digging out dry clothing for the pilot, Lieutenant Hamilton used his GPS to select a zigzagging course as they made their way through the forest toward the safe house, where they were to meet the contact. At least three of the SEALs had lost their night-vision glasses at the road, which slowed progress. Hamilton estimated their arrival at destination at about daybreak, just in time to avoid daylight movement.

Hamilton knelt next to John Nighthorse during a rest halt. They hadn't had a chance to talk before now. "What about the wounded Serbs?" he asked the linguist in a low tone.

"One of them might live. The other's a goner. I don't think they realized we were Americans, especially since I questioned them in Serbian. I let it slip, Skipper, that we were Serbs fighting against Milosevic. Serbs, not Albanians. Let Milosevic and his bunch chew on the idea of a Fifth Column at their next cabinet meeting."

"Good thinking. Did you ask them how they found out where the pilot was hiding?"

"The Serbs were nothing but foot-pounding

grunts, sir. All they knew was that somebody came running up and told them to saddle up. Are you thinking what I'm thinking, Skipper? That we definitely have a spy somewhere in higher-higher?"

Hamilton agreed. "And apparently well-placed."

"Within our own ops? We're so Top Secret even God doesn't have a need to know."

Hamilton let himself to the ground to rest with his back against a tree. "I think they received word about the pilot, but I don't think they knew about us."

"Yet," Nighthorse added ominously.

Again Hamilton agreed. "Yet," he said.

Nearby, Captain McMasters eased down next to Preacher Hodges. The wiry black man remained alert for danger, kneeling on one knee with his M16/M203 across the other knee, scanning the lifting darkness through night-vision goggles.

"Did you finally get warm?" Preacher asked him.

"Once I got into dry clothing," the pilot whispered back. "I heard the others calling you Preacher. Are you a minister?"

"I was. Once."

"You killed some men at the culvert."

"The Bible says 'Thou shalt not commit *murder*,' God Himself smited evil when he encountered it."

There was silence between them for a time.

"I believe in God," the pilot murmured presently. "More so now than ever."

"No atheists in culverts."

"You know, Preacher, I was scared, really scared. The one fragment of the whole event I cannot remember is pulling the ejection seat handle. God took my hands and pulled."

Preacher nodded, understanding.

"Preacher, what about you guys?" He paused. "Who *are* you guys, anyhow?"

THE REPORT

After Action Reports would have to wait until after they were extracted from enemy territory. Lieutenant Hamilton made the pilot memorize an abbreviated version of what he wanted Smith to know. Captain McMasters would surely be debriefed. It was a simple report: Seven enemy KIA at the rescue point, pilot recovered, no friendly casualties.

"Speak to a man named Smith," Hamilton stressed. "Smith. No one else. They'll know who he is. I'm sure he'll be wanting to talk to you too. Tell him the Serbs found out about you. He'll understand. Don't tell this to anyone else. No one. Understood?"

"You can count on it. You guys risked your lives for me."

Hamilton checked his watch, his GPS readings and his compass. So far, so good. He leaned his head back against the tree. He felt the rough bark even through his bush hat. He closed his eyes for a minute.

As he often did, he saw the face of his dead wife, Judith, on the inside of his eyelids.

3: DEEP WATER

PRE-MISSION

So far, NATO aircraft were only bombing under cover of darkness in an endeavor to cut down on friendly casualties. That meant Serbian troops would be on the move during the day. Lieutenant Hamilton picked up the pace as farms began to emerge out of shadow into the brightening dawn and they no longer needed night-vision assistance.

Twice on the way they came upon houses, one of which was unlighted and asleep, the other of which was undoubtedly occupied by Albanians, for it was in the process of being abandoned. The family had hooked a trailer to the back of an ancient farm tractor and was loading it with their belongings. Moving out under the false protection of night. What wouldn't fit in the trailer or on the tractor, they carried on their backs, en route to join a growing exodus fleeing Serbia and Kosovo for the relative safety of neighboring states.

"This could happen in the U.S. someday," Dog predicted, whispering to Preacher. "What with all our diversity bullshit."

"The Millennium is coming," Preacher responded in his best doomsday voice. " 'And behold a pale horse: and his name that sat on him was Death, and Hell followed with him.' "

"Sounds like us, Preacher," Dog said.

The team skirted the farmhouses and arrived in the predawn at a copse of trees growing on the lee side of a gentle hill. Hamilton's GPS advised him they should be within sight of their destination. Ahead of them, a rooster crowed clear and ringing, signaling both the presence of another farm and the nearness of dawn. Nighthorse leading on point dropped to one knee and flashed a signal. The other SEALs had already wilted to the earth, forming a 360-degree perimeter. One night on the ground together and they were already working like a finely oiled machine. Captain McMasters, startled, took a knee next to Lieutenant Hamilton.

Hamilton motioned for him to stay where he was. He slipped forward and dropped next to Nighthorse. The woods were too thick to see far through them.

There should be a split-rail fence at the edge of the woods next to the hill. There would also be a dug well with a high stone wall around it and a drawing pulley. If the well bucket were upright, it was safe to make the contact. If it were upside down or missing, that was the signal to fade away and launch into E&E mode—escape and evasion.

"I'll look for the well," Hamilton said.

The Kiowa rose silently to run backup. Chief Adcock moved up to assume his position on point. Hamilton and Nighthorse melted into the deeper shadows beneath the trees.

Sounds carried extraordinary distances on cool, clear nights; the rooster was farther away than he sounded. From the look of the wide band of red across the eastern horizon, the sun was only minutes away from popping out like a yolk from a busted egg when the two SEALs came upon the rail fence and the well in the clearing beyond. They crouched and observed the scene for anything out of the ordinary.

The farmhouse looked exactly as it had in photos included in mission target folders—whitewashed plaster over stone walls; two stories tall; red-tiled roof. Beyond a short distance stood the stone barn and several cows peacefully chewing their cuds. The rooster crowed again, warming up to his morning duties and undoubtedly anticipating the stirring of his hens.

The well bucket was right side up, signaling the all-clear. Hamilton's sharp eyes caught movement. Someone had been sitting on the hidden downhill side of the well. That someone now rose, an indistinct form against the reddening sky, and paced idly to one side. He leaned against the well. Obviously he was waiting for someone.

Hamilton nodded at Nighthorse, who faded back into the shadows to cover with his AKMS. The lieutenant stepped out of the trees into view. The figure at the well stiffened, stood watching intently as Hamilton advanced across the rail fence.

When the SEAL officer drew near enough to discern the other man's features, he froze in his tracks, surprised to find that the other man was not a man. The woman covered the remaining distance separating them. She wore a dark sock cap over her hair, but strands of long reddish curls escaped from around it. Baggy form-concealing jeans and a loose flannel shirt completed her attire. He could tell little about her face in the dim light other than that she seemed to wear an amused expression at his befuddlement.

The woman spoke in Serbian. Hamilton turned to bring Nighthorse up to interpret. The woman smiled slightly and repeated herself in perfect American English. "What are you looking for?"

"I am looking for my cow," Hamilton said, providing the code phrase.

"We have him in our pen," she responded correctly. "Hurry. It'll soon be full light."

"Who are you?" Hamilton demanded first.

"Call me Tori."

"Are you a spook?"

"You have no need to know, Solitary Elk."

"Okay, I'll call you Tori. You call me Elk. Look, I don't know what Smith was thinking, but we weren't expecting a woman."

"Then you got better than you expected," she jousted. "You're not one of the old-fashioned types who think women should bake cookies and drop puppies every other year, are you?"

"There's nothing wrong with baking cookies."

He could see her face better now when she turned slightly toward the sunrise. It was not an exceptional face, he thought. The nose was thin and flared at the nostrils. Her mouth was full but too wide. Her eyes were the color of green seawater over sand and went with her red hair. She appeared to be rather lean and fit underneath the baggy clothes. Hamilton guessed her to be in her early thirties. She still wore that bemused expression.

"What either you or I want or expect at this point doesn't make any difference, Elk," she said. "This is what we're stuck with. You have a package for me to get out of the country. I have a new mission for you."

THE BRIEFING

It was common practice for the United States to seed CIA operatives into foreign nations in which it had, or might conceivably have in the near future, a vital national interest. The spooks were competent professionals who formed intelligence networks, built up an underground, recruited assets such as safe houses and vehicles, manufactured PSYOPS, and established transportation and communications nets. Many of the best agents were women who understood how to work themselves around men. Only Mad Dog, typically, openly expressed his reservations.

"A broad?" he questioned. "There'd be a bounty on them if it wasn't for what they got between their legs."

Immediately after the team crossed the rail fence and entered the house, two kids and another woman wearing a long loose dress drove cattle around the yard to mask any scent or sign of the SEALs' presence—a precaution that greatly satisfied Hamilton's appreciation of planning and detail.

The house was typical in style and furnishings for what might be expected of a Serbian farmhouse: a bit rustic, well-used, and comfortable. It was occupied by two young men who spoke no English. One stood watch downstairs, the other on the second floor. The SEALs, always suspicious, a quality that lent itself to survival, searched the house thoroughly to make sure there were no further surprises. A secret radio, perhaps? Chief Adcock remained at an upstairs window, glassing the surrounding countryside for signs of trackers or troops.

Tori took the pilot aside and spoke to him a few minutes in confidence. She turned to Lieutenant Hamilton when she finished.

"Captain McMasters will be leaving with Oton and Josip as soon as he eats," she directed.

"Where to?"

"Call it an underground railroad. You've done your job, Elk. He'll be safe with us. He should be back in Allied hands before dark. Better you concentrate on your next job. I'll brief your team as soon as you've eaten and rested."

Captain McMasters bade the team an emotional farewell. He embraced Preacher and said, "I'll be praying for you."

To Lieutenant Hamilton, he said, "Whoever you are, I'll never forget what you did for me."

It was in the late afternoon, after the team had eaten and taken turns sleeping on 50 percent alert, that Tori called assembly for briefing. With the sock cap gone, her hair hung long down her back and reflected copperish undertones. Something about the color of her hair and her exceptional sense of confidence on top of a wry sense of understated humor unexpectedly reminded Hamilton of Judith. Judith too had sometimes chided him because of his old-fashioned attitudes about men being protectors and leaders and clan heads. Her death at the hands of terrorists had certainly done nothing to convince him that women should be in combat situations.

Tori tapped her teeth reflectively with a pencil

eraser. "Let me fill you in briefly on the international situation," she began, but was immediately interrupted.

"What we're most interested in," Chief Adock said, "is how the Serbs knew about that culvert."

Apparently, Smith had brought Tori up to date. "After first claiming to have received a tipoff," Tori responded, "Russia is now declining to make any comment about whether it does or does not have an infiltrator in NATO supplying intelligence on troop movements and missions."

"What I mean is," came Adcock's rejoinder, "do they know about *us*?"

"Don't let that concern you. You are insulated from exposure by several layers."

Dog oozed sarcasm. "Oh? 'I'm from the government and I'm here to help you.' "

"You need to concentrate on your mission and leave everything else to us," the redhead suggested tersely.

John Nighthorse slowly lifted his eyes. "We always concentrate, lady," he said in a low, challenging tone.

Up until now, Lieutenant Hamilton had remained out of the exchange. He now cut it short. "You were about to fill us in on the international situation?"

She tossed him a grateful look. "Yes. While we're attempting to keep the Serbs and the KLA from escalating this thing into a real ground war in which Russia will join, followed undoubtedly by one country after another, U.S.

Congressmen are introducing the Kosovo Self-Defense Act, which would allocate twenty-five million dollars to train and arm the KLA. Their idea is to let the KLA defend Kosovo rather than use U.S. and NATO ground forces. It's going to be harder than ever to keep Milosevic and Radovan Kradznic apart after this. Kradznic and the KLA have started gaining confidence."

She paused to let the team digest the enormity of what she had presented. During the pause she broke out a map and spread it on the kitchen table. The SEALs gathered around.

"This," she continued, pointing with her lead pencil, "is Zepadna Morava. It's a river, not as big as the Danube, but it's flowing pretty good because of all the spring rains in the mountains."

The lead pencil shifted.

"This is the town of Krusevac. There's a wide two-lane bridge crossing the river here. Ordinarily, the KLA are fairly scattered and disorganized. However, Kradznic has assembled and moved guerrilla forces into a staging area in the mountains south of the river. We believe his plan is to force a major battle with the Serbs during which he will demand ground assistance from NATO and the U.S. The Bay of Pigs fiasco in Cuba, during which President Kennedy declined at the last minute to send reinforcements to prevent the defeat of anti-Castro invaders, may be all too real in the current president's mind. We think the president may com-

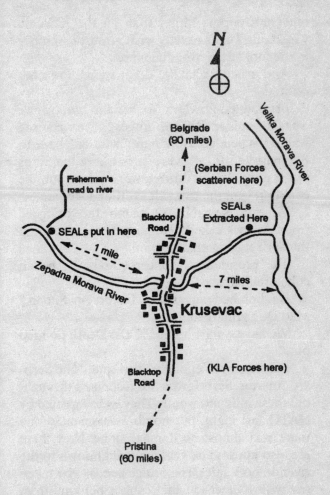

Blowing of bridge at Krusevac

mit paratroopers rather than let the KLA be wiped out. That's exactly what Kradznic wants."

She looked up from the map.

"And exactly what we don't want," Preacher offered.

Tori nodded gravely. "We send in paratroops, Yeltsin sends in Russian forces . . . you can see where it's headed. Now, here," she said, back to the map, "north of the river is where the Serbs are staging. If this bridge were taken out, we could prevent the two sides getting together."

"Why doesn't NATO bomb the bridge?" Chief Adcock asked. "Better yet, why not bomb the Serb staging area?"

"The president is concerned about civilian collateral damage."

"He bombed an aspirin factory in Sudan," Mad Dog grumbled.

"We have 'smart bombs,' " Dr. Death pointed out.

"But not smart enough," Tori said. "The Serbs are smarter. Serb forces are dispersed throughout these hills and woods. They were targeted by NATO last night, but bomb assessment shows there was almost no damage done. Now there are also houses and buildings right down to the river on both sides. The bridge needs to be taken out with a precision that cannot be done from the air without taking a chance on killing the populace. That's where Deep Water begins. It's up to you to take it out. I understand you are experts at demolitions, among other things."

Hamilton decided she looked better when she smiled.

"When?" he asked.

"Tonight. We've assembled a target folder with maps and charts and both aerial and ground photos. We have access to a certain number of assets. Work up a mission operations order and let me know what you need as soon as you can. Gentlemen, the KLA is patrolling one side of the river, the Serbs are on the other bank. You're right in the middle of them. If we can blow up that bridge, it'll delay the battle and give NATO more time—days, maybe even weeks—to bring Milosevic down and avoid the possibility of another world war."

THE TARGET FOLDER

There were topo maps of Krusevac showing a highway running through the town and down and around a covey of small house-dotted hills to the bridge. What appeared to be amateur snapshots showed the bridge and surrounding terrain, while aerial satellite photos provided amazing detail from the air. Tori remained at the table to answer questions.

"We've mustered a half-dozen military satellites to serve over Yugoslavia," she explained. "We've also found the U.S. Lacrosse satellite and the U.S. Landsat system useful."

Space spying got its start in 1960 with a 300-

pound U.S. satellite that took photographs of the Soviet Union, then returned from orbit with exposed rolls of film for a parachute descent to a recovery plane waiting below. Since then, the eyes of space had acquired far sharper senses and shifted to electronic imaging systems that could be downlinked instantly to receivers on earth. Apparently, that was how Tori had acquired these images.

"These pictures are from yesterday afternoon," she said, confirming Chief Adcock's speculation that the CIA had set up a secret and sophisticated ops center somewhere in the mountains. "Here you see a KLA staging area south of Krusevac. Those are old Soviet tanks, Chinese armored cars, and that's a U.S. 105mm Howitzer, Vietnam surplus."

"Fairly well armed," Lt. Hamilton observed.

"Bits and pieces," Tori said, tapping her pencil. "More and more small arms are coming in from China and Iran. The KLA wants U.S. armor and artillery from the Self-Defense Act."

"They're staging right out in the open," Nighthorse noticed.

"That's because NATO owns the skies and we only bomb the Serbs at this point," Tori said.

Aerial images of the north side of the river showed what appeared to be several noncamouflaged Russian tanks. Lieutenant Hamilton studied them closely before determining they were probably masqueraders set out as decoys to attract bombs away from actual targets. It was amazing, he thought, even scary, what governments could do with satellites on the eve of the twenty-first century. It was almost impossible to hide anything on earth, at least for long. Countries spying on each other, eavesdropping on radio communications, probing through clouds with radar, monitoring emanations of heat to indicate missile launches or even population concentrations . . .

But, of course, he thought wryly, there was also satellite television. Two hundred seventy-seven channels and nothing on.

Topos revealed how the river made a wide curve southeast, underneath the bridge and past Krusevac, before turning back northeast and flowing into another river, the Velika Morava. It was a relatively fast river with sharp, swift bends and twists. It would be a strong river now from high snow meltoffs in the mountains and recent rains. Hamilton conferred with Tori on transportation.

"It won't be the high tech you're accustomed to." She smiled. "Remember, you've faded to black. Your presence cannot be known. But we'll get you there and we'll get you out."

Preacher Hodges closely examined the shots of the bridge from the viewpoint of a demolitioneer. A pedestrian in one of the photos provided perspective. The bridge appeared to be constructed of reinforced concrete. It spanned about one hundred feet of river, was roughly twenty feet wide, and rested on massive concrete piers fully six feet in thickness and as wide as the bridge itself. It would take a B-52 full of 500-pounders to breach those pillars.

His long face dark and soulful, as though concentrating on palpating for weaknesses and points of greatest stress, he turned his attention to photos disclosing the underside of the bridge and its latticework of steel supporting girders. He had parachuted in with two MK-138 explosive packs designed especially for underwater demolitions. Each canvas pack contained ten two-and-a-half-pound Mark 35 charges of C4 plastic explosive, detonating cord, electrical and nonelectrical blasting caps, fuse igniters, crimpers, clothespins, and other tools of the trade, modified to fit his anticipated needs. From memory he quickly worked out a tentative formula based on material and tamping factors—$N = W/2R$.

Dog watched him. "Superheroes to save the world," he chided.

"Only the Second Coming will save the world," murmured Preacher in his solemn, distracted manner.

"Yes," Dog agreed. "Jesus is coming again— and, boy, is He pissed off."

"Can you do it, Preacher?" Lieutenant Hamilton asked.

"Here," Preacher said, pointing, "where the girders V and intersect. Charges placed in the junctures will direct most of their energy into the steel on either side. I can drop these large sections of the bridge directly into the river."

He looked up, his expression unchanged.
"All you have to do is get me there."

THE PREPARATION

Shortly after nightfall an ancient farm truck
rattled up in front of the safe house. It had tall
wooden-slatted sideboards with a scrap of canvas stretched over to provide some shelter for

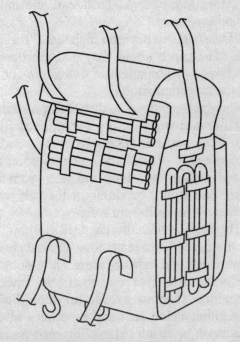

MK-138 explosive pack

its load of grunting, squealing hogs. The stench of the animals hovered over it like a noxious cloud. The driver, an elderly farmer wearing a straw hat and gnawing on a bread roll, went to the back of the vehicle and removed an end panel to reveal a dark crawl space hidden in the bed of the truck, directly underneath the swine.

Tori smiled, amused. "Gentlemen, your carriage."

The SEALs stared. Mad Dog balked. "What the fuck are we—pigs?"

"More likely asses," Dr. Death murmured in his hollow voice.

"I warned you it wasn't high tech," Tori chuckled. "The trip is about sixty miles through Serb territory—so you might as well get in and make yourselves comfortable."

She had wrapped a dirty scarf around her head and changed into a faded, patched dress that hung past her ankles. Rubbing wood ashes into the skin of her face accentuated lines and pores, making her look old and worn in the dark. She would be riding in the cab with the farmer, as his well-used wife.

The SEALs had also changed clothing, giving up their BDUs for jeans, long-sleeved chambray work shirts and light sneakers. They would be in the water much of the night. All other gear, including weapons except for their holstered P5K submachine guns and Preacher's satchel of explosives, were left behind. Tori promised everything would be returned to them upon extraction from Operation Deep Water. Dr. Death objected to parting with his Haskins 50-caliber rifle.

"I'm sure it's the only rifle of its sort in this country. I'll be needing it."

"I understand," Tori reassured him, turning away from his unblinking eyes with an inward shudder. This man seemed to exude death. "It'll be safe."

After some hesitation, the team steeled its resolve—for God and country—and squeezed into the crawlpace beneath the pigs, for all the world like sardines in a flat tin. Pig hooves rattled clacking noises above them. Liquid stench seeped down through cracks. Dog gasped in disgust. "Pig shit!"

They shifted around trying to find some comfort but ended up with sneakers in each other's faces, crammed so tightly together the movement of one required the dislocation of all. The farmer wordlessly replaced the end panel, trapping the men in total darkness and suffocating odor. They heard him smearing waste on the door panel to hide its presence. Tori's voice came from nearby.

"No more talking once we start," she said, "unless it's in squeals and grunts."

She laughed softly as she walked away.

"She's *enjoying* this," Chief Adcock growled.

Truck doors opened and slammed. The motor started. The truck lurched forward, throwing the pigs toward the tailgate. They recovered with tapping hooves and squeals of protest.

Lieutenant Hamilton had to chuckle to himself in spite of his discomfort. While all manners of assets were available to naval SpecWar groups—jets, helicopters, armored vehicles, automobiles, ships, submarines, SEAL delivery vehicles, SDVs—what made the SEALs really unique were the men. They were selected and trained to be independent thinkers, resourceful, and, most of all, adaptable. Jumping from perfectly good airplanes in flight or locking out of subs underwater was old hat. Being delivered on a mission in a load of pigs—*that* was being adaptable.

Oh, well. The only easy day was yesterday.

All the shocks on the truck must have worn out. It was rough riding on rougher roads. Although they were somewhat cushioned by being packed in so tightly, it was still a miserable ride in the dark. Every time they hit a pot hole, which was frequently, more pig shit dribbled down through the cracks on top of them until their clothing was soiled with filth. Mad Dog cursed and fumed inside his head. Dr. Death and Preacher endured it in typical stoic style. The worst part of it for Lieutenant Hamilton was having to give up control and depend upon someone he hardly knew to deliver them where they needed to go. It was like his SEALs were for all the world like a . . . like a load of pigs.

On the other hand, he reasoned, he often had to depend upon pilots and ship captains, whom he also hardly knew, to deliver them where they needed to go.

Prior to departing the safe house, they had traced out their route on a map and committed it to memory in the event something unexpected occurred en route. Hamilton kept track of where they were at any particular minute by timing their progress. By his calculations, they were more than halfway through the journey, uneventful so far, when the truck began braking. Hamilton tensed as the truck came to a halt with its engine roughly idling. The pigs grunted inquiringly. At least they could *see* what was going on, while the miserable cargo in the crawl space could only guess and depend on their hearing.

The engine died with a shudder and a sputter. A voice barked a command. Truck doors opened as the farmer and Tori got out. The resulting exchange was all in Serbian, so that only John Nighthorse understood. He stiffened, a tension that transmitted itself to his teammates. They had encountered a Serbian army roadblock.

Footsteps crunched on the road. Hamilton had his short submachine gun underneath his chin with his finger on the trigger, muzzle covering where the end panel would be removed if they were discovered. Hardly anyone dared breathe. Even the pigs went quiet except for an occasional interrogatory sound.

Tori spoke rapidly in a scolding tone, transmitting her impatience, indignation, and weariness. Whoever detained them had a flashlight. Glittering needles of light penetrated painfully into their hiding hole. A man's voice, as impatient as Tori's, gruffed back at her. She fell abruptly mute.

The footsteps approached the back of the truck.

"Phew!" That was decipherable in any language.

Preacher closed his eyes. Dr. Death's snake eyes almost glowed, catching a thin beam from the flashlight. Chief Adcock was afraid his legs had gone to sleep and he would be unable to react. Mad Dog sifted through options. Nighthorse listened.

The soldier rattled the sideboards. Pigs squealed in alarm and rushed to the other side of the truck. The soldier barked a question. Tori's reply came softer than before, conciliatory.

Their conversation lasted all of thirty seconds. Questioning by the soldier. Soft, confident answers by the farmer's wife. Voices and footfalls drifted back toward the front of the truck. Silence. Hamilton wondered if they were going to be detained. He had about decided they were when he heard more crunching steps. Truck doors opened and slammed. The engine started and the truck pulled slowly ahead. The truck resumed speed.

Even Mad Dog felt so relieved that he almost

appreciated having pig shit drip down on top of them.

THE MISSION

Sometime later the truck slowed again and turned onto a side road with even more pot holes and ruts than before. The crammed-in SEALs had it easier than the swine, judging from the volume of protest. So much for a clandestine approach. The truck stopped. The engine died. The pigs calmed. Someone fumbled at the rear panel.

"It's me," Tori said. "Last stop—Santa Fe, Albuquerque, and points south."

Judith had had a sense of humor under pressure.

SEALs scrambled from the crawl space and automatically formed a quick defensive perimeter even before stretching the stiffness from their bones. They were in dark woods. Hamilton smelled the river and heard its faint murmur and the lulling croon of frogs.

Without waste of time or unnecessary discussion, bicycle inner tubes, one for each man, were retrieved from behind the truck seat and quickly inflated with a small hand pump. So much for high tech. Preacher hoisted his canvas satchel over his shoulder by its carrying strap. They quietly set out for the river along a fisherman's path, carrying the inner tubes.

"They won't have to hear us coming," Dog complained. "They can *smell* us."

"The river'll wash it off," Preacher said.

Hamilton lingered behind a moment to speak to Tori. "What was with the stop on the road?"

"A checkpoint. We persuaded them we were pig farmers moving our crop to market."

He wrinkled his nose. "Wonder what finally convinced them."

She laughed softly and touched his arm with her fingertips. "You've watched me all day," she said. "I kept thinking I reminded you of someone."

That caught him by surprise. "It doesn't matter." He would never see her again anyhow.

"I suppose it doesn't. Well . . . Good luck, Elk."

"Jeb," he said, and left it at that.

"Good luck, Jeb," she said.

The river was so wide at the point they entered it, bellying down noiselessly into it like salamanders, that the inkline mark of the opposite bank was barely visible. No lights burned on either side of the river. North and deeper into the mountains, flashes like heat lightning marked where NATO was commencing its fourth night of air raids on Serb targets.

The water was cold but not unbearable as they pushed into the current. The inner tubes were sufficient to keep them afloat as they hugged the shadows of the near bank, only their heads showing above water. The bridge silhouette came suddenly into view as they rounded a bend in the river. It rose high over the surface of the river, providing a clearance of perhaps thirty feet, the height of a three-story building.

On prearranged signals, Chief Adcock and Dr. Death began stroking across the river to secure the bridge's south end, using the drift of the current to assist them. They were the team's strongest swimmers. There was no moon yet; they quickly disappeared into the darkness and rush of the stream.

Nighthorse and the lieutenant would secure the bridge's north end. They let the flow of water carry them on down. Mad Dog the mountaineer and Preacher broke off toward the bridge's first support column. Dog was an agile man capable of climbing like an ape; he would be of invaluable assistance to Preacher swinging among the bridge girders to lay charges. Floating the heavy load of explosives between them, they pushed it toward the target. Water hissed around the base of the pillars as they drew near.

There were buildings on both sides of the stream, all blacked-out against the threat night brought from the skies. Canines yapped at each other from bank to bank, carrying the ethnic feud down to basic levels. Otherwise, silence prevailed except for the mutter of the river and the slight ripple Preacher and Dog made as they maneuvered into the greater shadows underneath the bridge and tethered their inner tubes.

The vertical concrete columns were impossible

to scale. Preacher felt for the steel I-beam support braces that ran at angles from the bottom of the elevated roadbed to near where the bridge attached to land. When he found the nearest one, he swung up on it out of the current. He rested for a second, then monkeyed a ways up the forty-five-degree incline of the steel brace. It required unencumbered hands and feet to execute the maneuver without losing grip and falling back into the water, the splash of which was bound to alert sentries who might be stationed on either end of the bridge. Water draining off his body sounded like cave drip striking the river below.

Dog swung easily out of the river with the heavy demolitions haversack anchored to his back. Preacher reached to take it, but Dog indicated it was safe with him.

One behind the other, in darkness so dense they might was as well have been blind, they ascended into the tangle of steel. The river had been cold and the night was cool with breeze, but they were soon sweating. Preacher checked the glowing face of his watch. They had twenty minutes to set the charges before the team reassembled in midstream to initiate their exit and escape plan. He immediately went to work.

The bridge's stringers—longitudinal strength members—were also steel I-beam girders. There were five of them with about four feet of space between each. Attached to them were vertical straps about two feet high. Flanges extended two to three inches on either side of the straps.

These five stringers, their attached support, and a set of monster concrete piers held up nearly a foot of steel-reinforced concrete roadbed.

"It looks like it would be easier to reroute the river through Belgrade than to destroy this bastard," Dog whispered to Preacher.

"Nobody said it had to be easy."

Preacher had already decided where to make the cut. It didn't take much demo to do a job if you did it right. Old railroad men used to cut track with what they called a twister. It was like putting on a pair of earmuffs, crooked. One muff covered the front part of one ear, offset by the other which covered the back part of the opposite ear. The force of the detonations pushed right past each other and sheared the rail cleanly. The British used the technique to cut down the bridge over the River Kwai.

The darkness was so nearly complete they had to feel their way through the girders, depending on Preacher's having memorized the photos. They made their way to the first concrete pier, crawling belly against the girders and pulling themselves along with their arms.

"We're in luck," Preacher muttered. "I can divide the Charlie-4 to set twisters on each of these two girders and run the charges diagonally so the torque will twist the span off its foundations and right into the drink."

"That's easy?" Dog asked.

"Theoretically."

"Theoretically?"

"Open that bag and start passing the Play Doh."

The explosive was the texture of vanilla fudge. Dog recalled stories his dad's buddies told about how grunts in Vietnam pinched off small bits of it to make a hot fire over which to heat their canteen cup coffee. Plastic C4 would burn and not explode without the addition of a concussion. Dog knew an old SEAL at Little Creek who had no toes on his left foot. He had attempted to stomp out a C4 coffee fire.

Dog handed the cakes of plastic to Preacher, who worked quickly but exactly, molding ear muffs into the girders, holding them in place with duct tape. When he finished, he had four sets of charges.

From a roll, he secured the ends of detonating cord into each of the charges, again using duct tape to keep the cord from being jerked loose. He cut the cord with crimpers to lay out twin detonating cord ring mains for the nonelectric dual firing system he was building. He slipped the crimpers into his back jeans pocket. Although he was sweating, he shivered in his wet clothing from the breeze that played whining among the girders.

"Okay," he said. "Back the way we came, playing out the det cord and taping it to the girders as we go. You take the left one. I'll take the other. We still got ten minutes."

So far, no sounds had come from either end of the bridge.

Any noise they made was covered by that of the river rushing below. Preacher had to remind himself that it was nearly three stories down. If he or Dog slipped off the girders, the splash he made would be like that of a falling boulder, a sound sure to alert either the Serbs or KLA scouts. He wished he were as agile as Dog, who even in the dark swung from one steel to the other on his long arms like a great ape brachiating in the rain forest. The man was a hell of an operator for all his cynicism and outspoken opinions about everything.

Preacher's mind wandered, but only for an instant. Tears had come to Lateisha's eyes when he told her he would be gone again. She asked no questions about where, or how long, being the good SEAL wife. Maybe after this ops was over, Preacher speculated, he would leave the Navy and take that position offered him in Georgia as pastor of God's Grace Holiness Church. There were ways to serve God other than fighting evil hand to hand. Besides, in these strange days, it was getting harder and harder to discern between various evils. He truly believed they were living in the Last Days when Satan ruled the earth. Lateisha would be overjoyed if he quit. She always said she wanted their three daughters to grow up knowing their father other than from photos of him in his Navy uniform.

All this went through his mind with the speed of an electric spark. Then he was all focus and concentration again. He and Dog played out the det cord on the downward angle to where they had climbed up out of the river on the steel brace. Preacher took the two ends of the ring mains.

"Fuse," he said.

Whereas det cord burned so rapidly it was like part of the explosion—a length of it wrapped around a tree would fell it—time fuse, or primer cord, was supposed to burn about a foot a minute. Preacher tucked the two ends of the ring main det cord into his belt to hold them while he unreeled approximately ten minutes' worth of fuse. One arm's length measured from the center of the chest was roughly three feet, or three minutes' worth. He made sure both pieces were precisely the same length in order that all charges would explode simultaneously.

"Blasting cap."

He slid one end of the det cord and an end of the primer fuse into either end of a blasting cap and reached to his back pocket for the crimpers.

"*Tanks!*" Mad Dog hissed.

He heard them then. On the northern bank. A low, chilling rumbling sound like mechanical monsters emerging from the center of the earth. Serb tanks preparing to cross over on the bridge. Perhaps there had been activity over there all along, except he and Dog had been so concentrated on their job they had failed to notice. Awareness added urgency to their efforts.

Awareness was immediately followed by the magnified cloth-ripping burst from one of the little submachine guns the SEALs carried. Because of the darkness and the way it isolated, Preacher had lost his perspective on distance. He and Dog were in fact only mere yards away from the north shore. The submachine gun shredded darkness, muzzle flickering, almost within reach, it seemed, of where they worked to add the finishing touches to their charges.

They hadn't the leisure to figure it out tactically. They had their own job to do.

Lieutenant Hamilton and John Nighthorse had waited to open fire until they had no other choice. The Serbs had been moving up to their end of the bridge when the two SEALs slithered out of the river and crawled up to the road. They heard the tanks further away on a hillside. Out ahead of the tanks a platoon of infantry worked its way almost up to the bridge, then stalled for some reason—perhaps waiting for the tanks to catch up.

Once the infantry resumed movement, sending out an advance squad to secure the bridge, Hamilton made up his mind. He checked his watch. Five more minutes and Preacher should have the bridge wired. They could sow enough confusion to hold out that long. He notified Nighthorse of his intentions before unleashing a quick burst over the heads of the advancing patrol. The Serbs hit the dirt and ducked for cover.

Hell broke loose, not only from the Serb side of the river, but from *both* sides. Each camp apparently assumed it was being attacked by the other. Streams of tracer fire crisscrossed on top of the bridge, under and around it, bouncing and ricocheting in a crazy-quilt pattern and joining four times as many invisible rounds in a giant buzzing hornets' nest. Machine guns opening up in short stuttering bursts on both banks sent bright green tracers vaulting across the river.

The SEALs found themselves at the center of the maelstrom, caught in the crossfire and open to both sides. Dog and Preacher, trapped in the bridge girders, were especially vulnerable. Fire spanged against the girders and ricocheted in amazing patterns. If a bullet struck one of the charges . . .

After a moment of hesitation, Preacher returned to his work, not exactly oblivious of the firefight, but simply choosing to ignore the danger in order to complete his mission. His hands were cold and stiff from the water, cut and scraped from climbing around in the steel. He felt for the right place to crimp the blasting cap to join the det cord and primer fuse. Crimp the treacherous little thing too far *from* the open end and it might go off, too far *toward* the open end, and it might be crimped too loosely, allowing it to fall off or fail to detonate at the right time.

He found the right place and moved the

crimpers, the cap, and the cord down and away behind his best natural blast absorber, the cheeks of his ass. It was a useless gesture and he knew it, but somehow it felt better and it was habit. He had already attached the other end of the cap to the det cord and the det cord to the charges. If the cap went, so did the C4. *Nearer my God to Thee . . .* It was not good technique, but they were not working under ideal conditions.

A tank's main gun opened fire with a giant, shattering crack and a muzzle flash that, even from the distance, opened a momentary window to the night. It cracked twice more in rapid sequence. Three high-velocity rounds marked by green tracers sliced over the bridge. The muffled thump of explosions drifted across the river from the KLA side.

Preacher considered shortening the time fuse, then left it alone. The SEALs needed at least those ten minutes to make their escape. Neither side should be able to cross the bridge in so short a time period.

Numbed fingers fumbled with the little plier-tool crimpers. Dog felt the demolitioneer suddenly freeze.

"What is it?" Dog demanded.

"I dropped it. I dropped the crimpers."

"Now what?"

Preacher hesitated. "Old railroaders used to call it jawboning. Hand me another cap."

"Ho-ly shit!"

Preacher inserted the primer fuse into the shiny cap and stared at it, although he could not see it in the darkness. A green streak zipped between the two men. At Demo School, the instructor had placed a blasting cap inside a softball and lit it off. The explosion busted the ball and slung scraps of it all over the place. That could have been, he said, teeth, eyeballs, and face.

I want to go to Heaven, Lord, but not now . . .

He searched the cap gingerly with his teeth for the right place to crimp it. It felt as huge as a diving air tank stuffed into his mouth. His teeth found the rim. He slid it a minute distance out. Then he bit, slowly tightening his teeth until they ached. It tasted like aluminum.

He eased the cap out of his mouth and tested it. It was securely fastened. Dog seemed to be leaning away, his face averted.

"Want to give it a try, Dog?" Preacher asked, a rare joke for him.

"This what you Ne-groes call black humor? One lunatic is enough on this work party."

"Want to watch me do it again?"

This was the big one—attaching the time fuse and cap to the end of the det cord. If the cap exploded in his mouth, the C-4 went immediately afterward, taking both SEALs with it.

Preacher repeated the procedure. Dog held his breath, unmoving amid the mass of green supersonic fireflies shrieking about their heads.

"Okay," Preacher said. "Give me another cap."

He attached the second cap to the other det cord and time fuse the same way.

"Whew!" he said.

"We made it?" Dog asked.

"We made it."

On the bitter ends of the primer fuse he appended fuse ignitors and taped them together so they could be set off together. The two SEALs then played the lines down the bridge brace until their sneakers touched water. Dog used more duct tape to secure the ignitors to the steel. Preacher checked his watch. Everything was on go!

The flurry of initial shooting was gradually dwindling into a deliberate, measured duel across the water. Single rifle shots and bursts from machine guns erupted in random sequence. Neither Preacher nor Dog had heard American submachine gunfire since the opening round. Their guys were keeping their heads down. It was unlikely either side was even aware of the SEALs' presence.

"Preacher?" called a voice from the black water.

"Here."

Dog and Preacher joined the lieutenant and Nighthorse in the river, finding their inner tubes where they had tethered them. They held onto the bridge and treaded water against the current, waiting for the last two members of the team.

"What happened over there when the proverbial doo-doo struck the proverbial oscillator?" Dog inquired.

"They were starting across," Hamilton said. "How much time do we have, Preacher?"

"Ten minutes when I hit the ignitors."

"Then hit them," came a voice as Chief Adcock and Dr. Death rejoined the group.

"Stay together for the extraction," the Skipper cautioned.

They let go the bridge. The current was relatively swift in the narrows across which the bridge was built. It caught them on their bicycle inner tubes and swept them downstream. Behind them, the firefight continued in reduced mode. A parachute flare shot into the sky illuminated the bridge in an eerie liquid light, but by that time the river had already carried the infiltrators out of danger.

Within the ten minutes Preacher's fuse allotted them, they were almost a mile downstream and around several bends of the river.

"It hasn't gone off," Nighthorse worried.

"It will," Preacher said.

It went with a brilliant flash of light, like a lightning strike. Soon afterward the thunder of the explosion reverberated downstream, rippling the water and vibrating in the air and in their bodies.

"The world is safe for a few more days," Dog

quipped with sarcasm as ripe as the odor of the river.

POST-MISSION

The UH-1 Huey helicopter skimmed the river's surface, air-skidding around bends and following the stream in a dizzying carnival ride for Martin Smith, who rode alone in the troop compartment with both doors open. The Huey was small, quick, and so generic in the post-Vietnam era that many nations, including Serbia, owned and operated them. If one without markings were to crash, it could never be traced to a particular country. The two pilots forward were nonmilitary "company" workers, their clothing devoid of all markings and as generic as the bird they flew.

"There they are!" Smith piped through his helmet intercom.

Dit-dit! Two red flashes from the middle of the river. Smith replied in kind, adding a *dot. Dit-dit-dot!* The six Americans in the drink locked into each other's arms to prevent being separated by rotor wash as the small bird reined in and hovered above them like a windy black cloud.

Smith tossed a line and reeled the men in with a winch while the Huey hovered with its skids slapping the surface of the river. Within seconds, all "fish" were aboard. Smith tossed them wool blankets to wrap themselves in. Their teeth were chattering. The helicopter nosed down and shoved in full throttle, returning downriver, then taking to a valley that headed easternly toward Romania, flying underneath Milosevic's radar.

"What's your scrawny professional ass doing away from a desk?" Mad Dog asked Smith.

"I wanted to see how the other half lives," Smith said, unoffended. "Hold on to your jock straps. It's a wild ride, but we'll be over the border and into Romania in twenty minutes."

THE REPORT

Martin Smith held the team debriefing in a room of a remote police outpost not far inside Romania from the Serbian border. Satellite surveillance had confirmed that a large chunk of the Krusevac bridge had been dropped into the Zepadna Morava, thereby delaying a clash between Milosevic's forces and Kradznic's KLA rebels. Serbia was blaming the bridge on KLA saboteurs; Kradznic claimed his forces were prepared to defend the homeland and that the bridge must have been targeted by NATO bombers.

"Captain McMasters is safe in the United States," Smith reported to the team. "He's been debriefed to say nothing to no one, not even the president of the United States, on how he was rescued or who rescued him. Not that he ever really knew."

Lieutenant Hamilton's brow furrowed. He thought it odd that the president would be out of the loop, but he said nothing.

"He's being feted and dined as a national hero," Smith went on. "The president will receive him at the White House this week."

"He'll be the only hero to pass through the White House under this administration," groused Mad Dog, who never let up.

Smith chuckled drily. "Milosevic is stewing over how the rescue was accomplished, snatching the pilot literally out of his hands. From what we gather, he thinks the rescue was conducted by anti-Milosevic Serbian elements. You men did a good job."

He paused to change directions.

"As for the bridge—another good mission accomplished. There are reports of light casualties on both sides."

"None inflicted by us this time," Lieutenant Hamilton pointed out.

"Unless some of those poor souls were on the bridge when it blew," Preacher commented. "I'll pray for their souls."

"You do that," Smith said. "You have twelve hours. Eat and catch up on your sleep. I'd like to give you more time, but things are speeding up out there. Russia may be mobilizing troops. Yeltsin has filed a resolution in the United Nations calling for an end to NATO bombing. The UN is debating right now on whether to indict Milosevic and his top aides and generals for war crimes. Your job is not over in No Man's Land. We have to keep hammering until Milosevic is brought to his knees."

Mad Dog shook his head over an old saying from Vietnam: "We have to destroy the village in order to save it."

Smith looked at the big man. "Something like that," he acknowledged.

Dr. Death paused in cleaning the Haskins that had been returned with the other gear left behind at what the team now referred to as the "pig farm." As usual, he had little to say.

"We've utilized Preacher Hodges' special talents at the bridge," he said in that voice so without inflection that it could have come from a corpse. "When will we have use for mine?"

These were odd men, Smith thought to himself as his eyes took them in, but truly they were also special men. They probably should be locked up during peacetime and only let out when there was a war.

Perhaps they were.

"There will be a time," Smith promised Dr. Death. "Soon."

4: SNOW FIELD

PRE-MISSION

By 1000 hours of the beginning of the fifth day of
Operation Allied Force, the air war against Serbia that was not being called a war, the SEALs of
No Man's Land had risen, showered, and break-
fasted at the police outpost in Romania. All felt
rested and renewed from the rigors of the past
few days operating inside Yugoslavia. The police
post had a gym of sorts. Lieutenant Hamilton led
his men in a rigorous workout on a worn heavy
punching bag and a partial set of rusted weights,
followed by karate sparring bouts during which
each man went at least six two-minute rounds. A
SEAL had to stay in shape.

They were just finishing up, all of them dripping with sweat and the black hair on Mad
Dog's bare back matted down like a wet ter-
rier's, when Smith the spook entered the gym.
Dog looked up. A challenging grin crossed his
broad face.

"*Doctor* Smith," he greeted. "You got here just in time. How about going a couple of rounds?"

Smith smiled. "Do I look suicidal?"

"Actually . . ." Dog drew out the word into a pause, still wearing the sarcastic grin. "Actually . . . you look chickenshit."

Smith blanched, but otherwise retained his composure. Lieutenant Hamilton started to intervene, then decided to let the challenge ride. Might as well find out now what Smith was made of; he had, in a way, become part of the team. The rest of the SEALs slowly gathered round, silent and curious about how the spook would react.

"Surely you can take on a man with only one nut," Dog chided.

The young agent calmly searched the circle of expressionless faces. Finding no honorable way out, he shrugged noncommittally, and wordlessly began removing his shoes, socks, and sports shirt. He was lean and wiry with thick, muscular shoulders. Dog outweighed him by at least fifty pounds.

"I'm too big for you," Dog conceded reluctantly. "Why don't you take on Nighthorse or the Preacher instead?"

"*You* extended the invitation, Boats," Smith said, smiling a little himself now.

Dog bark-laughed in that humorless way of his. "It's your funeral, professor. The rules are: Use open hands and pull your punches and kicks by at least half."

They squared themselves off on the mat in the center of the floor. Dog seemed a bit disconcerted by the spook's cheerfulness.

"Let the games begin, sir," Smith said.

They felt each other out with left jabs and quick front kicks, circling like wary game cocks. Smith proved to be surprisingly nimble on his feet; he had quick reflexes and an adequate defense. Chief Adcock looked impressed.

Dog scored first. He feinted with a left jab and followed with a blazing right cross. It caught the Casper a ringing blow on the left cheek. He faded out and to his right in time to block a strong flurry of round kicks by his smaller opponent.

With a bellowing *Ki'Y!*, he closed in on Smith, attacking with a flying spinning round kick that could have near-decapitated an enemy had it connected and had Dog not pulled its power.

Instead of scoring the point as he expected, however, and landing on his feet prepared to finish the fight, he fell flat on his back, the result of Smith having countered with a feint and a left leg sweep. A look of astonishment took the place of the contemptuous sneer he had started with. John Nighthorse whooped in surprise and appreciation. Lieutenant Hamilton grinned.

Dog arched his back and vaulted in one movement back onto his bare feet. He closed in on Smith, only with more respect now. In a *real* fight, it was evident Dog would have disabled, even slain, the agent. Nonetheless, Smith proved himself to be no slouch. He was a competent martial artist capable of holding his own against anyone short of a trained SpecOp SEAL who depended on such deadly skills for his survival. Smith's stock suddenly went up in the eyes of the SEALs, especially in Dog's. Dog grinned broadly, genuinely, when the round ended with Smith still on his feet.

"Smith!" he roared. "You, sir, are no chicken-shit after all."

"You're not so bad yourself, Bos'n Gavlik, for a one-balled man."

He sobered as he wiped sweat from his face with a towel.

"Mission briefing in one hour, men," he announced. "The band plays on."

THE BRIEFING

"Here's the skinny," Smith said, once more the physics professor lecturing. "U.S. Congress is coming close to passing the Kosovo Self-Defense Act authorizing the United States to supply arms to the KLA. The president can go either way—"

"—because *he's* chickenshit," Dog opined with acerbic conviction.

Smith went on. "Italian and Czech authorities have come up with good evidence showing KLA connections to weapons and narcotics trafficking with Arab hostiles and China. It's being suppressed in Washington in order not to sour the American public against the air war on Milosevic. It's going to blow Washington wide open if we arm and equip the KLA and *then* it comes out about this narcotics trade."

Lieutenant Hamilton held up a hand to stop Smith. Something about all this troubled him. He racked his brain for words to spell out his as-yet-unformed misgivings.

"I'm trying to get this straight," he said. "I know it's up to you civilians to handle the politics of war, the military being simply one arm of diplomacy and all that. But it seems to me that the U.S. government is split wide open on how to conduct this campaign. While the White House is bombing Serbia, Congress is trying to pull the rug out from underneath the president and arm the KLA to fight their own war. The Pentagon wants to go in with guns blazing and the Eighty-Second Airborne Division. I take it No Man's Land is a CIA ops. Where does this leave *us*? In the middle?"

Smith held fire for a long few seconds. Then he responded in a crisp voice. "No Man's Land was assigned to make sure this war is cut short and does not end up in World War III."

"Does Congress know about No Man's Land?" Hamilton asked bluntly. "Does the president?"

"I hope not," Dog interjected before Smith had a chance to speak. "If they know, you might as well tell the press because everybody's gonna know and Russia won't need a spy in NATO. The president would gladly trade us for"—his voice lowered mockingly—"the 'peace process.'"

Smith took a deep breath. He reminded Hamilton of a professor being challenged by some bright but obnoxious student in the front row who reverts to authority when persuasion fails.

"You are covered through the Defense Department," he said vaguely. "That's all you as soldiers need to know."

Hamilton withdrew, although he was still puzzled. A military man's duty was to follow *lawful* orders.

Smith, satisfied, returned to the mission briefing.

"Your team, Lieutenant Hamilton, is being reinserted immediately on Snow Field. Tonight. The Czechs snatched a drug runner from Iran on his way to Bulgaria and then into Serbia. He's talking. This seems to be sound intelligence. According to him, the drugs-for-arms trade works through Saudi billionaire terrorist Osama bin Laden. Terrorists supply heroin and cocaine to the KLA. The KLA funnels it to America, the 'Great White Satan,' then uses money from the drugs to buy arms through Iran and China."

"Where do we come into the equation?" Chief Adcock wanted to know.

"I'm getting to that. There's going to be a big exchange of 'snow' and money tonight between bin Laden suppliers and representatives of the KLA."

"Where?" Hamilton asked.

"Just inside the Serbian border."

"I suspect we're going to be there?"

"You'll not only bust up the exchange, you'll take photographs and samples as proof positive of KLA complicity in drug running. Along with Italian and Czech evidence, that should be enough to persuade Congress that arming the KLA is a bad deal."

"One more step," Nighthorse said.

"Yes," the spook said. "One more step in shortening the war."

THE TARGET FOLDER

The drug-money exchange was supposed to take place on a flat mountain top ten miles up the Timok River from where it junctioned with the Danube in the tricountry border region of Serbia, Romania, and Bulgaria. Terrorist drug runners would arrive on the mountain by helicopter at 0200 hours, to be met by a KLA patrol. Flying this region underneath the radar curtain was relatively easy, as the SEALs had already discovered in their chopper extraction from the Zepadna Morava after the bridge.

Satellite photographs revealed the general terrain: rugged country. Topographical maps showed all contour lines converging into a near-solid line running adjacent to the Timok River at the base of the mountain. The solid line encompassed three sides of the mountain.

An asset, Smith said, would show them the way.

"An asset?" Hamilton inquired suspiciously.

"Call him Rashish."

"The captured dope runner?" Chief Adcock guessed.

"He's the best we have."

Lieutenant Hamilton looked at the map. "Why do we need a guide? Locating that mountain is like finding Denver on U.S. 40."

"You'll need him for on top of the mountain. There's a small clearing where the meeting will take place. He can't find it on the map or photos, but he knows how to take you there."

Mad Dog groaned. "Another ride in a pig truck."

Rashish was escorted into the room. He reminded Hamilton of a swarthy rat out of a kids' cartoon. Quick paws, sharp face, twisted mustache and dark beady eyes. The lieutenant immediately distrusted him.

"Better tie a rope around his neck and stuff some C4 in his pockets," Preacher suggested.

"What about his soul?" Dog teased.

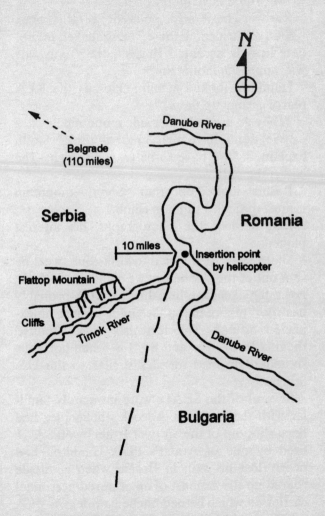

Ambush of KLA/Terrorists
at Cocaine Exchange

"May God have mercy on it."

Rashish hesitantly pointed to the map. "You . . . must climb there," he squeaked in broken, heavily accented English. "It is only one way approach mountain."

Hamilton looked at him. "How is the KLA patrol getting up there?"

"They go around other side mountain."

"We don't have that kind of time," Smith explained. "We have to be on top tonight. The cliff is the only way."

Rashish looked uncertain. "She the mountain is most difficult I think to climb."

Dog studied the photographs, his interest piqued.

Smith said, "If we tried to air-assault, we'd be shot out of the sky before we could reach them. For a big exchange like this the KLA probably has the mountaintop secured against unexpected aircraft. The terrorists have supplied them with SA-16s and SA-18s—man-portable, shoulder-launched missiles similar to the U.S. Stinger."

Several of the SEALs were intimately familiar with the weapons. Adcock's helicopter had been shot out of the air over Israel by an SA-16 fired by one of Arafat's PLO. Hamilton had nearly lost his skin in Bosnia when a missile roared up the exhaust of an armored personnel carrier on which he had hitched a ride.

"We don't dare come in hot," Smith continued, "and chance it being misinterpreted as an invasion."

"This cliff?" said Mad Dog, still studying the map. "How high did you say it is?"

THE PREPARATION

The governments of Romania and Bulgaria both kept low profiles in the NATO air war. They had to accommodate and live with Russia, who had dominated them as the United Soviet Socialist Republics before the Wall crumbled. Any overt violation of their territorial integrity brought required and expected protests. At the same time, however, what they didn't know *officially,* they didn't know. And they didn't know, *officially,* about the black dual-rotored CH-47 Chinook helicopter that took off in Romania and low-contoured the Danube, flying southerly with the flow.

It was the sixth night of air raids against Slobodan Milosevic. The bombing had intensified and was concentrating on the capital of Belgrade. Along the triborder area where the Danube flowed out of the Carpathians, the night went unmarred. There were no air raids in the vicinity, as there were no known major military targets. There would not be a moon tonight because of the cloud cover. The night threatened rain.

The Chinook pilots flew with night-vision goggles. When landmarks told them they were approaching the point where the Timok River converged with the Danube, they buttoned on the green "Get ready!" lights in the troop bay. Six SEALs and their reluctant guide, Rashish, scrambled to make last-minute preparations.

The SEALs were as heavily laded with rucks, gear, and weapons as when they were first inserted into Serbia by parachute, including holstered pistols and submachine guns. All that was missing were the parachutes. They expected to remain behind enemy lines for an undisclosed period of time.

A fully inflated RPB, Rapid Penetration Boat, formerly known in simple Navy nomenclature as an RB-6, a rubber boat for six passengers, waited on the helicopter's rear loading ramp. It was the ideal craft for special ops troops approaching a target from the water. With its outboard motor muffled by a jacket of rubber insulation, it made only a whisper of noise while reaching speeds of about 20 knots. Its major drawback was its limited fuel supply. It had to be transported as close to the objective as enemy radar and other defensive measures permitted. Fuel would not be a factor tonight. The objective was only ten miles away up the Timok, then another sixty feet straight up the sheer wall of a cliff.

The team piled into the boat where it rested on the closed ramp. Chief Adcock would operate the motor. Lieutenant Hamilton shoved Rashish into the prow of the boat and got in behind him.

"Get down," he ordered, "and stay low."

The rest of the team positioned itself inside the rubber craft on either side. In addition to his ruck and weapons, Mad Dog carried a heavy canvas bag. He made room for it between his crossed legs and gripped the painter rope that threaded around the boat's gunnels as the Chinook bled off speed and began settling through the night toward the surface of the river. The men in the boat waited expectantly for the ramp to open.

Lieutenant Hamilton bent toward Rashish. That the man was a known terrorist repulsed him even more than the stale spicy odor that seemed to ooze out of his pores.

"If anything goes wrong," he whispered in a low threat, "*you* won't be coming back."

The little man recoiled. "No, no. Everyt'ing all right, all right," he protested.

The big aircraft hovered inches above the flowing river. Water lapped at its sides. The loading ramp lowered quickly and smoothly with the boat and men on it, flooding the ramp. The chopper crew shoved the boat out into a black night whipped by spray and hot rotor wash. As soon as it floated free, the Chinook rose tail first to gain forward speed. Water taken on during the insertion cascaded from the rear and through drain holes in the fuselage.

The boat floated deep and heavy because of its overloaded seven-man crew and gear. It rode the churned river wildly for an instant before the chopper was gone with its windmilling blades. It shot free onto the river. Chief Adcock had the engine purring.

They had been dropped on the Danube near the mouth of the Timok. A tumbled rock slide marked the wide entrance into the lesser stream. The team had eschewed the cumbersome night-vision goggles, as they would be more hindrance than help in the spray from the river and the likely advent of rain. Adcock almost missed the rock slide in the dark, but could not miss the Timok's mouth and the strong current sweeping out of it. He turned upstream.

The current was strong, reducing the RPB's top speed by nearly half. That was expected. They ran the middle of the river with Lieutenant Hamilton in the bow keeping a sharp eye peeled for obstacles. Not that he could see that far ahead. The banks of the river were merely darker ink marks in a giant puddle of spilled ink. No lights penetrated the darkness. There were few dwellings on these high and mountainous slopes.

The low steady hum of the motor, the cloaking darkness, lulled the senses. The chief's mind drifted momentarily, unintentionally, into Marge's parting words.

"Gene, I don't know how much longer I can take your disappearing like this for weeks at a time to God only knows where. When you're gone, I seldom know whether you're alive or dead, whether you'll ever come back again. Do you know what that does to me, to our son?"

"He's wanting to join the Navy next year when he's out of school."

Poor choice of words. "*I* didn't join your damned Navy, Gene," she snapped.

"You did, Marge. When you married me, you did."

"Gene, I'm going to tell you this now because it's how I feel. If you leave this time, I don't know if I'll be here when you get back. *If* you get back."

The teams had a phrase that purportedly expressed a SEAL's relationship with women and the Navy. "There is only *one* Navy." It was simplistic and used mostly by unmarried younger operators like John Nighthorse or cynics like Mad Dog Gavlik. SEALs was not a home for family men. You weren't special operations–qualified, it was said, until you were divorced at least once. *Four* women had divorced Mad Dog. The only good woman he ever knew, he said, was his mother.

Sounds made by the river narrowing and running between steep banks on either side wrenched Chief Adcock's mind back on track. The darker ramparts of the mountains closing in rose slightly darker against the lowering blackness of the starless sky.

It began to rain. Drizzle quickly turned into a cold downpour hissing deafeningly against the surface of the river. Wind moaned deep in the canyon's throat. It howled as it escaped along the river's course, driving sheets of rain like icy needles into the tiny band of waterborne infiltrators. No rain gear was dug from rucks; they needed to be unencumbered for the job ahead. They were soaked immediately and shivering from the plunge in temperature. Water sloshed in the boat around their feet.

Lieutenant Hamilton considered scrubbing the mission and reverting to Plan B. No helicopter could fly in this weather. He checked his watch: 2200 hours, ten P.M., still four hours ahead of the rendezvous on the mountain. Area studies he had digested on the flight from D.C. reported that rain like this, this time of year, seldom lasted long. In that case, there was still a chance the party would go down.

They were going to be there to crash it if it did.

At least no near lightning accompanied the storm to flash them out of their cloak of obscurity. Amidships, Preacher bowed his head against the downpour. It stung his face and eyes. He silently asked God to grant them success and good hunting against the evil that beset His word, and he prayed for the souls of those who might be taken tonight. Dr. Death stared ahead, immobile and seemingly unblinking in the maw of the tempest.

THE MISSION

The river narrowed and came bellowing white-flecked against them out of the canyon ahead. The little boat dug in against the force of the heavy water. Escarpment to starboard steepened until the team was beating alongside what best appeared in the poor visibility to be a sheer cliff of stone with only a gravelly toehold of beach at its foot. Cascades of runoff water pushed small boulders splashing into the river below.

Rashish suddenly gripped Lieutenant Hamilton's arm and pointed. "It is there!" he squeaked above the thunder of the rapids and the slash of wind-driven rain that shredded voices before they could reach the length of the RPB. Rashish's eyes were white-rimmed with fright.

Chief Adcock nosed the boat onto a narrow gravel bar. Men jumped out and quickly pulled it out of the river against the base of the cliff. Wind howled and shrieked around them and the blinding rain continued. Worse conditions could not have been imagined. Dog stood in the open and craned his neck for a look at the top of the cliff while the others sought out a jutting of rock that offered some protection.

"Can you do it?" Lieutenant Hamilton asked him.

"If this job were easy," Dog answered, "everybody would be doing it and SEALs would be Boy Scouts."

"Can you *do* it?" the lieutenant repeated, annoyed.

"Did the president get a blowjob in the Oval Office?"

"I take that as an affirmative."

Sometimes Mad Dog Gavlik was not an easy man to take. He squatted on the gravel with his back hunched against the rain and wind while he extracted from his heavy canvas bag a special short-barreled object that resembled a 60mm mortar tube, only smaller. He arranged next to it a box of coiled nylon rope, one end of which he secured to a grapnel with its hooks compressed against its shank. He charged the mortar and dropped the shaft end of the grapnel down the tube.

He moved the base plate as near the river's edge as he could to get the angle on the cliff. If he had one of these gadgets with him on his assault of K-2 in the Himalayas, that poor bastard from England would probably still be alive. The wall there had been like this one, only of pure ice. Sir Roger had panicked on the ascent, missed a piton, and plummeted to his death. The poor bastard was perfectly preserved in an ice crevass for eternity. He might have a little freezer burn if and when future archaeologists found him and claimed he was the missing link.

Satisfied with his aim, Dog triggered the mortar. It emitted a pneumatic sound immediately swallowed by the wind. Rope hissed from the box as the grapnel rocketed toward the top of the cliff, the hooks automatically opening in flight. The rope slackened. Dog gave a yank to set the grapnel's hooks.

The rope went limp. Dog shouted a warning.

The falling grapnel bounced off the face of the

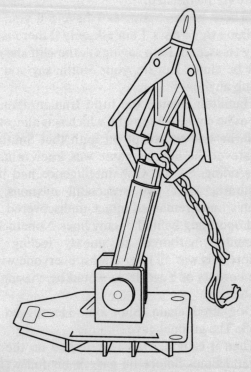

Grapnel Mortar

cliff and the wind carried it into the river. Dog recoiled the line as he reeled it in. He recharged the mortar for a second shot.

"This ain't like them goofy SEAL books where everything always goes exactly right every time because SEALs are supermen," he commented to Dr. Death in a wry aside.

Lieutenant Hamilton had Rashish cornered against the cliff. "There has to be a better way to the top," he insisted.

"There is, sir . . . But as I have tell you, it is walking three days. I am ask only if there is fast way to ascend. I am saying . . . the cliff she cannot be climb. But he, your Smith, say you will climb anyhow."

Hamilton trusted the little Iranian about as far as he could see tonight, which was almost nil. Still, he had to accept on faith that Smith, or whatever the hell his name was, knew what he was doing. So far, CIA intelligence had been accurate. After two successful missions, No Man's Land remained intact, undiscovered, and still operating behind enemy lines. Nonetheless, Hamilton harbored an uneasy feeling that before this was all over almost everyone within the borders of Yugoslavia would be chasing the SEALs.

Dog fired again. Shot out. He tugged the slack. The grapnel gave.

Then it caught. Mad Dog jerked on the line several times before he gave it his full weight. He bounced flat-footed off the base of the cliff to test its hold. When he was satisfied, he placed his ruck against the cliff and took a long coil of climbing rope from the canvas bag and slung it over one shoulder and around his torso.

"I'm going up, Skipper," he said to the lieutenant. "When I tug on the line, send the chief up next. He's the biggest and strongest. We'll rig a safety line and haul up what gear we'll need. There are carabiniers in the sack and enough short rope to make everybody a Swiss seat."

He had already rigged his own rope seat. He snapped a carabinier into the rope twist at his crotch and gated it in a wrap to the climbing rope. The rope was wet, but it was good rope and not too stiff. Without another word, eager to test his skills, he disappeared up the line, short legs bracing against the rock face and long arms reaching for the next byte.

Gusts of wind tore at his body and threatened to tear him loose from the wall. The rock was slippery underfoot and hissed angrily at the rain slapping against it in torrents. Runoff water like waterfalls cascaded around him. He heard boulders and rocks crashing and bouncing past on either side, but kept his concentration and ignored them. Stinging rain all but blinded him, but it was too dark to see much anyhow.

He climbed without gloves, the better to feel his way. The nylon rope was slick. Knuckles and joints in his hands ached immediately from the stress. It was one hell of a climb—and Mad Dog loved it. His lips ripped back from his teeth, grinning and squinting as he went up the rope like the great ape he resembled in dark profile.

Halfway up, he faltered. A sudden strong gust of wind blasted him off the rock like a fly blown off a window pane, hurling him wide into dark wet space. He lost his grip on the rope. He felt it ripping through his carabinier as he plummeted.

He swept his arms wide, desperate but still in perfect control of his wits, and found the wet rope. It burned through his hands. He caught himself. He crashed backside against the cliff with a force that all but knocked him breathless. He bounced off once with an agonized grunt of pain. Twisted in midair. Caught his boot soles against the rock on the next contact. He hunched his shoulders into the driven rain until he recovered his breath and equilibrium. Then he continued swiftly until he reached the top.

Had it been daylight or had there been a full moon, the view would have been spectacular. Tonight, however, there was only the black and the wet howling at him. He attached a pulley to a tree and to one end of his spare climbing rope; he lowered the other end down the cliff face. With this he drew up Chief Adcock. Together they pulled up weapons and other necessary gear. Everything else was left cached with the boat on the beach.

It took nearly two hours before the team and a frightened Rashish were on the top. The storm blew over during that time. Rain diminished to a misting drizzle and finally stopped altogether. Starlight played hide and seek through tattered clouds.

Lieutenant Hamilton placed Rashish on point with John Nighthorse to lead the way.

"If anything goes wrong," he said to the Kiowa, making sure Rashish overheard, "the raghead is the first to go."

Traveling light, carrying only weapons, the team moved noiselessly through the wet forest toward the interior. Rashish nervously indicated that the rendezvous site lay just ahead. Nighthorse approached the edges of the clearing with caution. The KLA patrol was likely already in the vicinity awaiting the drug chopper's appearance. The SEALs would have to be in place when the helicopter arrived and prepared to act swiftly and decisively. The exchange would take no more than three or four minutes—only enough time for contacts in the bird to pop out and unload a few kilos of raw cocaine, receive a bag of cash from the KLA, and then back into the air. Hamilton wondered what methods the KLA then used to dispose of the drug for even higher profits, how it eventually reached the United States and up the noses of American cokeheads.

The initial task in the ambush belonged to Dr. Death, the marksman. He would place an armor-piercing 50-cal round through the chopper's engine housing in order to disable it. He selected his hide and almost disdainfully opened the carrying case that contained his Haskins. He assembled the rifle. At this range, less than 200 meters at most, depending on exactly where the chopper chose to land, it would be a ridiculously easy shot, even in the dark, almost insulting to a shooter of Dr. Death's caliber. He assumed his talents would eventually be utilized for something other than pot-shooting machines on the ground.

Preacher partnered with Dr. Death. His duties were relatively simple compared to the bridge. He laid out for easy access a bandoleer of 40mm fragmentation anti-personnel grenades for the M203 grenade launcher mounted like the barrel of a very large shotgun underneath his M16 rifle. The weapon operated like a pump shotgun, except it only loaded one round at a time. He slid one of the short, heavy little rounds into the chamber and eased the mechanism closed on it. A good shooter could lay down a solid wall of exploding steel.

The rest of the team split to either flank to lay a crossfire on the target. Lieutenant Hamilton and Dog went left, taking Rashish with them. They tied his hands behind with cord, wrapped a length of it around his neck as a leash and taped his mouth to keep him from having a change of heart at the last moment, then left him tied to a tree slightly to their rear. Nighthorse and Chief Adcock assumed their positions on the right flank.

They burrowed into their ambush sites. So far,

there were no signs of the KLA greeting party. The rain stopped completely, along with the wind. Torn fragments of clouds raced past the face of a low waning moon that lit up the clearing at fleeting intervals. More banks of clouds in the distant west threatened additional rain later in the morning.

There was nothing to do now but wait. Waiting for men of action was always the hardest part.

An hour later, Dog touched the skipper's arm. Lieutenant Hamilton nodded; he hoped the other SEALs were also observing the arrival of the KLA greeting party. He need not have worried. They were alert men with senses fine-honed from working on the knife's edge of danger. Shredded clouds parted around the low moon, whose fading light provided sufficient illumination to reveal two figures materializing out of the forest halfway around the clearing from the concealed Americans. The two men walked out into the opening. Through his rifle scope, Dr. Death watched them gaze up into the skies. It was obvious they were waiting for something. Manna from heaven.

A third man came out, spoke briefly to the pair in the open, then returned to the forest and disappeared. It was impossible to ascertain how many of them there were—a small party of six or eight, or a platoon. In these woods, on this night, a company could hide in reserve security to prevent exactly what the SEAL team intended doing when the cocaine chopper arrived.

Hamilton contemplated sending Nighthorse to check out the situation. But good as the Kiowa was at moving in the brush, he would be apt to stumble over the men before he saw or heard them. Better to wait it out and see what developed.

Three more armed men emerged from the timber and started on patrol of the clearing's perimeter. Lieutenant Hamilton cast a suspicious glance toward Rashish. He touched Dog, whose entire body had tensed, and indicated with a gesture that he would check on the Iranian. The ground and foliage were soaked from the recent rain and absorbed sound like a sponge soaked up water. The American slithered noiselessly through the undergrowth.

Rashish gave a start. The rodent appeared edged out, hyped up, about to freak. Was it because he had intentionally led the SEALs into a potential trap? Or was it because he had snitched on his buddies and was contemplating his contribution to their violent demise?

Whichever, he had to be kept perfectly silent until the patrol passed. Using the same cord with which the snitch's hands were tied, Hamilton made snugger the loop around Rashish's neck and secured the loose end around the tree trunk against which the Iranian sat. Rashish could turn his head neither to the right nor the left without the cord cutting off both blood and air.

Rashish groaned and mumbled through his gag. Hamilton pricked the septum of his nose with the point of his knife, drawing blood. Rashish's eyes crossed toward the middle and he stared at the blade.

"We don't need you anymore," Hamilton whispered harshly. "Understood?"

When the patrol drew near, Dog melted low into shadows and breathed soft and shallow. Lieutenant Hamilton lay on his belly next to Rashish's tree and twisted his blade into the Iranian's crotch, just to remind him.

The three KLA men were talking in low voices as they approached. They continued to talk, unaware as they passed by that mere feet away two of the deadliest men on the continent were prepared to snuff out their lives if they so much as faltered. Talking, they proceeded on their rounds, paying little attention to anything other than each other. And in that neglect of their duties they sealed their fate and that of their comrades.

No further patrols were sent out. The SEALs waited, watchful and ready. They remained hidden almost within sound of the chattering Kosovars, but the patrol remained unaware of their presence. Expecting nothing, it looked for nothing.

At 0200 hours, Lt. Hamilton began checking

his watch at five-minute intervals. They would have to be back off the mountain by 0400 at the latest in order to make their escape via the river without being exposed by daylight.

At 0230 hours he was to the point of deciding they had drawn into a dry hole when Dog's hand shot up in an alert. Hamilton heard it then—the thumping drone of an approaching helicopter. The sound drew rapidly near until the bird itself appeared low and fast-shadow-flitting across a slightly lighter sky. A flurry of activity erupted on the ground as those men hiding in the forest poured into the clearing to join the two already there. A red-lensed flashlight caught the approaching aircraft and guided it in to a low hover. Its skids gently touched the receiving drenched earth.

That was Dr. Death's cue.

The cracking sound of a weapon as large as a .50-cal was something felt in the air as well as heard. The power of that big bullet seemed to suck the surrounding air into its vortex. It was a good shot; Hamilton expected nothing less from his marksman.

The helicopter's blades were still turning at two-thirds RPM when the bullet struck. The housing assembly at the base of the main rotor blade exploded in a tremendous shower of sparks and electrical energy, accompanied by the screeching and tearing of metal against metal. The dying bird flung pieces of itself against the night. The long blade whipped loose and shrieked like an incoming Howitzer round before it struck the forest and ripped through it like a manic giant with a scythe.

The rest of the team opened fire simultaneously. Machine-gun fire in a lethal crisscross from Dog on the left flank and Chief Adcock on the right raked the clearing, chewing into the surprised men who had circled around the chopper in anticipation. Lieutenant Hamilton and John Nighthorse fired deliberately on semiauto, picking off shadowy targets one by one, aiming quickly and instinctively and dropping men before they could react. Death flew unseen because the SEALs did not need tracers to shift and guide their firepower. The only glimpses the dying men may have caught were of flickering muzzle flashes from the forest and the fireballs of a string of deadly giant firecrackers let loose among them by a Kiowa Indian with an M203 who cranked, loaded, and fired, cranked, loaded, and fired.

No matter how many ambushes Hamilton participated in, he never failed to be amazed at how quickly and violently they began and then how quickly they were over. A mad minute of bedlam followed by silence even more deafening by the contrast.

Hamilton and Dog leaped to their feet as soon as the firing ceased and raced toward the dead helicopter and the awful hush that enveloped it. Chief Adcock and Nighthorse converged from the right flank to form the other half of the assault-and-search element. Preacher and Dr. Death maintained outer security and kept watch over the trussed-up Iranian snitch. Hamilton hoped the bastard had been watching.

Hydraulics fluids and hot oil and hot spilled blood mingled in a nauseating odor. Hamilton and Chief Adcock rushed directly for the helicopter, leaping over bodies crumpled in the grass like old lifeless bags of clothing. Dog and the Kiowa darted among the corpses on the killing field, checking them for life and therefore threat. Only one was alive, but unconscious. Nighthorse rolled him onto his back and used a red-lensed flashlight to inspect his wounds. There were a dozen tiny holes in his chest, each ringed in blood. His face, unrecognizable, resembled bloody ground hamburger. It looked like he had been bending over when one of Preacher's 40 mike-mikes detonated in his face.

"This guy's heading for the Happy Hunting Grounds," the Indian said to Dog.

"You ain't gonna scalp him, are you? Put the bastard out of his misery."

"No. Let him use what awareness he has left to make his peace."

"You are one sentimental redskin, Nighthorse."

Everyone in and near the chopper was dead. Bullets and exploding M203 grenades had shattered all the glass from around the cockpit. The pilot's body, minus its head, sat slumped against its seat harness. Something, perhaps from the engine when Dr. Death exploded it, had severed the head cleanly from its shoulders. The SEALs did not look for it. The red beam from their flashlights probed the cockpit only to make sure no one alive was lurking there. From the cargo compartment they jerked another corpse out and onto the ground, out of the way of their lights inspecting the interior.

"Holy shit!" the chief breathed.

Strapped to the steel deck of the helicopter were a half-dozen boxes. Adcock vaulted into the bird and ripped open one of them with his K-bar, spilling out a miniature snow avalanche that glinted crystalline underneath their red light beams. The chief gutted the rest of the boxes, creating a knee-high pile of cocaine. Hamilton broke out the special camera Smith had furnished them before they left Romania.

It was a miniature 8mm TV infrared with a maximum ten-minute run. It broadcast images in real time to a relay space satellite, which could then be downloaded at CIA headquarters. CIA Director Louis Benefield or anyone else with a "need to know" would be viewing the scene and recording the images at almost the same time they were being filmed. Along with actual samples of the cocaine and a report the lieutenant would later relay via code-burster, this was solid evidence that the KLA was involved with drug-running Muslim terrorists.

Let the U.S. Congress tamp *this* into its Kosovo Self-Defense Act and smoke it.

The lieutenant filmed the helicopter, cargo, and surrounding area. He made sure he included several of the dead men wearing partial uniforms that included red-and-black KLA shoulder patches. He also filmed a suitcase full of U.S. currency Dog and Nighthorse found among the dead guerrillas.

"This looks like a million dollars in here!" Dog gasped. "What are we gonna do with it, Skipper?"

"Toss it in the helicopter."

Dog did, with an uncomprehending shrug. Chief Adcock was scooping cocaine into a plastic baggie.

"How much we need of this shit, Jeb?"

"That's enough. Let's get out of here."

He ripped an M34 white phosphorous grenade from his fighting harness. He pulled the pin but held onto the handle. "This is one load of nose candy that won't snow on American streets," he said before dropping the grenade into the helicopter's gas tank.

"What are you doing?" Dog cried in alarm. *"The money!"*

"It's only paper," the lieutenant said, breaking into a run for the woods.

The fuse delay on the grenade was about five seconds. Willie Pete, white phosphorus, burned at over 4,800 degrees Fahrenheit. It formed a sort of napalm when mixed with aviation fuel.

There would be virtually nothing left of the helicopter within five minutes, nor of the cocaine, nor of an estimated one million dollars in U.S. cash.

"I was a millionaire there for about two minutes," Mad Dog lamented as the helicopter went up in a brilliant gaseous display of blue flame.

POST-MISSION

Dawn was arriving by the time the team with Rashish returned to the river, descended the cliff, and motored the RPB another five miles upstream, where they let the air out of it and sank it in the river weighed down with rocks. Banks of clouds from the west eased over the sky again, turning the morning gray and cold. Hamilton shot a GPS azimuth off the river leading into the relatively uninhabited Balkan Mountains. They climbed hard for several hours, avoiding occasional villages and farms. Their clothing and gear were already soaked from perspiration and the previous night's rainstorm when rain started falling again, a slow steady drizzle that would have dampened the spirits of lesser men.

Rashish stumbled from fatigue. "I cannot go on, please?" he protested in his squeaky voice.

"Would you rather I shot you?" Hamilton asked.

They stopped in a deep copse of woods at

noon to rest and eat cold rations. Afterward, they climbed even higher and came upon a large cave whose mouth was almost concealed by newly leafed aspen. It was an accident they stumbled upon it. Lt. Hamilton looked it over while Nighthorse scouted out an escape route.

The front of the cave provided a breathtaking view of the entire valley below and the Timok River winding through it. Nighthorse returned to report that more timber lay on the hillside beyond, good cover. There were no trails leading to the cave. Hamilton made his decision.

"We're to make commo with Smith at 1500 hours for further orders," he said. "We'll hole up here. At least it'll be dry in the cave."

Dr. Death looked at the cave, then looked at Mad Dog and his long, powerful arms, bandy legs, and hairy, low-browed face. "You should be right at home here," he commented in another of his rare efforts at a joke.

Dog swung into his Neanderthal role, hanging his arms, grunting a long line of guttural noises and pounding his chest. Chief Adcock rolled his eyes in mock horror.

"With clowns like these," he said, "we're expected to save the world?"

5: SKY HOOK

PRE-MISSION

Few understood the political side of warfare more completely than CIA Director Louis Benefield. He first learned about war the bloody way—on the battlefield. A 1966 graduate of West Point, third in his class, he commanded a company of airborne infantry in Vietnam for one tour before extending to serve on General Westmoreland's staff. It was there while confronting the daily frustrations of a war micromanaged from Washington that he came to understand that when it came to warfare, some of the most ruthless battles were fought in politics. Actions down to even platoon level often had to be cleared through the Pentagon and the Defense Department. President Johnson himself sometimes gave the final go or no-go on minor operations. If anything, Vietnam proved politicians couldn't fight wars and win them. Hell, they couldn't even pass a balanced budget.

Director Benefield was convinced that, left on their own, Washington politicians of the current administration, almost none of whom had any military experience, were going to screw up the Kosovo affair and mire America in another Vietnam—or worse. He could not let that happen, no matter what was required to prevent it.

In his office at the "Puzzle Palace" in Langley, Virginia, Director Benefield swiveled his chair away from his desk, leaned back with his feet propped on a corner of his desk and his hands tented underneath his chin, and gazed reflectively out the window over the manicured grounds of the CIA compound. General Roger Norman, Chairman of the Joint Chiefs of Staff, and Assistant CIA Director Mark Goodson let him think it through in silence. They were the only two other men in the office.

Benefield rubbed his face hard with both hands, as though attempting to massage something into his mind—or something out of it. He dropped his feet off the desk and swiveled his chair to face his visitors. The hard-sad eyes probed into theirs. General Norman took it as a sign to continue.

"So far," he said, "the Joint Chiefs are split fifty-fifty—hell, the whole of Washington is split fifty-fifty—on whether and how far to support the administration's conduct of the bombing campaign. There's a lot of under-the-table fighting and maneuvering for power and position."

Mark Goodson snorted in disgust. "In the

White House, it's 'The Gang That Couldn't Shoot Straight.' There's talk up on the Hill of impeaching the president if he screws this up and we end up with another Somalia or Haiti or egg on our faces from bombing an aspirin factory like we did in Sudan. One good thing—Congress is pulling back its support of arming the KLA after we showed that film from No Man's Land of the KLA drug deal. It is still considering passing the resolution to withdraw funds to support the bombing."

"I'm afraid that if the resolution comes up for vote," General Norman put it, "it will force the administration to step up the bombing campaign to the next level. We received orders yesterday to begin moving two troops of Apache attack helicopters to Italy, along with support forces. Apaches are not *air* assets, they're *ground forces*. Boris Yeltsin is threatening to send Russian helicopters to Belgrade to beef up Milosevic and General Krleza."

"How is Russia finding out all this so quickly?" Benefield boomed, slamming his hand palm down against his desk.

"There's a leak, sir," Goodson said, then felt foolish at pointing out the obvious.

"It's not a leak. It's a pipeline!"

"We're narrowing it down, sir."

Benefield exploded. "*Narrowing* it down? They know our bombing targets and flight routes almost as soon as we do. We've already lost one stealth fighter because of this guy. I want him ferreted out of the ground and . . . I want the sonofabitch *eliminated*. Damn him! Damn him to a Stalin's hell."

"We're working on it, sir."

"Work harder. This war is going to escalate, I promise you that. Before the summer is over, there's going to be a ground war in Yugoslavia unless we can contain it now. Vietnam was a walk in the sun compared to what we're going to see here. Tito held out against Hitler in the Balkans for four years. We're stretched too thin for a war in Europe. This administration has 'peacekeeping' forces spread out all over the damned globe."

Director Benefield sighed deeply, his hands once more tented underneath his chin, a sign of deep and troubled thought. He turned to again look out the window.

"Everything depends on No Man's Land," he stressed. "If it's exposed, we can give up the whole ship."

"I don't see how it can be, sir," Goodson countered. "The three of us in this room—"

Benefield cut him off. "We three *in Washington*," he snapped. "It takes support to keep these guys in Serbia and operating. Within a five-day period, these SEALs rescued one pilot, blew up a bridge, and fucked up a drug deal by killing seven KLA militiamen and three Iranians on a mountaintop. How long do you think we can keep things like that hush-hush? Whoever this spy is, he's high-placed and he's bound to figure it out. There are already rumors floating around about 'secret commandos.' Everybody all the way to the White House suspects *something* is happening. It's just that nobody knows *what*, or *who*."

General Norman said, "The longer they're in there, the more pressure there's going to be inside Serbia and out to identify them. If we leave the SEALs in much longer, we may as well write them off. They'll be history."

"A history that can never be written," Benefield said.

He paused to light a cigarette, concentrating totally on the process. His cop's eyes lifted to his second-in-command.

"Mark, we have to have a UN war crimes indictment against Milosevic and his minister of state, General Krleza. Krleza may be even more heavily tied to Russia than Milosevic. He's the one behind the military campaign against the Kosovo Muslims. Nobody will much question their deaths after they're officially branded as war criminals."

Both men knew what he meant.

"We don't dare move the SEALs on them until they're indicted. Twist arms on everybody you know with influence to make it happen. I have a meeting with the president today. He's ready to go along with it now to assure his legacy as the world leader with the balls to stand up to the 'second Hitler.' "

He emitted a sharp derisive bark of bitter

laughter, the characteristic response by military and ex-military men over a president who evaded the Vietnam draft but was now showing "balls" by sending other men to fight.

"In the meantime," he continued, "keep No Man's Land busy applying pressure. It seems to be having an effect." He paused, as though in afterthought. "There's one small problem we need to handle tonight."

"Sir?"

"Iran is making noise about one of its citizens being detained in Czechoslovakia. Yeltsin is applying pressure to the Czechs to either charge the man with a crime or release him, and to our State Department as well."

"Sir, he's not in Czechoslovakia. He's in Serbia with—"

"I *know* where he is, Mr. Goodson. I want him out of there ASAP. Tonight. The Czechs must agree to charge him and hold him totally incommunicado until everything settles down. He must not be allowed to expose No Man's Land. Those SEALs' lives depend on that. *Everything* depends on it."

"What if he never made it out of Serbia?" Goodson suggested.

"We can't have the Czechs out on a hook with Yeltsin, or the White House asking questions. We have to get the Iranian out."

General Norman looked uncomfortable. He was a large buff man with gray hair cropped so short he looked almost bald.

"We've got a problem there," he said, apologetically. "We can't take a chopper in to pick him up."

"Why not? We've been using choppers in that area."

"Yeltsin again. Russia has strong-armed Romania and Bulgaria to close down our military and covert access across their borders into Serbia. The president has ordered us to withdraw our assets from those two countries and relocate in Tuzla or Macedonia. We can no longer support you with helicopters for insertions into or extractions out of Serbia on the eastern border."

"That Iranian has to be immediately pulled out of Serbia—"

"Hold on, Louis. I didn't say we couldn't do it. It's risky, but there is a way . . ."

THE BRIEFING

"Skipper, we're receiving SAT commo."

Chief Adcock punched in the code on the radio's miniature abbreviated keyboard. Thus cued, it decoded the incoming message, reading it out on a tiny computer screen. Adcock handed the entire machine to Lt. Hamilton.

It was a remarkable device. Classified "Secret" by R&D, it was about the size of a transistor AM/FM radio worn by joggers. It contained a "code-burster" the size of an audio cassette. When properly keyed, it automatically encoded messages and burst them through a dedicated satellite at thousands of words per second, far too rapidly to be triangulated by enemy RDF. *Ri-i-i-i-i-ppppp!* And a multipage message could be hurled into space in unbreakable code, routed through satellite and, in this case, sent and picked up between a field post and a secret ops center in Aviano, Italy.

"Looks like we've got a job," Lieutenant Hamilton commented.

For the past two days, the team had remained holed up in their cave. Other than daily SITREPs, situations reports, which amounted to little more than radio checks, the only orders the SEALs had received from Smith was "Stand by." They had been standing by, waiting, with little to do other than keep watch and guard Rashish, whose rodentlike demeanor and squeaky voice grew more offensive by the hour. At least it was dry in the cave, and easily warmed with a small fire.

NATO bombings had apparently expanded from nights-only raids into a twenty-four-hour-a-day campaign to hammer Milosevic into capitulation. In the early afternoon of their first day in the cave there had been banging explosions beyond the mountains. That same night, dropped bombs flickered on the horizon beyond the river, but were too far away for sound to carry. The SEALs were unable to determine what the targets might have been.

"Mission briefing," Hamilton said, looking up.

"Hallelujah!" Mad Dog cheered drily. He was leaning against the cave wall at the entrance, glassing the valley below with binoculars. He was a man easily grown restless by inactivity.

Preacher thoughtfully closed his Bible. Dr. Death looked up from cleaning and oiling his Haskins. John Nighthorse sat cross-legged outside the cave, lost in the vastness of his "inner space" while enjoying the sunset that painted the valley below with a red-glowing wash that pleased his ascetic nature; the skies had only started clearing that afternoon. He turned an inscrutable expression toward the team's leader.

"Control wants our guide back," the lieutenant said.

Dog cast a baleful glance at the little Iranian watching from the shadows at the back of the cave. "They don't want the dude back nearly as much as we want to give him back," he said.

"Helicopters are no longer available and Control doesn't want to run the risk of exposing us by walking him out," Lieutenant Hamilton said. "That means extraction by Skyhook. Times, grid coordinates, and other data are included in the message. We'll be resupplied at the same time Skyhook picks him up. We'll move out as soon as it gets dark."

Mad Dog walked back to the Iranian. He chuckled. "Rashish, ol' raghead, are you ever gonna get the ride of your sorry life!"

THE PREPARATION

They traveled through a cool, clear night following the past two nights of intermittent and sometimes heavy rainfall. A positive side of the weather was that it had washed away all signs the team might have left both upon entering and leaving the ambush site on the mountain and during its cross-country escape to the cave afterward. Lieutenant Hamilton found it curious that there had not even been search parties; of course, this was Serbian territory and why should the Serbs be worked up about the wiping out of a few more Muslims? The KLA would be upset, but they probably blamed the massacre on the Serbs.

Lieutenant Hamilton punched in the numbers on his GPS and followed it southerly to a small clearing on another mountaintop. They moved with their usual stealth, crossing several fenced pastures so much like ghosts that the cows barely noticed the intrusion. An occasional farm dog barked in the near distance. They reached their destination at midnight as planned and code-bursted Smith a SITREP. All ready.

Obviously Smith had used a satellite to select the site for its remoteness and lack of heat signatures indicating concentrations of people or machines. Dog and Nighthorse ran a quick security patrol to make sure. They had barely reported back an "all clear" when the drone of a heavy aircraft announced its low-flying approach; it was arriving precisely on time. A U.S. Air Force C-130 Combat Talon winged into view in shadowy silhouette, like that of an ominous giant owl swooping low. Chief Adcock flashed it a signal using his red-lensed flashlight as the bird roared over them low enough to ruffle grass and rustle leaves on trees.

The pop of the parachute was clearly audible. The 'chute opened, oscillated once or twice, then settled in the clearing not thirty feet from where Chief Adcock stood. Dr. Death, of whom Rashish was terrified, kept guard on the Iranian, a rope around the prisoner's neck, while the rest of the team jumped on the air bundle and began taking it apart even before the parachute collapsed. Rashish had to be rigged up for Skyhook within five minutes. Although the C-130 flew NOE, nape of the earth, to place it beneath radar, it dared not remain long over enemy territory at such low altitudes. The longer the mission took, the greater its risk.

"Get him in the harness!" Hamilton ordered.

Dr. Death jerked Rashish into the clearing like a balky poodle on a leash. Rashish looked alarmed, suddenly aware of what might be in store for him. "What? *What?*"

THE MISSION

In addition to a resupply of ammo and food, the air drop contained a baggy nylon suit, a parachute harness fastened to a nylon lift line, a reserve parachute, a helmet, 500 feet of special nylon rope, a balloon twenty-three feet long, and helium tanks with which to fill it. Hamilton tossed the reserve 'chute aside while Mad Dog and the Kiowa inflated the balloon. He didn't think Rashish had the balls to cut away from the lift line during extraction and actually use the 'chute, but he was taking no chances of his escaping to compromise the team's presence in Yugoslavia.

Preacher and Dr. Death tossed the frightened and struggling Iranian to the ground.

"You're going one way or another," Preacher told him. "Cooperate and you'll survive. Otherwise, it'll break your neck. Do exactly as we tell you. Do you believe in Jesus?"

"I . . . I am Muslim."

"Too bad. Sit still. Don't move."

In short order they had him garbed in the nylon suit, helmeted, and snugged into the parachute harness. As instructed, he sat on the ground with his helmeted head lowered until his chin pressed hard against his chest, arms crossed tightly and his legs straight out in front of him with his ankles crossed—frozen there by fear.

He trembled violently when he heard the airplane returning.

"I hear it," Dog responded to Lieutenant Hamilton's unspoken question. "He's ready. Go!"

Hamilton snapped one end of the long lift line

to Rashish's harness. The helium-filled balloon jerked the other end of the line 500 feet into the air. Flashing colored bulbs on the line, like a string of Christmas lights, marked its length for the C-130 pilots.

The object of the Fulton STAR, Surface-to-Air Recovery system, otherwise known as Skyhook, was for the C-130 flying at about 120 knots to meet the lift line just below the balloon that held it aloft. A V-shaped apparatus fixed in the nose of the aircraft guided the line toward a clamp in the center. Breakaway cords let the balloon snap free. Force exerted on the man being picked up caused him to rise vertically for the first 100 feet, greatly reducing his danger of colliding with trees and other obstacles. At first, because of stretch in the nylon line, the acceleration was smooth and gentle. Once the stretch was exhausted, however, the resulting jolt was powerful enough to break bones. Lieutenant Hamilton had been Skyhooked out of Iraq; it had felt like his body was being wrenched apart.

Once the pickup was being towed through the sky, aircraft crew lowered a hook out the tail ramp of the C-130 to catch the nylon tether trailing close to the plane's belly. They pulled the line into the plane and attached it to a winch that reeled the man in like a perch on a fishing pole.

Mad Dog bent down to the Iranian. "Rashish? Have a good flight. Don't forget to write."

The roar of the aircraft's four great turboprops drowned out the terrorist's screams. One moment he was sitting on the ground trembling. The next instant he was jerked up so abruptly it was almost like a vanishing act. Only his screams remained, but they thinned out rapidly. Rashish was gone.

THE REPORT

The team concealed the discarded reserve parachute and other unneeded items before breaking down the resupply bundle among the team members. Chief Adcock code-bursted Smith that the mission was successful. Smith's only reply was a grid coordinate, a date three days hence, the hour of contact, and a code name: Play Golf.

"Saddle up," Hamilton said. "We're back in the game."

6: PLAY GOLF

PRE-MISSION

The GPS, Global Positioning System, was a remarkable instrument for being no larger than a man's hand. It triangulated off three or more satellites in order to provide a present location as well as destination and fastest route to it. It also tracked your route as you traveled, recording it in the event you had to backtrack. Twice during the three nights the team trudged southwesterly toward Kosovo, it had to backtrack and select an alternate route.

The first time was because of a NATO air raid on a target near the city of Nis. The SEALs, traveling only under cover of darkness and holing up during daylight, had ascended a distant hilltop overlooking the city and halted to compare GPS readings to the map and their own scrutiny of the terrain. Bombs suddenly exploded in the night, opening a bright glimpse into the universe. The aircraft that dropped them flew too high to be heard or observed, as usual, but anti-aircraft batteries nonetheless fed the sky with their heavy bursting fire. A SAM streaked from ground level and turned into a shooting star.

"It's like the end of the world." Preacher breathed in awe. It was the first SAM he had ever seen fired.

After the bombing, there would be too much activity in the city to pass near it. The team backtracked and skirted wider to the west.

The second backtrack occurred because of refugees on a major road the team had to cross. Under moonlight, the road appeared clogged for over a mile either way with humanity all moving the same direction and utilizing every form of locomotion imaginable—walking with packs and bundles weighing heavily upon their backs; riding tractors pulling trailers loaded down with possessions; riding horses or wagons pulled by horses and sometimes oxen; peddling bicycles; pushing carts and wheel barrows. They migrated almost without human voice, the collective sound being only that of their conveyances and their feet, emphasizing the sorrow and desperation of their exodus. Behind them an entire village seemed to be burning, searing into the horizon a blood-red glow.

People disrupted by a war that was not being called a war, dislocated and uprooted, flung about their own countryside like roadside trash blown by a foul wind. Judging from the number of ethnic Albanian refugees being driven south into Kosovo and then, presumably, exiting out of

Kosovo into neighboring countries, Milosevic's Serbian army had been little deterred by nearly two weeks of NATO air strikes.

"Fucking politicians!" Mad Dog spat out the bad taste the word left in his mouth. To him, politicians and lawyers were the collective curse of civilization.

"The love of and seeking of power is the root of all evil," Preacher always said.

The team withdrew and again skirted to the west.

For all the sophistry available to Special Operations forces, they still often had to depend upon the basic human form of transportation while operating behind enemy lines: walking. War fighting at its most fundamental level. Even though SEALs trained extensively in operations in small units, on foot, the longer they were on the ground, the more they moved about, the greater their risk of being detected.

During a rest halt, John Nighthorse whispered to Mad Dog, "My last tour before I volunteered for BUD/S training and SEALs was aboard the aircraft carrier U.S.S. *Abe Lincoln*. The longest distance we ever walked was from the main flight deck to the mess galley."

"You ain't in Kansas no more, Toto," Mad Dog said.

"Oklahoma," the Indian corrected him.

Late into the third exhausting night of the trek, the team approached its destination. Hamilton called a stop alongside a rocky stream bed gurgling full with rainfall. Exactly *what* the objective was had not been provided in the SAT message, but the GPS would direct them to within three steps of whatever it was. The SEALs had to trust Smith knew what he was doing.

"We're within three hundred meters," Hamilton whispered to Nighthorse. "Check it out. We still have an hour."

The Kiowa eased his ruck to the earth. He melted into the forest, taking only his AKMS. It was late enough that the moon had gone down. There was heavy dew.

Nighthorse returned as noiselessly as he departed. "It's a small country church. It looks abandoned. The road up to it is overgrown."

"Take Preacher and set up security on the other side," Hamilton instructed. "The rest of us will wait here until contact time."

The four remaining SEALs burrowed into a dark thicket to wait. Hamilton rested his long legs by elevating them over his ruck. He closed

AKMS "Assault Rifle"

his eyes and tried to picture Judith's face in his memory. It disturbed him that another face kept blending into Judith's. He recognized the other face with a start. It was so much like Judith's. The too-wide mouth, the flared nostrils, the sorrel hair, and the dry sense of humor under pressure. Dismay opened his eyes for him. Why could he recall *her* face with such clarity while the face of his dead wife continued to fade with each passing day?

It occurred to him that the reason he saw Tori's face was because he was hoping she would be the contact. He closed his eyes again. That was too much to expect. He forced a blanket across his mind so that he would not think. He let the minutes pass and thought of nothing.

When it was time, he rose from the ground, shouldered his ruck, and checked his rifle. He indicated to Chief Adcock that he and the others were to cover him from far enough back that they would be out of a potential kill zone. They moved out in the silent darkness toward the church.

The contact was waiting for him by the church door.

"We're going to have to stop meeting like this," she said with her quirky sense of humor.

"Tori!" He was surprised, but not that surprised. "I was just thinking—" He broke off.

"Thinking what?" she teased.

"Actually, I was wondering if it'd be you."

She laughed softly. "Why break up a winning combination?"

"Not another pig truck," he said.

"I promise. Not another pig truck."

THE BRIEFING

The team members rested inside the abandoned church the rest of the night and until noon the next day, all of them except for rotating sentries sleeping soundly. After they awoke, they ate plastic-packaged MREs, Meals Ready to Eat, before the lieutenant assembled them for Tori's mission briefing. Hamilton sat with Tori to eat, chatting easily with her but avoiding anything of a personal nature. As he knew virtually nothing about her, she likewise knew nothing about him, the team, nor their missions beyond the current one. She didn't know if they were SEALs, Army Special Forces, CIA, or what. She assumed they were Americans, but couldn't even be certain of that. She provided Hamilton with his current mission and his next contact. Beyond that—nothing. The more they knew of each other, the greater the threat they posed if they were captured.

"Are you going to keep cropping up like this?" Hamilton asked her.

"I'm given only one mission at a time because of security precautions," she said. "I assume it's the same with you. It's good to see you again, Elk."

Had she forgotten his name? She was teasing him. She smiled. "Jeb," she added.

"It's good to see you again, Tori."

He wondered what her real name was. He hoped it was Tori. He liked it.

As before with Deep Water, Tori came prepared with maps, ground photos, and satellite images. The CIA had pulled out all plugs in support of No Man's Land. She assumed a position at the pulpit with a map of Kosovo on the wall behind her and the SEALs clustered on the front pew before her. The pew was a worn, dusty bench, gray and splintery with age. The church had not been used in a long time.

"If I get a splinter in my ass, will you pull it out with your teeth?" Mad Dog asked her.

Tori smiled. "Face to face with that ass would be like coming face to face with the monster from Boggy Creek."

The cheeky retort drew laughter, but they soon settled down.

"So far your presence in Serbia is still in the black," she began soberly. "The situation is this: We have loosed a sledgehammer on Serbia when we could have used a surgical instrument instead. We went directly from a breakdown in negotiations with Milosevic to bombing him. The result is a gradual escalation of the war. Targets are being hit twenty-four hours a day now. U.S. Apache attack helicopters and their ground support have already arrived in Italy and are preparing for commitment in Kosovo. As a result of the escalation, the possibility of nuclear confrontation and some sort of terrorist attack on the United States has been significantly increased."

She let them digest that before continuing.

"The proliferation problem related to nuclear-biological-chemical munitions is a dangerous thing to America and to the world. Russia right now does not have control over even half its 152mm nuclear artillery shells or over the 'suitcase nukes' once under the control of the KGB. There are all kinds of nukes being run around and sold commercially. The American public would be horrified if it knew the extent of loose NBC weapons."

She had captured the team's full attention. Play Golf obviously had something to do with nuclear weapons.

"Detonation of a half-kiloton nuclear device at five to six stories high on Wall Street would take out a trillion dollars of our economy in a nanosecond. Electrical magnetic impulses would fry every computer in New York."

She paused to let the enormity of all this soak in.

"We're down to Play Golf," she said, "and it's eighteen holes in the rough. As you probably know, the KLA has ties to Iranian terrorists. Iran has many of the old USSR nuclear weapons. The KLA has obtained one of the KGB suitcase nukes, which Kradznic planned to use in Belgrade to force Milosevic and General Krleza to grant sovereignty to Kosovo. However—"

She walked to the map and pointed.

"This is the town of Gracanica. Serb forces attacked and occupied the town four days ago. We have reports—we don't know how accurate they are—that as many as two hundred ethnic

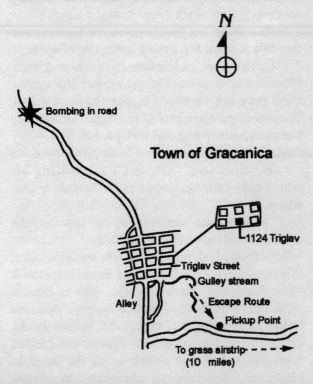

Recovery of Suitcase Nuke

Albanians living there were massacred in their homes and buried in mass graves. Suspected KLA guerrillas were either captured and executed or forced to withdraw south. One of the survivors now in our custody told of how they hid the nuke in a house with the intent to return for it after the Serbs moved on."

" '*Suitcase* nuke'?" Dr. Death interrupted. His white hair caught a ray of sunlight from a dusty window. "How much does the thing weigh?"

Nukes from his viewpoint were missiles the size of a Kansas silo arcing down out of space.

Preacher the ordnanceman answered him. "Plutonium is relatively heavy, but the device itself may not be much bigger than a softball. The whole package probably weighs somewhere between twenty-five and fifty pounds."

Mad Dog whistled.

"Yes," Tori said. "You get a lot of bang for your buck. That thing can easily be taken anywhere."

"I assume our mission is to recover the nuke?" Lieutenant Hamilton said.

Tori looked at him. "You can imagine what this thing can do in the wrong hands," she said. "The Serbs also know that the nuke is hidden somewhere in town. They're going house to house looking for it. If they find it before we do, we can expect it to be used against the United States in a terrorist attack or in the least as blackmail. We have an advantage. We know which house the nuke is in. They don't."

"Again, I don't want to be the one to ask the obvious question," Chief Adcock said. "But why doesn't NATO bomb it? Civilian collateral damage?"

"That's part of it, yes. The other part of it is that the arming device may be such that it could explode from even a grenade concussion. It would take out the entire town. Russia and Serbia would claim NATO dropped a nuclear bomb. You can imagine world opinion after that."

In the deep hush that followed, the rustling of her handing out Play Golf file folders sounded like the crackle of gunfire.

"Target folders," she explained. "You know the routine. Memorize everything, then we burn the folders."

She looked them in the eyes one by one, ending with Lieutenant Hamilton, where she lingered longer than necessary.

"The bottom line," she emphasized, "is that NATO cannot take the chance of that thing getting out of Gracanica and into the U.S. Tee-off in three hours. You'll have nine hours after that to locate the weapon, secure it, and get out. There'll be a vehicle waiting for you on the outskirts of town to take you to a grass airstrip ten miles away, where you and the nuke will be picked up. You're to be there no later than 0200 hours. It's all in the target folder. The execution of the mission is up to you."

She paused, as though finding the next part painful.

"If you're not at the airstrip by 0200 . . ." She took a deep breath and avoided Lieutenant Hamilton's inquiring eyes. "At 0200 hours, the town will be targeted for a major air raid to destroy the nuke, if possible. It sounds cruel, but it has been decided that more lives will be lost if the nuke falls into Serb hands than if it explodes in Gracanica. That's the way it has to be, so don't fail."

"We *are* expendable!" Dog cried triumphantly, looking around with an "I told you so" expression.

THE TARGET FOLDER

Satellite closeups showed the entire town, neighborhoods surrounding the targeted house, and the house itself. The town seemed typical of those the team had encountered so far in this region of the Balkans. A single main street, the road going in and out, bisected what was in effect no more than a very large village. Mortar-sided houses, most painted white, with roofs either of burned-red tile or weathered cedar shingles, squared off from a main street in neat blocks. Black smoke drifted from some of the houses, while others appeared to have already burned.

"When were these photos taken?" Lieutenant Hamilton asked Tori.

"We down-linked yesterday afternoon. You can see damage done by the Serbs. They're torching some of the houses."

"How can we be sure the Serbs haven't already found the nuke?"

"We've had constant satellite surveillance on the house."

The house even had an address—1124 Triglav. There were no ground photos of this target; they were all from the air. It was a single-story building with a red-tiled roof and a front porch facing a side street. Houses adjacent on either side were snugged close to it. What in American suburbs would be known as a privacy fence surrounded the tiny backyard.

Streams of humanity, on foot and in a variety of vehicles and conveyances, clotted the highway leading into town and out again on the other side—refugees fleeing toward the south. It seemed the entire population of Kosovo might be on the move. They gave Hamilton an idea of how the team might enter Gracanica undetected.

"Tori, we'll need civvies again—something farmers might wear. Include a dress for a woman."

She lifted an eyebrow.

"Six men together might be suspicious," he partially explained before continuing with his thought. "We'll need a big wheelbarrow or a cart . . . A bale of hay . . . ?"

"They may be a little more difficult, but we have local assets."

Working together, the six men hammered out an execution plan. As commander, Hamilton had the last say, but he respected the opinions and expertise of his teammates. SpecOps on a practical level rarely followed the military protocol of conventional units. Members of SEALs and Army Green Berets were in effect associations of equals, no matter what rank they wore on their collars. What counted more than stripes and bars was the individual's capabilities, ingenuity, courage, adaptability, and imagination.

THE PREPARATION

Tori guided the team from the church through a cedar woods to an isolated country road where transportation awaited. Mad Dog drew up in dismay when he spotted the same rickety old farm truck they had used before. This time there was a black white-faced cow in the back, along with a wooden two-wheeled cart. The cow was haltered and tied to keep her from eating a bale of hay inside the cart. A farmer-driver waited alongside.

In spite of the gravity of the mission, Tori laughed softly. "I promised you it wouldn't be another *pig* truck. The cow was my idea. She'll provide good cover."

In keeping with their refugee disguise,

Preacher was garbed out as a woman in a long farm dress and a Muslim shawl. He protested, but since he was the smallest man of the team he was the logical choice to go transgender. He was light-skinned enough that his chocolate complexion would go largely unnoticed when he pulled the Muslim shawl over his lower face. He wore jeans and a shirt underneath the dress, along with his combat harness and holstered weapons. A woman and a cow among the group would make it appear much less conspicuous.

"You look *good*, Preacher!" Nighthorse approved. "Dog'll be hitting on you."

"Dog'll be hitting on the *cow*," Preacher countered.

"That cow is *pretty*," Dog rose in his own defense. "You, Preacher, are one *ugly* woman."

Tori was not accompanying them this time. All they took with them were weapons; Tori said they would be resupplied after this mission.

"Will you be at the airfield?" Lieutenant Hamilton asked her.

"No." She shook his hand and let hers linger in his a heartbeat longer than required.

"Until next time then," he said.

She nodded. "Nine hours."

He looked at his watch: 1700 hours, five P.M. "We'll be there," he promised.

"See that you are." Still she lingered. "Jeb, you have the saddest eyes of any man I've ever known."

Then she turned and was gone into the trees while the sun still touched their tops. Sunset was still two hours away.

The team sighed collectively, resigning themselves to the inevitable, and looked at the truck. Hamilton grinned, saying, "You guys know the drill. Climb in."

The SEALs had barely settled into the truck's sardine-can false bottom when a drawn-out gaseous whoosh erupted from above, followed by a liquid splatting and a ripe digested-grass odor. Dog groaned.

"You might have known the bitch would have diarrhea."

The truck transported its mixed cargo via a roundabout route to a deserted country road off the main highway leading toward Gracanica. When the false door was opened and the SEALs let out, there was a bruised reddish color high in the sky from the setting sun. It was nearly seven P.M. Seven hours to go. The cow was unloaded, despised though she now was, along with the cart and hay. Weapons were piled into the cart and covered with loose hay. The truck drove off. The SEALs would see it again after midnight on the other side of town.

Refugees had thinned out some on the main road with the purpling approaching of nightfall. The team casually joined one of the smaller groups which included a farm wagon pulled by a team of skinny gray horses. Furniture was piled in the back of the wagon, on top of which rode three ragged urchins.

Mad Dog pushed the cart. Preacher, disguised as a woman, led the cow with John Nighthorse walking by his side.

"Lovely evening, miss," Dog whispered to Preacher. "Wanna go to the bushes?"

"Are you, sir, speaking to me or to the cow?" Preacher replied with pretended offense.

There was a Spanish word for refugees used when Nighthorse was running operations in Latin America. *Displacedos*. It applied here. Truly these people were "the Displaced." The long sad stream of them plodding, seemingly organized to the procedure, reminded Nighthorse of old movies he had seen of people fleeing ahead of the nearest advancing armies during World War II. Surely these people and the generations that preceded them had developed a gene by now that predisposed them to survive as refugees. The invasion of this part of Europe so many times, from so many directions, accounted for the diverse ethnic mix.

A woman with wild hair and wilder eyes came running from behind, waving her arms as though she were about to take off flying. She screeched something in Albanian as she flew past the undercover SEALs.

"What's she saying?" Preacher asked Nighthorse.

" 'They can torture me, they can kill me, but please don't let them massacre me.' "

"Poor frightened soul," Preacher sympathized. "I'll pray for her."

"Better pray for us." Nighthorse said. "What frightened her was a Serbian tank."

It was a common ploy for armies to mask troop movements by mingling with refugees. The Russian-made tank followed by a truck loaded with armed Serbian troops dressed in camouflage barreled past the little procession of SEALs. Lieutenant Hamilton stiffened, but the Serbs kept going, heading toward Gracanica, undoubtedly part of the search force to find and capture the nuke. The TC—tank commander— had his head stuck out from the open turret hatch and was yelling at people to get out of the way. One of the soldiers in the truck pointed a rifle at the crazy woman. He made a shooting sound with his mouth and his buddies all laughed.

Three minutes behind the first tank and truck came two more tanks. Gracanica must be swarming with armed Serbs.

"We could let them have the nuke if they promised to use it on Washington, D.C.," Dog proposed.

Hamilton shot him a hard look but said nothing. He recalled that Mad Dog's father had won a Congressional Medal of Honor in Vietnam, posthumously. Mad Dog despised politicians, all politicians, especially the current administration. Dog's outspokenness was all right in the team, but Hamilton would have to keep a rein on him when they were among others. Soldiers could be court-martialed for criticism of the commander in chief. An admiral, an army general, and a number of lesser ranks had either been recently court-martialed or forced to resign from the service for badmouthing the administration.

Ahead, a wide curve in the road climbed to the top of a hill before dropping into a straight run for the town that lay in a wide valley. Full darkness had settled by the time the SEALs with their cow and hay cart reached the top of the hill. The wagon with the gray horses was pulling out ahead of them. Although they were now in Kosovo, Gracanica had gone into blackout mode, all lights extinguished, probably because the town was occupied by Serbian soldiers searching for the hidden nuclear device. Only the tongue-flicker of flames as a house burned or the glowing coals from a building that had already burned marred the night.

"Once more into the Valley of Death—" Preacher softly commented.

Nighthorse took over: "—but verily we shall fear no evil for—"

And Mad Dog finished it: "—We are the baddest motherfuckers in the valley."

Although vision was now limited by the advent of nightfall, Hamilton made out refugees starting to clog the highway ahead. Probably a Serb checkpoint. They were being diverted at gunpoint to a side road that went around the town instead of through it. The outskirts of Gracanica still lay more than a mile in the distance.

"Shit. *Shit!*" he murmured under his breath.

Plan B. The team, still walking, congregated around the cart to discuss options. The cow lowed mournfully and tugged at her lead trying to get to the hay on the cart, and the wooden cart wheels rattled against the road. They couldn't go back, and they couldn't split off into the meadow without risk of being noticed. They would have to bluff their way through the checkpoint.

"Can you wing it, Nighthorse?" Hamilton asked.

"Do we have another choice?"

At the moment, no. But then, unexpectedly, events changed as they often did within the uncertain fog of war.

They were tramping down the hill toward the town with tension riding around them like bad air when a sound enveloped them like that of a fleet of Volkswagens falling out of the sky. Those who have ever heard it never forget it, and when they have heard it once it will forever chill the spine of even the bravest man. Forward of them by a half-mile a series of bright balls of instantaneous flame ate into the road with a booming rumble that cracked the sky into splinters and charged the darkness with electric energy. They reminded Dog of old Vietnam vets telling about B-52 Arc Lights raids which left moonlike craters in the earth and whose detonations trembled the earth for miles around.

Bombs charged up the road toward the SEALs, running like the footsteps of a terrified giant whose feet exploded each time they touched the earth. The strobing effect of the raid flickered startled faces in and out of relief, black and white, black and white . . .

The bombing ran through the team and continued up the road, shredding the earth and trembling it in manmade earthquakes. Howling shrapnel ripped the cow into bloody parts. Her torn body fortunately provided a shield against the blast for both Dog and Preacher, who hit the ground with the dead cow almost on top of them.

Seemingly on its own volition, the hay cart leaped high into the night, splintering and raining weapons into the middle of the road. Chief Adcock and Dr. Death threw themselves face down into the bar ditch. Shrapnel whizzed overhead and thunked into the earth all around.

A force like a giant hand picked up Lieutenant Hamilton and tossed him into the middle of the dead cow. Momentarily stunned, he quickly recovered and rolled into a ball next to Dog and Preacher.

The bombing passed on up the road and ceased as quickly as it began, as though the racing giant had reached the finish line. The gray horses were unleashing unearthly screams of pain and panic. Somewhere else, a woman screeched a single syllable that rose in volume and decibels until it seemed no mortal could have issued such a forever note of despair and agony. The night returned unblemished except for the moans, cries, and screams of the wounded, both human and animal.

"Our own people bombed us!" Dog cried angrily.

"It was an accident. We don't bomb civilians," Preacher said.

"Then what's all that hollering you hear?"

Lieutenant Hamilton was on his feet, looking around. "Keep your voices down." He quickly went through the roster—Dog, Dr. Death, Preacher, Adcock . . . Only Nighthorse failed to respond.

"Find him."

The Kiowa was sitting up by now in the middle of the road, having regained consciousness. He held his head and moaned. Lieutenant Hamilton dropped a knee next to him. "John?"

"Excedrin headache number nine," he replied after a moment. "I'll be all right."

Adcock found the shattered parts of the cart. He and the others were scrabbling around in the wreckage on hands and knees, gathering weapons and battle harnesses. Everything was soon accounted for. Unbelievably, nothing was damaged. The wooden cart had absorbed most of the blast and shrapnel.

The time for disguises was over. Preacher

eagerly shucked his dress and shawl. Dr. Death
inspected the case containing his Haskins for
damage. Finding it intact, he slung it over his
back by its carrying straps and kept his shotgun
ready for action. The team peeled off the road in
tight combat formation and cut through woods
and fields toward the darkened town. Preacher
assisted Nighthorse with an arm around his
waist until the Indian's nausea and dizziness
lessened.

The Serbs were too busy with their own problems to worry about refugees scattering all over
the countryside, escaping the din and carnage
left behind by the air raid. The voices of the
wounded and dying pursued the SEALs until
they reached the first building of Gracanica. An
image of the Picasso painting "Guernica," de-
picting the bombing of a village during the
Spanish Civil War, flashed into Hamilton's mind.

He shook his head to clear it. Later, but not
now, he would deal with the fact that NATO had
deliberately bombed civilian refugees. Acci-
dents happened; miscalculations occurred. He
knew that. Nearly a third of all American combat deaths during the Gulf War had been inflicted by "friendly fire." But, somehow, he thought
this raid was no accident. The refugees had been
targeted because they were being used as cover
by Serbs entering the town. A cold, calculating
decision through NATO, in spite of all the talk
about avoiding "collateral damage," to try to

limit the number of Serbs entering the town to search for the nuclear device. Kill 'em all and let God sort 'em out. Everything justified because of the nuke.

Okay, think about it later. In less than six hours, more bombs would start raining down, this time on the town itself. If the nuke went off, which it probably would, you could dump Washington, D.C. into the crater it left.

THE MISSION

The town was darkened but not entirely dark. Nor was it abandoned, although the only people about the streets were Serb soldiers. Firelight in eerie restless patterns illuminated armed shadows flitting and rummaging about, like rats allowed to breed in a food warehouse. Gruff shouts echoed along the narrow main street. There was the brittle shattering of glass, the crashing of doors being kicked in, running boot-falls—a kind of *Krystalnacht* under Hitler's shadow.

The SEALs used alleys to traverse the town, employing a street map to work their way toward Triglav Street. A Russian-made tank nosed its low, rounded profile into the end of the alley, like a cat hunting. Backdropped into silhouette by the glow of distant flames, its main battle gun lowered ominously, sniffing. The SEALs dived for whatever cover they could find. They burrowed into trash and garbage left behind shops and hardly dared breathe lest the tank detect their location.

Dog lay half-buried in decaying meat and rotted cabbage. Pig shit, cow shit, now *this*. Where, he wondered, was all the glamor supposedly associated with being an elite, stalwart, highly trained kickass hero of the U.S. Navy SEALs?

The tank crouched motionless blocking the alley, its engine rumbling in idle, a predator watching and waiting for prey to flush. Minutes passed. Minutes dragged into a half-hour. Still it blocked the alley, engine growling in its deadly steel throat.

Its powerful engine revved as it ended the standoff. It suddenly lurched forward into the alleyway, nose gun swinging back and forth, searching, suspicious. Sniffing toward the hiding SEALs.

Heart pounding, Preacher worked two Willie Pete grenades, white phosphorus, free of his battle harness and arranged them next to his face. They were insufficient against a tank, but if the tank wasn't buttoned up, if it didn't see them until the last second, and if God were with them . . . A small chance, but it was better than no chance.

Mad Dog shifted slightly to reach his own grenades. Should he die in Kosovo, he reflected idly, would the Navy Department award him a medal posthumously to go on his mother's wall next to his dead father's Congressional Medal of

Honor? Probably not. No one *officially* knew he was even in Kosovo. The Navy would tell his mother he got drunk and died in an auto crash or a barroom brawl.

I regret that I have but one nut left to give for my country . . .

Dr. Death's cold eyes watched the tank's approach as though it were *his* prey and not the

M34 White Phosphorus
("Willie Pete") Grenade

other way around. Lieutenant Hamilton ran his quick gaze along walls searching for a way out. He concluded they were going to have to take a chance fighting the monster hand to hand. Running away was out of the question. It had them under its gun.

He bunched his muscles. Thirty more feet. The growl of the engine vibrated off the alley walls, a deep-throated sound not unlike that of some giant mechanical cat.

Rifle fire cracked from a street behind the tank. The monster braked and rocked back and forth on its faulty suspension system. It rumbled there for long seconds, as though trying to decide what to do. Then, mind made up, it reversed itself and scooted backward out of the alley the way it came. It roared away in the direction of the rifle shots. Soon even its sound was nothing but a haunting echo.

John Nighthorse drew in his first deep breath in over a half-hour. It tasted of garbage and slops, but he thought it the sweetest breath he had ever taken.

Lieutenant Hamilton leaped to his feet. "Three hours," he reminded them.

The bombing on the road would be nothing more than the harmless popping of fireworks at a Fourth of July celebration compared to the bang when NATO hit Gracanica and the nuke went off.

They crabbed to the end of the alley and

looked up and down the darkened street. The gunfire had ceased. A riderless horse trotted their way, its hoofbeats drumming on cobblestones. It nickered and burst into a gallop when it saw them. Blood streamed from a wound in its hindquarters.

They crossed the street into another alley and worked down it, crossing two more intersections. Once more there was rifle fire, but it came from behind them. Most of the fires still burning were to their right flank. Only darkness lay ahead and to the left where they were heading. So far, they had encountered neither foot soldiers nor town residents. The inhabitants were apparently either in hiding or had joined the exodus toward the south.

"The map shows Triglav to be the next street," Lieutenant Hamilton whispered to Chief Adcock. "The house should be about halfway down the block."

They would recognize it by an antique street lamp erected in its front yard.

"Piece of cake," Adcock said.

Dog snorted softly. "I've heard *that* before."

The team split to either side of the street when they reached Triglav. Dr. Death, Dog, and Preacher took the far side. There was a hardware store on one corner whose windows were busted out. It appeared to have been looted. Broken glass crunched underneath their feet. A bakery next door remained intact. The aroma coming from it reminded Dog that he was hungry.

On the target side of the street, Hamilton, Chief Adcock, and Nighthorse slipped past the cold ashes of a burned-down building and continued upstreet, moving like shadows blown through a graveyard on a soft breeze. The street looked abandoned. Serb searchers either had not been through this part of town, or they had been here and gone.

They swept onto the next block. The house should be immediately ahead.

Midnight.

Two more hours.

A partial moon had risen while the tank held the team trapped in the alley. Now it shone low down the street into their faces. From its pale illumination, Hamilton picked out the antique lamp post standing like a stick of shadow. He increased his pace, almost running.

They were within two houses of the target, within sight of its windows reflecting moonlight, when they heard a truck coming. Coming fast. Hamilton threw himself onto his belly, a SEAL on either side of him.

They watched, tension mounting, as a troop truck turned into the silence of the dead street from the intersection ahead. Its lights were extinguished. It roared purposefully toward them. It was on a mission. It sped up, gears grinding, then came to a brake-screeching halt directly in front of the lamp post. Troops noisily unassed the truck. Boots pounded on the road.

An officer turned on a flashlight and jerked its beam in erratic patterns. It passed over the lamp post, then leaped toward the house containing the KLA's nuke. He shouted orders.

This bunch *knew* where they were going and why they were here. Somehow, the Serbs had received a last minute tipoff, as they had about the pilot in the culvert.

They must not be allowed to find the nuke.

Hamilton had hoped to sneak into Gracanica and then sneak out again without confrontation. That was not going to happen now. He pushed himself to one knee, shouting, *"Go! Go! Go!"*

Startled Serbs hesitated on the house's dusty front yard. The officer's light beam froze. That instant of indecision was all the SEALs required. Stationary targets.

Hamilton's assault rifle flickered flame and death. He saw the nearest man take rounds full in the chest. It was like the bullets lifted him off the ground and deposited him on his back.

From across the street. Mad Dog's light machine gun came violently alive. Dr. Death pumped double-aught from his twelve-gauge, spraying the truck and the men around it with a deadly hail of buck. Six weapons in the hands of men who knew how to use them with maximum effect. Screams froze in the throats of the Serb soldiers as they fell like wheat under the scythe. Not one managed to get off a defensive shot.

Lieutenant Hamilton rushed toward the house ahead of his assault team. Dr. Death sprinted across the narrow street, his shotgun booming as he raked fire across the fallen soldiers to make sure there was no fight left. The officer's flashlight lay on the ground in a pool of its own light.

A single soldier crouching behind the truck survived. He jumped up, unnerved by the wild men charging toward him. Wrenching free of the truck's shadow, he broke for the opposite corner of the house and the safety it offered beyond.

Dr. Death drew down on him with his shotgun. Like popping a flushed rabbit. Except his shotgun was empty. Chief Adcock started in pursuit as Dr. Death reloaded.

"Let him go!" Hamilton shouted.

What difference did it make now whether one escaped or not? The ambush itself was bound to attract more Serbs. Additional troops were probably on the way.

Hamilton was already at a full run toward the house, leaping over fallen bodies as though he were back on the football field with the Fighting Irish, breaking through the defensive line. He hit the front door without slowing down. The door crashed in, bringing the lieutenant down to one knee. He was back up again as Nighthorse darted past him, his flashlight beam probing.

A fifty-pound bomb couldn't be *that* difficult to find.

"I'll start at the back of the house!" Hamilton shouted, lighting the way with his own flashlight.

The house had five rooms—a living room, two bedrooms, a kitchen, and an enclosed back porch. The two SEALs went through the first time quickly, hoping to find the device in plain sight. No such luck.

"All clear!" Chief Adcock called out from the front porch.

So far, Hamilton added mentally.

They forced themselves to disregard the expected arrival of enemy troops and go through the house a second time systematically and thoroughly. Nighthorse tore open a box of old clothing. Hamilton ripped apart a suitcase full of homemade biscuits. The kitchen reminded the lieutenant of his grandmother's kitchen in the 1950s: old-fashioned and functional. Pots and pans and other items littered the floor, as though discarded in haste when the owners fled.

They looked in cabinets, inside an ice box that used chunks of ice for refrigeration. It was full of spoiled meat. They stamped the wooden floor listening for the hollow of a trap door.

Hamilton moved to the back porch. Nighthorse reached the living room and the front bedroom.

"Nothing," he reported. "Maybe the Serbs have already found it."

"Couldn't be—or they wouldn't still be looking."

"The KLA?"

"I don't know."

There was nothing in the last bedroom either.

"Go through it again." Hamilton instructed. "It has to be here. This is the right house."

Chief Adcock stuck his head through the front doorway. "Jeb? I hear trucks coming."

They tore the house apart, overturning furniture, ripping apart mattresses with their K-bars, throwing clothing out of closets.

"We got company!" Chief Adcock warned.

They *couldn't* leave without the nuke.

Mad Dog's HK-11A1 opened up in measured three-round bursts, rockin' 'n' rollin' in rhythm. Chief Adcock's machine gun joined his from the front porch. The range was too great for Dr. Death's shotgun, but Preacher started lobbing grenades from his M203. Hamilton heard them banging like giant firecrackers as he worked.

The Serbs were fighting back this time. Judging from the deep-throated sputtering of AKs, there must be at least a platoon down there. Rounds thudded into the house like wind-driven hailstones. Green tracers penetrated the

HK-11A1 Light Machine Gun

walls, zinging about in the darkened house like atomic-powered fireflies and lending impetus to the search.

"We've got their heads down!" Chief Adcock reported, his voice thin and strained. "It's not going to take them long to maneuver to envelope. I think I hear tanks too. How much longer?"

The clock was running out. Last minute of the fourth quarter, third down, six yards to go—and the opposition had a copy of their playbook.

The chief sprawled belly down in the yard next to the concrete porch, laying down a field of fire with his light machine gun. Bullets snapped off the porch and dusted in the ground around him as the Serbs zeroed in on his position. Fortunate for Marge that she hadn't divorced him yet; she was going to have a good time spending his GI insurance.

It made Lieutenant Hamilton furious to think terrorists might end up with the nuke and do to other innocents what they had done to Judith.

"We have to find the sonofabitch!"

Enemy fire continued, ventilating the house. One lucky round was all it took. They wouldn't have to wait on NATO bombs.

"Mr. Hamilton!"

Nighthorse dragged a large piece of luggage out from behind a loose panel in the master bedroom closet. He unsnapped the lid and shone his flashlight into a mass padded in Styrofoam and surrounded by intricate coils of wire,

microtubing, and other electronics. Nighthorse
stared.

"So this was how the Cold War played?" he
breathed, awed.

"Learn your history later." Hamilton
slammed the lid and secured it. He wrested the
bag up with his free hand and broke for the
front door.

"What if a round hits it?" Nighthorse worried.

"None of us will ever know it. Let's hope
Preacher has prayed for us."

They paused at the door to take deep breaths.
Continuous muzzle flickers on the other side of
Triglav Street marked Dog's position where he
was hammering away at muzzle blasts winking
at him from downrange. Adcock continued to
spray bullets from next to the porch. Between
them, they kept the undisciplined Serbs ducking
and dodging and robbed them of much of their
potential effective firepower. The lieutenant
yelled at Adcock.

"We got the football! We're heading for
goal!"

Adcock lay on his trigger, melting the barrel.
"Go!"

Nighthorse grabbed one handle of the luggage, sharing the load with Hamilton. Together,
they sprang from the doorway and off the porch
and past the lamp post, vaulting bodies, racing
around the dead truck and across the street,
running through the steel and lead raindrops.
Tracers streaking green and whining through

the night, seeking flesh and howling when they could not find it.

Miraculously, they reached the other side unscathed. Chief Adcock folded in close behind them. They heard Preacher reciting the Lord's Prayer as he fought, his M203 blooping as fast as he could fire, reload, and fire again.

Hamilton and Nighthorse continued running with the ball. The others lay down a fierce final volley of fire to pin the enemy in place, to make him think more about saving his own ass than about pursuit. Dog was the last to break contact. He emptied a full mag, then jumped up and ran. Enemy fire heightened for another thirty seconds after the SEALs broke contact.

By the time the Serbs realized they were shooting at nothing but shadows and that the nuke was gone, the team was already hoofing it out of town. Rifle fire spattered into silence. Hamilton knew the enemy's next step was to attempt to ring the little town in steel to prevent the thieves escaping with the suitcase. *So solly, Milosevic,* he thought. *Too late. Better luck next time.*

POST-MISSION

Running hard, panting from exertion and excitement, the six Americans reached the far edge of Gracanica ahead of their pursuers. The darkened houses thinned out. They raced across a meadow as they heard trucks, and perhaps tanks, on their back trail.

They came upon a woodlot and turned down a small gully exactly where it was indicated on the map. They followed it south, no longer concerned with noise discipline, only with speed. Water chuckled through the creek at the bottom of the gully, but it was shallow and easier to run in than along the brushy banks. Sheets of water flew from their passage. Mad Dog, incongruously, was laughing from the thrill of it.

They burst out onto a gravel road. Where was the truck?

Preacher pointed. "There!"

The engine was already running, the driver behind the wheel. SEALs tumbled across the sideboards, not bothering with the secret compartment. Dog slipped in cow manure and sat down in it—the dead cow having her revenge.

It was a wild and reckless flight, more like rowdy boys fleeing the scene of a Halloween prank than well-disciplined SpecWar operators who had just snatched a nuclear bomb from beneath the bad guys' noses. It was an incredible high for all of them, even for Hamilton, who was usually taciturn and contained. The truck careened along little-used side roads, without headlights, and made the ten miles to the grass airstrip nearly an hour ahead of schedule.

The driver attempted to leave them at the strip, but Lieutenant Hamilton told Nighthorse to advise him to stay until the airplane arrived. They drove and pushed the truck deep into a thicket and kept watch on the road. Then it was dark and quiet. This was the part Dog always hated—the waiting. He hadn't the patience of the Kiowa, who could stay on a track for days and miles at a time, or of Dr. Death, who had hid in a treetop for three days once in order to get a kill, defecating and urinating in his pants rather than move and chance missing his shot.

The partial moon provided light enough that a pilot practiced in night takeoffs and landings without NavAids could make the strip okay. Night flying onto darkened grass strips in mountains was always risky business, a definite insurance risk, but the CIA had men—and women like Tori—who thrived living on the blade's edge. Hamilton was developing increasing respect for "Martin Smith" and the in-country support he had recruited to make sure No Man's Land both succeeded and survived.

On and off ever since the operation began, Hamilton had pondered over its organization and chain of command. The fact that Smith had remarked at the beginning that it might be necessary to "eliminate" Slobodan Milosevic, a foreign head of state, made him think No Man's Land may be more secret than any of them imagined. Assassination was against U.S. law. No politician, especially the batch of them currently wielding power, would ever stick out his neck to authorize such a measure, even if it was the right one to save the world from war and prevent thousands, even millions, from dying.

Then *who* had authorized No Man's Land? *Who* was responsible? How high up did the chain of command go?

The irony of it did not escape the lieutenant's analytical mind. If No Man's Land succeeded, the U.S. president and his administration would be lauded in the media for their shrewd, brilliant, and courageous leadership in preventing ethnic cleansing in Serbia, winning the air campaign, and maintaining the "peace process." No one would ever know the role the SEALs played in it.

On the other hand, if No Man's Land failed ... Could Hamilton and his men claim they were merely "following orders"? Or would they be branded war criminals and tossed to the UN for trial?

It was indeed, as Mad Dog frequently observed, a mad, mad world.

THE REPORT

The C-47, an ancient transport from World War II that may have flown over the Hump to Burma or air-dropped supplies to Tito behind Hitler's lines, came in through the dark low and fast to the airstrip. It touched down in the ankle-deep grass, rolled out, then started taxiing back to the downwind end in preparation for immediate takeoff. Hamilton's team had run alongside and pulled themselves in through the open cargo door. To their surprise, Smith helped yank them inside.

The heavy suitcase sailed through the door and landed on the aircraft's deck. Hamilton followed it.

"Is that it?" Smith asked, anxious.

"We need some answers," Hamilton barked as, the team all aboard, a crew chief pulled down the door and the C-47 nosed back into the wind, big engines roaring, revving. The plane shuddered.

"There isn't time." Smith shot back.

"Make time."

Smith pulled the lieutenant into the web seating and they buckled up for the takeoff run. Hamilton shouted to be heard above the engine. "What's going on, Smith? Somebody told the Serbs where it was. You have a spy, Smith—and the spy is going to get my men killed. On top of that, NATO is bombing refugees—"

Smith cut him off. "Mr. Hamilton, you have new rucks and equipment. Everything is already rigged. You have a half-hour to climb into a parachute and prepare to bale out of this airplane. You'll receive further instructions once we're on the submarine. Maybe we can talk then."

7: GOODWOOD

PRE-MISSION

It was midafternoon in Belgrade. Although, these days, air raid sirens could begin howling at any time of the day or night, normally they were silent until after nightfall. In a loft on the west side of the Sava River from the Kalemagdan Fortress, Ned Cosic pushed glasses up on his forehead and rubbed weary eyes. Cosic was a Yugoslav Internet provider and peacetime graphics designer who now spent up to twenty hours a day working on what amounted to an anti-NATO early warning system and intelligence net. E-mail warnings and messages began coming in early each afternoon, typically from other Serbs or former Yugoslav residents in Slovenia, Hungary, and the Czech Republic. They provided a pattern by which Cosic predicted targets and time-over-targets with amazing accuracy. Because of that, and particularly because of one unusually reliable anonymous correspondent Cosic had dubbed Cyber Phantom, he was provided twenty-four-hour direct access to President Milosevic's minister of state, General Yevgeny Krleza.

We can hear the idiots flying toward Yugoslavia, warned an e-mail sent from Slovenia hundreds of miles away. *Good luck, Serbia.*

They're starting early today, advised another about an aircraft coming from the north.

From the border town of Bijeljina came the notification, *They are flying very high up. Shoot down the bastards.*

Planes flying high over Banja Luka. Brothers, hold on.

The pace picked up as the evening progressed. Cosic opened new mail every few seconds on his computer and kept a phone line constantly busy to General Krleza at Command Headquarters. The chronology of raids on towns and suburbs around Belgrade progressed with the evening.

We in Zemun hear planes and several detonations from the direction of Belgrade . . .

Loud explosions and planes flying over toward Belgrade. Our air defense is fighting back. Good luck, fellow Serbs . . .

Many bombs falling in Pancevo . . .

Someone at Batajnica, the military airfield north of Belgrade, had a bad case of the jitters. *About eight bombs were dropped. I didn't count them well. I was confused and lying on the floor. The whole sky above the airport is red . . .*

Then came the message Cosic had been expecting. Cyber Phantom was almost always correct. It was he who had provided both the location of the downed American stealth pilot and the location of a nuclear device hidden in a suitcase in Gracanica. Unfortunately, in both instances someone else got there first. Phantom e-mailed that he was trying to find out *who* got the jump on Serbia and how they were doing it.

Targets for tonight are as follows, the e-mail began, then commenced to list them . . .

In a TV address to Americans before attending a NATO summit held in Washington, D.C., the president of the United States, frustrated over how little damage the bombing campaign was inflicting on Serbia, urged patience for his strategy.

"We're not drifting. We are moving forward with a strategy that I believe strongly will succeed. Two weeks of air strikes against Serbia might seem long to some, but remember that the Allies bombed Iraq for forty-four days before beginning a ground assault. It takes time to force Serb forces from Kosovo. We Allies must be willing to prosecute the campaign with determination and pay the price of time. We are acting to save hundreds of thousands of innocent men, women, and children from humanitarian catastrophes, from death, barbarism, and ethnic cleansing by a brutal dictatorship."

The NATO summit was held behind closed doors, but the agenda became public almost as soon as it ended. Assembled politicians from the different nations no more than let their shirttails flap their backsides before they started posturing their respective cases. Although Russia was not a member of NATO, a representative from that highly vocal nation had been allowed to attend the summit. In Moscow, President Boris Yeltsin stridently warned that the world was "slipping toward a third world war, the final war."

In Serbia, General Krleza accused NATO of intentionally bombing civilians using cluster bombs on a road near the town of Gracanica. NATO spokesman Jamie Shea, an Englishman, countered by saying that NATO had bombed a Serb military convoy that was using that road to invade the town to plunder and kill; he denied any civilians were injured. The U.S. president insisted such bombings were necessary because "over three hundred thousand ethnic Albanians have either been mass-executed or are being driven from their homes. Entire towns are being burned. Civilians are being targeted along roads by Serb forces, not by the Allies."

The main agenda for the summit had to do with oil. Officials were seeking strategies to stop oil imports from reaching Yugoslavia via Montenegro on the coast of the Adriatic Sea. Montenegro along with Serbia/Kosovo formed what was left of Yugoslavia at the end of the Cold War. They finally agreed on an oil embargo.

"Why are we doing this?" rhetorically asked Jamie Shea at his news conference. "Essentially because without oil, the Yugoslav military machine will come to a halt, and very quickly. The Allies will do whatever is in our means and capabilities. I hope it will not be necessary to challenge Russian ships."

The U.S. president said it was unreasonable to ask NATO pilots to risk their lives attacking oil depots when Milosevic could get fuel from ships.

"I do not expect that sea searches will lead to violence," he said, clenching his jaw and compressing his lips and looking determinedly into the camera the same way he had when he denied receiving a blowjob in the Oval Office from a White House intern, "but we have to be firm about it and take every reasonable means to ensure the embargo's success."

French President Jacques Chirac expressed reservations. "According to international law, it is an act of war to stop and search ships on the high seas. So we must be very cautious."

Angry over the days of air strikes against Serbia, President Yeltsin said Russia would ignore any NATO decision to impose an oil blockade against Yugoslavia.

"According to international law," he fumed, "sanctions cannot be imposed unless they are approved by the UN Security Council. We abide by the international law and not NATO decisions. We will continue delivering oil in keeping with our international commitments."

The Adriatic Sea was less than two hundred miles across at its widest point. At 0300 hours of a morning now cloudy over the water, a C-47 flying at one thousand feet ASL dumped seven parachutists out its doors one hundred miles off the southern coast of Montenegro. Instead of the square canopies used for HAHO and HALO, the men jumped standard Dash-One parachutes, minimally steerable but more than adequate for a "hop and pop." The CIA agent known as Smith accounted for the seventh man.

The 'chutes blossomed like mushrooms in a cellar. There was a whisper of wind through risers. Rucks rigged for flotation were dropped on lowering lines. To prevent entanglement in their parachutes in the water, the jumpers quick-released from them at the last moment and plunged into the sea, ankles hooked over one another, chins down and arms crossed to protect their faces. Parachutes floated gently away before settling on the sea to resemble giant jellyfish.

Jumpers bobbed in the cold water only a short time before being picked up by a waiting U.S. nuclear-powered submarine, the U.S.S. *Louisville*, SSN-724. Sailors aboard the sub were waiting for them with dry dungarees and blanket wraps. They were immediately escorted to a wardroom in officers' country. A man who introduced himself as "John" awaited them. He was a fragile twig upon which hung a pair of thick eyeglasses. He looked like he should have had a pocket protector full of ballpoint pens. Next to him, Mad Dog resembled a walking man mountain with his thick shoulders, Neanderthal jaw, and short quills of black hair driven like nails into his scalp.

"I take it we're paying Papa Milosevic another visit?" Lieutenant Hamilton asked.

"That's not to be discussed until I tell you it's time to be discussed," the nerd snapped in reply. Evidently he was having a bad day. But his could be nothing compared to what the SEALs had gone through in the past twenty-four hours. None of them were in a mood for his petulance.

Dog stepped close into his face, towering over him. "Twiggy," he growled, "you don't speak to the skipper in that tone. He's the best goddamned operator in the SEALs and the SEALs are the best goddamned operators in the world. So don't get snotty or I'll drown your skinny ass."

Martin Smith smiled behind his hand as Twiggy blanched and backed off. "What I meant was, I'm sure you'll want breakfast and some rest first. We thought you might want some coffee."

"Fucking Christians in Action," Dog scoffed,

only marginally mollified. He poured himself a cup of coffee and cupped his hands around its warmth.

"This is your warning order," Smith put in. "You have another mission tonight. John will give your briefing after you've eaten and slept."

Dr. Death slowly shook his head. "Life is a study in contrasts," the sniper said in an infrequent philosophical display. "At the beginning of the night, we were riding in a two hundred–dollar farm truck and getting shit on by a cow. Now we're on a billion-dollar underwater marvel carrying enough firepower to annihilate half the earth's population and getting shit on by a bureaucrat."

Twiggy shrank even farther into the walls to escape this strange, white-haired man's pale unblinking eyes.

"I love the SEALs," Dr. Death added. "We get all the best war toys."

THE BRIEFING

Cooks prepared a hot breakfast for the visitors in the boat's galley. Eggs to order, hot links and bacon, hashbrown potatoes, gravy, grits and biscuits, French toast, milk, orange juice, and as much hot coffee as they could drink. Other sailors, curious about the men who arrived so dramatically by air, came into the galley for breakfast, a cup of coffee, and a look-see at the strangers. Although the team members were curious about what mission had once more led to their being jerked out of Serbia, they did not, could not talk about it when others might over-hear. Even their control spook did not yet know the details of the mission.

"I purposely refrained from being briefed on it because I was flying in to retrieve you," Smith explained. "In the event the plane should go down or something."

He looked across the table at John Night-horse. "How's the head?" he asked. "I under-stand you were wounded. Better let the corpsmen check you out just in case."

The lieutenant stopped eating. In a lowered voice, he said to Smith, "That's something we need to talk to you about. How can we tell the good guys from the bad guys when even the good guys are bombing civilians?"

"I know. Word's already gotten out. It's offi-cially being denied."

"It *happened*," Hamilton insisted with unchar-acteristic passion. "We were there. We saw women and kids being killed by American bombs. Don't you tell me that was a mistake or a miscalculation."

"I don't know what it was," Smith admitted. "I'm not asking you to forget it. What I'm saying is that there's nothing we can do about it right now. We have a much bigger job to see that it *all* stops before the world gets out of hand. Con-centrate on that."

Hamilton was tired. Perhaps that was clouding his perspective. Smith was right. They had a job to do. Everything else would have to wait. He rubbed his face wearily with both hands. He knew enough about war to understand that *things* happened on both sides; the winner was the one who dictated the terms afterward.

"All right," the lieutenant conceded. "But how about this? Somebody on our side tipped off the Serbs about where the package was hidden. If we had been ten minutes later, we wouldn't have gotten it."

"But you *did* get it," Smith said, keeping his voice low and looking about at the other tables to make sure no one was listening. "It's safe in our hands now. That's what counts."

"It also counts if everywhere we go the Serbs also show up."

"They don't know about *you*," Smith argued. "They only know about what brought you there. We've increased security all the way up and down the line."

"Yeah?" Dog said sarcastically. "You're the government and you're here to help us?"

Smith smiled. "Something like that. Now let's all get some rest."

The team, in fact, felt much better and ready for action after sleeping and putting on dry, clean dungarees. Twiggy, dressed in shirt, sweater, slacks, and deck shoes, received them in the

wardroom for the briefing. He seemed less con-
stipated than before. He rubbed his hands
together with the subdued relish of a neighbor-
hood gossip.

"Gentlemen . . ." he began.

"I ain't no gentleman. I work for a living and
my parents were married," Dog retorted, not
ready to forgive him.

Twiggy cleared his throat. "You are about to
embark on one of the most significant missions
of your military careers to prevent a standoff
the outcome of which only God knows. The
world may be only days, even hours, away from
nuclear confrontation."

Dog nudged Chief Adcock. "Who *is* this asshole?"

"That's your new lord and master."

Martin Smith stood up. "John, these men
don't need the pep rally. Get down to the need-
to-know."

"Fine. You're the boss, Mr. Smith," Twiggy
puffed, throwing up his hands like a schoolgirl.

"Don't ask—don't tell," Nighthorse stage-
whispered.

Twiggy glared but held his tongue, intimidated
by these rough men and their banter. He spread
a map on the conference table so all could see it.

"Gentle—" He broke off, rephrased it. "This is
the seaport of Kotor in Montenegro. You can see
it is surrounded on three sides by towering mountains while most of the city is spread out along the

shoreline. The entrance to the harbor starts here, then dog legs back to the right. You're interested in those piers at the end of the dog's leg."

"And why are we interested?" Lieutenant Hamilton prompted.

"There's a Russian oil tanker tied up there. The *Lenin*. It arrived last night and will probably start offloading oil tomorrow—"

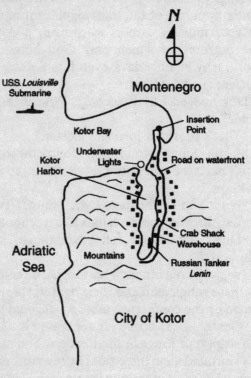

Sabotage of Russian Tanker *Lenin*

"And it can't be bombed because of 'collateral damage,' " Dog interceded with his typical cynicism.

"Not only that," Twiggy replied with forced patience. "The situation is much more complicated. We're not bombing Montenegro to the extent that we are Serbia and Kosovo, nor could we bomb a Russian ship even if we were. Russia is deliberately defying NATO by continuing to deliver oil to Milosevic. Yeltsin is attempting to force a confrontation between Russia and the U.S. in order to give Russia an excuse to intervene. He may get what he wants. Right now, a U.S. carrier group is moving in the Mediterranean to block off the Adriatic at the Straits of Otranto. It intends to stop and board all ships, including Russian."

Chief Adcock gave a low whistle. "Another Cuban missile crisis."

"The analogy is close," Twiggy said. "Step by step we're moving toward a confrontation. We have to stop it—or at least delay it. We stop it by sabotaging Russian oil ships that have already reached Yugoslavian ports, starting with *Lenin* tonight. The ship sinks, NATO and the U.S. can claim plausible deniability by letting the KLA take the blame, and Russia gets the point. We put off confrontation for at least another few days and buy us more time."

Lieutenant Hamilton was studying the map of Kotor. "And our job is to take out *Lenin?*" he said.

"Tonight," confirmed Twiggy, opening a briefcase from which he extracted target folders. He
slapped them on the table. "It must be tonight."

THE TARGET FOLDER

In the photographs, craggy mountains soared
above the harbor and the picturesque little town
hugging the relatively level land around the
water. The SEALs were little interested in the
postcard that was Kotor. Rather, they looked on
it as a puzzle to be solved tactically.

Closeups revealed a rusted tanker at port at
the end of the dog's leg. The SAT photos were of
remarkable quality. The Russian flag could be
identified. Frowns were seen on the faces of sea-
men working on the raised bow deck. Hauser
lines linked the floating derelict to the wood-
and-concrete pier.

Hamilton was particularly interested in the
entrance to the harbor where it narrowed and
twisted to the right out of the bay and into the
elbow of the dog's leg. Blown-up views of the
geography revealed armed patrol boats readily
identifiable as old-style Soviet Komars cruising
the harbor's mouth. In addition to the prowling
boats, night shots disclosed where a string of
lights had been stretched underwater completely across the narrows, making the clear seawater glow like a translucent diamond.

"It's a 'frog trap,' " Twiggy explained. "Serbs are afraid the KLA might try to send frogmen swimmers in to sabotage the port. The water is lit up like a carnival midway to a depth of about sixty feet. It's an obstacle you have to consider."

"Plus I'm sure the patrol boats have 'frog gigs,' " Dog noted.

The team studied the photos and maps for nearly an hour, passing them around with their comments, suggestions, and questions. Hamilton concentrated totally upon them and the job at hand, clearing his mind of everything else. Like most men engaged in hazardous occupations, he possessed an uncanny ability for total focus. Only at such times, it seemed, was his mind clean and sharp and completely free of the past.

"How close to the harbor can the sub put us?" he finally asked.

"There's a deep current at the mouth of the bay," Twiggy explained. "We can lock you out there. You'll have to swim nearly a mile before you reach the lights at the dog's leg. It's another thousand yards from there to the target."

The barrage of questions continued from all the SEALs. What was the depth of the water? Which direction did the currents run, and how strong were they? What was the seafront like? Were the patrol boats armed other than with small arms? Were troops guarding the piers?

Hamilton digested the answers carefully, gradually constructing a plan in his mind. To his way of seeing it, it was a relatively simple problem requiring a simple solution. The KISS principle—Keep It Simple, Stupid. Finally he made his decision.

"I'll take two men with me—"

Chief Adcock's head ratcheted toward him. "But, Skipper—"

Hamilton stopped his expected protest with a quick gesture. "I realize you all want to go. Let me explain. First, I don't want to risk the entire team. Second, the more swimmers we have in the water, the greater our chances of discovery. Besides, it only takes three men to do the job."

"But if you should run into something . . ." Dr. Death pointed out.

"We'll have to make sure we don't."

Reluctantly, the men accepted their leader's reasoning. They knew he was right, but they didn't have to like it.

"I'm taking Preacher to handle the explosives and John Nighthorse because his speaking the lingo might come in handy."

The chief gave it one last try. "Jeb, let me go instead of you. You're more valuable to the overall mission."

"I'm taking it, Chief, but thanks. Preacher, John, this is how we'll do it. Give me your input . . ."

THE PREPARATION

Even though Twiggy was an office schmuck and not a field operator—"He's still somebody we can trust," Smith explained—he came with the proper equipment and enough of it to service all six SEALs.

Twiggy cast a wry grin in Mad Dog's direction. "Mr. Smith warned me if I wasn't prepared you'd drown my 'skinny ass.'"

Clearly disappointed at being bridesmaids instead of brides, the stay-behind SEALs nonetheless assisted their comrades in inspecting gear and getting it ready for the night's mission. Twiggy produced six sets of dive equipment: black wetsuits in proper sizes along with state-of-the-art fins, masks, and support dive gauges. Hamilton was especially pleased to see the Draegers.

The Draeger closed-circuit breathing apparatus emitted no telltale bubbles to dimple the water's surface and give away a diver's presence. The concept of the closed-circuit system was simple. As the diver exhaled into his mouthpiece, the air was forced into a canister containing a soda-lime mixture that absorbed carbon dioxide. The cleansed air then moved to a flexible bladder, where it mixed with oxygen supplied by a high-pressure tank. The amount of oxygen the diver received was controlled by a valve that sensed the reduction of volume in the bladder as he inhaled. The apparatus provided the diver with approximately four hours of oxygen. That was more than enough for the estimated two hours it would take the SEALs to swim into the harbor, do their thing, then swim back out again to rendezvous with the *Louisville*. The system's major drawback was that it restricted divers to depths shallower than forty-

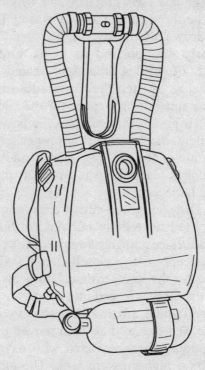

Draeger Underwater Closed-circuit
Breathing Apparatus

five feet, as pure oxygen under pressure of deep water became toxic.

Tonight's dive would be shallow, no more than thirty feet or so—unless things went to shit somewhere along the way. In any plan, you always had to consider Murphy's Law: Anything that could go wrong, would.

Twiggy had also brought serrated dive knives; .38-caliber Colt revolvers in black rubber holsters with water-proofed ammo; three SPUs, Swimmer Propulsion Units, that could drag divers through the water at speeds greater than five knots; and, of course, explosives for taking care of the tanker.

The two mines were especially designed for use by swimmers. Each included its own air chamber for neutral buoyancy in the water, a timing device, and magnetic adhesive strips for attaching it to the metal hull of a ship. Preacher looked them over and declared them good to go.

Hamilton decided to leave the SPUs behind. It would be a relatively easy swim without them. Besides, as a gesture to Chief Adcock, he indicated the chief might need them for a fast rescue effort in case something went bad. Lieutenant Hamilton trusted every man on his team to go through hellfire to reach the others should the feces strike the fan.

After everything was ready for lockout, there was only the waiting. The *Louisville*, submerged to periscope depth, maneuvered north through the Adriatic Sea toward H-hour and debarkation. She cruised the last leg of her journey at a distance of about two miles off the coast. Crowded around the periscope in the con, the SEALs took turns observing the shoreline of Montenegro. A few trucks, buses, farm trucks, and even fewer passenger cars raced the highway that ran along and around the beach toward Kotor.

When the sun left, the coast blacked out and there was nothing to see. Now there was only the waiting. Dog napped; Preacher studied Revelations in his Bible; Dr. Death cleaned his Haskins; John Nighthorse read *Don Quixote* from the boat's library; Lieutenant Hamilton and Chief Adcock, the team's leadership, spoke quietly of contingency plans with Martin Smith and Twiggy.

"There can't be a hitch," Smith warned. "If things should go bad, this sub will immediately go off-station and return to the carrier group. The U.S. cannot be implicated in this in any way."

Chief Adcock looked hard at Smith. "This sub will go off-station *only* after it has released the rest of us to go after them."

Smith said nothing. He suspected the chief meant exactly what he said.

Lieutenant Hamilton and Chief Adcock made one final check of the gear and the sub's airlock. The chief appeared to be mildly distracted, as though he had something on his mind.

"Your wife?" Adcock finally said, a puzzling question.

Hamilton stiffened and became guarded. He didn't like to talk about Judith. "What about her?"

Adcock retreated. "Sorry, Skipper. It's . . . uh, it's nothing . . ."

Hamilton turned to face the other man. His voice softened. "No, *I'm* sorry, Chief. It's just that it's . . . it's still hard to talk about her."

"I understand."

Then Hamilton understood. "Are you and Marge having problems?" he asked.

The chief looked away.

"Gene, you didn't have to come on this ops," Hamilton reminded him gently, letting a hand fall on the CPO's shoulder. "Any SEAL can decline any mission at any time, no questions asked, no stigma attached. You know that."

"If it wasn't this one, Skipper, it would be the next one. I don't know what's come over Marge lately. I'm afraid she might have . . . a lover . . ."

"Gene, I can have you pulled and sent home."

Adcock's head snapped up. "I'm needed here, Jeb."

"I also need your head clear. If you're thinking of home—"

"I can handle Marge, Skipper. We've got leave due after this. That's not the reason I'm telling you this."

Hamilton waited.

"I only wanted you to know, Jeb, in case . . .

Well, in case something happened. Don't be too hard on Marge if she's already filed for divorce."

"I'm pulling you, Gene."

"Don't do that, Jeb. I can still operate. I see you doing it, thinking of your wife, but you don't let it interfere."

Lieutenant Hamilton finally let it ride. If anyone did, he understood how a man could close off a portion of his life and still function. He had done it himself these years after Judith's murder. He was even doing it now as H-hour approached, shutting out everything in his life not relative to tonight's mission. He would have to trust his second-in-command to do the same thing.

THE MISSION

They locked out of the submarine shortly after good nightfall at a depth of forty feet. Whenever a sub dived, a bubble of air remained in the escape trunk just outside the airlock door. The three divers bobbed up into the air pocket together. It was so dark they felt and heard each other, sight being useless. Hamilton felt around for the intercom. Finding it, he contacted the bridge to report they were safely out and to ask for any last-minute SITREP.

"The only activity we're picking up are the patrol boats at the entrance to the harbor," Smith informed him.

"Good. We'll be back in time for another one of those great McBreakfasts. I'll have my eggs over easy."

The boat loomed a barely discernible darker smudge in the sea behind them as they finned free of it. The *Louisville* would lay in the trench off Montenegro for the next four hours, if that much time was required, waiting to recover them. After that, it would depart, with or without them.

Even at only twenty feet below the surface, which was the depth Hamilton chose on his gauge, the stars were mere pinprick refractions that served no more than to help them maintain equilibrium in a weightless liquid universe. Visibility was a matter of inches at most. Even with the luminous strips taped to the arms of their wet suits, they had to stay close to maintain contact.

Lieutenant Hamilton led the way, using his wrist instruments—watch, compass, depth and air gauges. Preacher and the Kiowa arrowheaded off him to either side, almost beneath his wings. Each of the two SEALs swam with one of the mines carried in a canvas bag secured to his waist. The sea was their element. They swam in long mile-eating kicks, using their arms primarily for steering. The water was cold this time of year, but the wet suits and exercise kept their bodies at a comfortable temperature.

While the luminous dial of the compass provided direction, they confirmed location periodically by angling toward the surface, breaking water gently and looking around. They made their way toward the sheen of city lights shimmering on the liquid horizon, using the city as a reference point. There was no need for blackout curtains in Kotor; NATO had not been bombing here.

Currents running crossways inside the bay forced them to compensate in order to avoid the line of submersible lights that protected against frogmen. They worked toward the darker strip of beach that lay outside the lights to the east. They surfaced to take a look deep into the harbor once they were at the correct sight angle, feeling secure in the darkness.

At the far end of the dog's leg, a number of piers extended in loose lips from shore. Two freighters of uncertain registry, having arrived after SAT photos were taken, were tied to the right, bathed in light. Lieutenant Hamilton swept his eyes back and forth until he located the Russian tanker tied up broadside to a long wharf, exactly where it was supposed to be. It too was bathed in light. Clearly no air raids were expected.

Hamilton pointed to the target and received answering nods. He took a fresh compass reading to their rally point on the beach, one that would lead them past the narrow mouth of the harbor and its Christmas illumination of underwater light. He tapped his companions on their heads to make sure they saw and understood their destination. Again they nodded as gentle swells bobbed them into each other.

The lieutenant adjusted his mask and was about to go under again when Preacher grabbed his arm and pulled back reflexively, treading water. Instinctively, Hamilton turned toward the lights, the most likely avenue of enemy approach.

Silhouetted against the harbor light appeared a pair of stocky, high-browed Komar patrol boats. They were coming toward them and coming fast. Somehow the patrol boats must have spotted something and were speeding out to investigate. Impossible! Hamilton's first thought was: *Have the Serbs been tipped off again?*

Distance can be deceiving at night. One moment the Komars were moving squares of shadow and the high-pitched predatory drumming of engines. The next moment, they loomed near, their black V-hulls shooting off phosphorescent wakes. Hamilton expected machine guns to start chewing the water red with the first loss of SEAL blood.

"Dive! Dive!" he hissed around his mouthpiece.

He upended himself, kicking furiously with his fins to drive deep into the sea, below the Komar's deadly prop blades. He felt the other SEALs diving with him. Then the three of them huddled like a school of stunned tuna, looking up through their masks with fearful darting eyes. They would be unable to see grenades falling on them through the dark sea.

The boats cut a wide glowing pathway across the surface directly above them. Preacher's adrenaline-spurred brain computed the timing of how long it would take before the grenades went off. Nighthorse waited for his ears to blow, his mask to fill with blood. Lieutenant Hamilton expected the final experience of his life to be someone driving an eggbeater up his ass with a wild man on the crank. Two faces flashed before his eyes. One was Judith's, the other Tori's. They merged into one and he held his breath to listen for the liquid whisper of grenades sinking through the water.

Nothing happened. The Komar engines faded to a distant humming. The SEALs surfaced briefly for a quick look around. Nighthorse with rare dry humor spat out his mouthpiece and eased the tension with, "Boss, do you reckon you might take out your knife and loosen up my asshole before it strangles me?"

They went under again, leaving only a trio of brief dimples on the water. They covered the remaining distance submerged to a depth of thirty feet, following the compass needle. They were not racing, but neither were they out for a lazy swim. They surfaced a final time as the bottom angled up beneath them toward dry land. Heads above water, they glided through the gently lapping shore surf and slithered onto hostile soil like amphibians breaking free of primordial muck.

Quickly they stripped down to black shorts, T-shirts, and water shoes, and strapped pistols and knives around their waists. They had previously smeared their faces and exposed arms and legs with a mixture of iodine and glycerine to cover the sheen of their skins under the wan moonlight. After wiping out their tracks and caching all their equipment except for masks and snorkels, fins, and mines in a driftwood deadfall where they could recover it afterward, they climbed up the short steep bank to the dead end of a narrow street. Retail businesses as well as residential areas lay farther back; this street appeared deserted with only the pale bug-filled cone of a streetlight here and there. Dilapidated warehouses and other run-down buildings lined either side.

Carrying masks and fins, they hugged the deeper shadows on the water side of the street, guiding on the distant glow of pier light where *Lenin* rode her moorings. The night was ripe with the mixed odors of the sea, fish, and rotted wood. They passed the narrow point of the harbor where the underwater lights were and approached a small weathered building on stilts over the water. It was attached to a tiny wharf on pilings. The door was open into the darkness. The SEALs darted inside to get their bearings and establish a temporary command post.

The single room was open, about twenty feet long, and narrow enough to induce claustrophobia. It smelled of wood rot and fish guts, hemp and seaweed. Old fish nets and fish traps, buoys and canvas and rope were piled everywhere. There was only the one door with a window on the opposite side of the room that provided a view of the upper harbor and let in the weak distant light from the enemy ship.

The tide was out. Crabs rattled their quick legs from the crawl space underneath the building and side-legged across the wooden floor, sounding like eager hangmen. Lieutenant Hamilton kept surveillance on the target and the approach to it, detecting no activity, while Preacher and Nighthorse scouted out the vicinity. They returned to report an all-clear.

"This looks *too* easy," Nighthorse whispered, squinting, looking for the hidden threat.

Deep into the harbor, yellow light reflected off the water where the Russian tanker was tied off to her long concrete-and-wood pier. Other lights draped over the tanker's side and shining into the water were apparently supposed to discourage underwater saboteurs. Two more chunky Komars rode at anchor in the harbor's channel, their machine guns looking unmanned. The SEALs detected *no* security. Hamilton had been in officers' clubs with more action.

Suspicious, they kept surveillance for another quarter-hour. When still nothing moved, they eased up the street toward a three-floored warehouse crouching in self-created shadow alongside the waterfront. There were still no sounds, no signs of movement other than their own. It was like all the crews had gone on liberty to get drunk and to get laid. Either the Serbs expected no infiltration this far from Kosovo and its troubles or there was security somewhere other than the patrolling Komars. Perhaps a stakeout in anticipation of a sabotage attempt.

This complete lack of enemy security unnerved Hamilton. Nighthorse was right; this *was* too easy. For a second he entertained a disturbing thought that the spy had compromised the mission and they were being lured into a trap. He shook it off. Martin Smith promised he was on top of the situation. You had to trust the people you operated with; there was no one else to trust.

They hid in the darkness of the buildings across from the warehouse for another quarter-hour, watching, before Hamilton nodded at his comrades and led the way across the empty street. Revolver in one hand, mask and fins in the other, he inched silently along the warehouse wall, using it as a cover to approach the waterfront and the tanker.

Lenin sat heavily in the water a football field's length away. Between them and it was moored or anchored a variety of other smaller watercraft ranging from pleasure boats to fishing boats and ferries. At the shoreline, low wharves and the clutter of timbers supporting them created a dark, forbidding labyrinth. In that maze lay both concealment and cover for the job ahead.

Preacher touched his arm. Hamilton nodded. He had heard it too. A skiff with a single dark figure huddled over the outboard engine burbled slowly upchannel, apparently returning from night fishing in the bay. Perhaps *he* was who the Komars had been rushing to check out earlier.

Flattened against the warehouse wall so they nearly melded into it, the SEALs watched cautiously as the fishing boat nosed into a pier this side of *Lenin*. The occupant stood up in the boat to tie off. He unloaded items onto the pier, presumably his fishing gear. Then he clambered out onto the pier, gathered his belongings, and soon disappeared into the dark, walking slowly the way an older man would. He was not challenged.

They waited another five minutes. Time was closing in on them. They were approaching the halfway mark of the four-hour period at the end of which they either rendezvoused with *Louisville* or were left behind. It was time, as Hamilton's dad used to say, to either cut bait or fish.

Easing to their bellies to reduce their profiles, the three infiltrators slithered to harbor's edge and slowly sank into it until only the no-glare faceplates of their masks were visible on the surface. They used silent breast strokes to slide through the sea. No sound betrayed their progress. They paused in the deep shadows underneath a low wharf at the ship's stern.

Lenin rose above them. Close up, it appeared much larger than in the photographs or from their first view of it outside the harbor. Schools of fish attracted by the lights swarmed in the water. There were no lights off the fantail, however, and the water there was black and oily. It lapped gently at the ship, making that nibbling, hollow-vessel sound.

Preacher quickly set the timers on both mines for 120 minutes. Two hours should give them plenty of time to escape Kotor and catch their ride. Placement of the mines had already been decided during the mission's planning stages. One would go aft and starboard of the keel while the other would go portside. The explosions would rip the stern off the tanker, sink it, and spill a few hundred thousand barrels of flaming oil. Environmental wackos were going to love this one.

The SEALs dived deep to traverse underwater the flood of light between the pier and the ship. They resurfaced together in the dark at *Lenin*'s stern. Preacher and Nighthorse quickly activated the mines and peeled the backing strips from the adhesive. Preacher stuck the blade of his dive knife between his teeth to have it ready to scrape away barnacles for a place to attach his mine. Nighthorse followed his example. Hamilton kept a sharp eye out for danger. He tapped his watch. Go!

Preacher glanced at Nighthorse, who nodded. They dove, each with a mine clutched between his elbow and body, careful to avoid the primed adhesive backing. They could hold their breaths free-diving for approximately three minutes. Not much time, but an eternity underwater without air.

The hull deeper down was surprisingly free of crustacean crust. Preacher worked by feel since visibility was all but nil in spite of the glow of light in the water to his side. He cleaned a place on the hull and pressed the mine to bond glue to metal. The placement was not that crucial. What with the tanker's cargo, anywhere along here would be like igniting dynamite in a gas tank.

Nighthorse finished first. His masked face appeared next to Hamilton's to gulp silent air, followed seconds later by Preacher's. The three saboteurs immediately dived back to the low pier and swam away in the shadows created by wharves and moored boats. The Kiowa found it difficult to maintain the careful noiseless pace set by the lieutenant in the lead; he wanted distance between him and the explosives in the event they somehow detonated prematurely. When the ship went up, folks in Italy would think the resulting fireball was the sun rising.

It had taken them sixty-eight minutes to swim in to the beach outside the lighted harbor entrance, another forty-seven minutes to make their way along the waterfront, reenter the water, and set the mines. One hour and fifty-five minutes.

When they emerged from the water at the hut on the wharf, which Lieutenant Hamilton now thought of as the "crab shack," eighteen minutes had expired off the mines' timers. In only one hour and forty-two minutes, things were going to start going thump in the night.

They made faster time trotting along the beach in their lightweight footgear. When they reached the band of submerged lights, they found a Komar patrolling it at idle speed. They couldn't waste time waiting for it to go elsewhere. They crept by close enough to watch as one of the boat's crew members lit a cigarette, cupping his hands around the match so that the glow lit up a circle of his face and momentarily destroyed his night vision. He propped an elbow on the mounted machine gun and leaned against it to smoke. His companion at the helm said something. Voices carried long distances at night across water.

Then the SEALs were safely past what was hopefully their last major obstacle and on their way home. It had been an unusually easy mission, what with the marked absence of security. Nothing lay ahead but the black spit of land and an easy swim off its point back to the *Louisville.*

They heard voices as they drew near the dead-fall where they had cached their tanks and other equipment. Laughter and casual chatter. It sounded like three men, maybe more, and a woman, all with slurred speech like they had been drinking. Nighthorse made out enough to identify the men as a roving patrol taking an unauthorized break with a bottle of *lovavacka* and a woman they had picked up somewhere. From the sounds of them, they were going to be in place for a while.

Nighthorse chuckled underneath his breath. "They're trying to decide who goes first."

Lieutenant Hamilton checked his watch: ninety-six minutes till showtime. They could not afford to await the amorous outcome of the present situation. They would have to go home without their Draegers. Hamilton motioned to his teammates and led them back into the sea from which they came. They would have to make the return trip surface swimming and hope the patrol boat crews were likewise engaged somewhere with their own *lovavacka* and sweet thing. It was risky, but not as chancy as hanging around on foreign soil waiting for trouble to develop.

POST-MISSION

They swam for nearly an hour against the current. It was a hard swim against the clock. As soon as they reached the open Adriatic, Hamilton turned on the homing device to summon Mom to come pick them up. They treaded water, waiting, held together by the jack stay line they intended using to snag the submarine's buoy when it was released to guide them back under into the *Louisville*. They faced a forty-foot free dive without air in order to reenter the boat.

"What if she doesn't come back?" Nighthorse worried.

"We swim out to sea and drown."

"Suppose we'll all go to heaven, Preacher?" the Kiowa wondered.

"That's your choice, John. Do you know Jesus?"

"I thought I met him once. Turned out to be a reborn hippie on crack."

Two things happened almost simultaneously. *Louisville*'s buoy popped up within twenty feet of them—and the Komars returned. The distant humming whine of their engines came their way with purpose.

"Rescued by the last hair on our macho asses," Nighthorse said in relief.

"We're not out yet," Hamilton cautioned.

Snagging the buoy with the jack stay line was the easy part. Getting inside the boat without their air tanks was going to be a bit trickier. Fortunately, the airlock at the forward escape hatch was roomy enough to accommodate all three divers at the same time. Sucking deep gulps of air, they dived for the airlock, going down the buoy line hand over hand, one after the other. Pressure seemed to want to burst their lungs.

The line led them through the liquid darkness

to the overhanging lip of the escape trunk. Hamilton let go of the line and ducked underneath it, bobbing up inside into the trapped air pocket. His teammates appeared immediately after him. Hamilton contacted the bridge on the intercom.

"Get in!" Smith urged. "Patrol boats are coming like bats out of hell."

No shit, Dick Tracy.

It took time to enter a submarine underwater. First, lock into the chamber. Blow the water, replace it with air, equalize pressure. Enter the sub, relock the inner hatch. All except the first step could be accomplished with the boat underway.

"The Komars are almost within machine-gun range—"

"Roger that!" Hamilton snapped. "We're starting to lock in now. Give us one minute— then get the hell outta here."

THE REPORT

None of the SEALs felt anything when the explosions finally came; they were several miles into the Adriatic and submerged, on their way to join the U.S. Sixth Fleet. Martin Smith reported to Jeb Hamilton that the submarine's sonar picked up a heavy explosion, followed by an even heavier secondary explosion as the gases trapped inside the *Lenin*'s tanks went off.

Mad Dog slapped Preacher on the back. "Good job," he growled. "Glad to have you back. Affirmative action wasn't the same without you."

"You SEALs really *can* go anywhere, anytime, and accomplish any damned thing for your country," Smith beamed.

The three exhausted warriors barely heard him. Wrapped in wool blankets, they were already dozing off.

8: UNDERLORD

PRE-MISSION

Night had settled purple and star-studded over the northern Adriatic. From the bridge of Aegis destroyer U.S.S. *Gonzalez*, Mad Dog Gavlik cracked, "To sir, with love," as a barrage of Tomahawk cruise missiles blasted free of the ship's two MK41 Vertical Launching Systems. These systems contained ninety cells, which meant a hell of a lot of firepower.

The missiles, six of them on this, the night's first fire mission against Serbia, whistled a deadly subdued tone underlying the roaring *whoosh!* of their rockets as they shot into the night sky with their tails on fire. They streaked easterly in a blazing flock. To Dog, they resembled giant bottle rockets shot off during a surreal July Fourth celebration.

The sea was awash with sky glow, which silhouetted the scattered ships of the U.S. Sixth Fleet's carrier battle group. Cheering slapped

echoes across the water from sailors crowding
the decks of their warships to watch tonight's
show. Lieutenant Jeb Hamilton and his men
had the best seats in the amphitheater on the
bridge of the *Gonzalez*, having been invited
there by the destroyer CO, Captain Joe Murphy.
They watched until the Tomahawks' red ex-
hausts blended with the canopy of stars and vanished into them.

Hello, Milosevic.

"That's it for now," Captain Murphy said. "It's
nothing like you see on the History Channel
with battleships softening up Tarawa or Iwo
Jima."

For the past three days, following the sabotage
of *Lenin* in Kotor Harbor, an event that caused
some ripples diplomatically, the SEALs of No
Man's Land had been on stand down aboard the
Aegis destroyer. They had little to do other than
eat, sleep, read, watch TV in the officer's lounge,
and work out in the ship's gym; their karate
sparring bouts always drew a crowd of specta-
tors wondering exactly *who* these fierce-looking
men were. Smith said subsequent missions
depended on political and diplomatic developments. He promised they would be back in
action soon.

Each afternoon an air of excitement began
spreading throughout the warship as the *Gonzalez* prepared for the launching of her missiles
that night. This was the kind of battle Americans

loved, Hamilton thought—sterile and high-tech without all that messy business of having blood and gore spread all over the TV screens at dinnertime. What made it even better was that, so far, America had suffered not a single casualty. Even the one pilot shot down in his stealth fighter, Captain Ron McMasters, was mysteriously rescued and whisked out of harm's way. Few knew the story behind his recovery—and Captain McMasters wasn't talking.

"What effect are we exerting on the outcome of the war so far?" Lieutenant Hamilton asked Smith during one of their strolls together around the *Gonzalez*'s main weather deck. Over the past days the team had spent a lot of time with the bookish-looking spook; their grudging respect for him continued to grow.

Smith stopped walking and the two men stood at the ship's fantail gazing out over the gentle cobalt sea at the outlines of a carrier, three or four cruisers, and a gaggle of destroyers spread out gray and formidable in battle formation.

"Commandos blowing bridges, stealing nuclear weapons, sabotaging ships, busting up drug deals, creating havoc . . ." Smith mused, with a sour smile. "Disorientation can be a very good thing. Each side feels it is being targeted by the other, but neither understands how. That makes everybody more wary. Will it work?"

He shrugged and left it at that.

"It seems to me," Lieutenant Hamilton ventured, more and more entertaining the thought that No Man's Land was a clandestine last resort against what *someone* in the United States felt to be a gigantic strategical mistake in the Balkans, "that we also have disorientation in Washington. Almost like a struggle for power."

"A republican form of government is always a struggle for power," Smith said, not intending to be condescending, and Hamilton didn't take it that way. "It's happening on both sides. Russia has deployed a small number of troops to Belgrade, but so far they have not left the capital. U.S. Apache helicopters and support troops have moved forward into Macedonia, but there doesn't seem to be a hurry to use them in Kosovo yet. I think we're all dangerously aware of the escalation possibilities, but it's going to be done anyhow. That's what happens when you mix politics and ego."

During the team's hiatus aboard the *Gonzalez*, Smith daily downlinked summaries and precises of the international climate prepared by CIA analysts in Langley and presented them to the SEALs to keep them updated. It was clear through this intelligence that a major schism between lawmakers and policy makers was tearing Washington D.C. apart. Everyone was choosing sides and attacking those who disagreed with him. One hot issue centered on how the KLA was being viewed.

After receiving fresh evidence implicating the Kosovo guerrillas in drug smuggling, U.S. Congress withdrew its Kosovo Self-Defense Act for rearming them. However, the more Congress backed off the KLA, the more the president and his administration scrambled to support these "freedom fighters." The president, who had fired his special envoy to Kosovo for referring to the KLA as a "terrorist group," gave a speech in which he ignored KLA ties to Middle East terrorists and spoke of how the U.S. needed to "develop a good relationship as the KLA transforms itself into a politically oriented organization. We want to develop closer and better ties."

Smith emitted a bitter sound that could not be called laughter as he gazed out to sea toward Serbia.

"Do you recall how the 'Sandalistas' in the U.S. supported the Nicaraguan Sandinistas?" he asked—a rhetorical question since SEALs kept constantly abreast of world hot spots. "It was anti-American Marxist chic. The same thing is happening again when it comes to the KLA. The hard-core, sandal-wearing groupies who followed around the Central American Marxists, whose heroes petered out with the end of the Cold War, have turned their sights on the Kosovo rebels."

Smith was lecturing, reverting to his professor character, but Hamilton was interested.

"Similar myths are being created in the U.S. to explain the KLA struggle as the same one that made the Viet Cong so cozy in the 1960s to draft dodgers and readers of *The New York Times*. Supporters of the KLA in Washington aren't too anxious to shatter the image. 'Don't confuse me with the facts, my mind's made up.' Anyone who points out the KLA's shadowy past and links to Marxist-Leninist groups is silenced. NATO *needs* the KLA as an excuse if it becomes necessary to deploy ground forces."

Discord and discontent were sweeping the globe like an angry tsunami wind, driving the world closer and closer to the edge. A Spanish pilot participating in the air campaign denounced NATO bombings as "one of the biggest savageries of history. NATO's repeated bombings of civilian victims and nonmilitary targets were not 'errors,' " he claimed. "There is a coded order of the North American military that we should drop antipersonnel bombs over the civilian localities of Pristina and Nis."

Former U.S. President Jimmy Carter published an article in *The New York Times* also condemning NATO bombing, calling the "destruction of civilian life . . . senseless and brutal."

While the International Ethical Alliance, IEA, supported the prosecution of President Slobodan Milosevic and General Yevgeny Krleza as war criminals, it also charged that war crimes committed by the president of the United States should be prosecuted. Russia likewise insisted that if the UN indicted Milosevic and Krleza, it should indict the U.S. leadership.

NATO seemed to be splitting apart at the seams. Russian overtures in forming anti-U.S.

coalitions with non-European great powers like China and India also held particular interest to European countries like France and Germany that saw their own interests threatened by American dominance.

Hamilton couldn't help thinking that Smith was providing a parameter for an upcoming mission.

"So where does all this politics leave *us?*" he asked the agent.

Smith turned to face him. "Right where we've always been—balancing on the high wire. If we keep hammering away, we may be able to end this thing without foolish men plunging us into hell without a back door."

THE BRIEFING

Hamilton was right. There was a purpose for the background intelligence Smith fed the SEALs about the international political weather. He realized it as soon as "Professor" Smith gathered the team in the captain's wardroom aboard the *Gonzalez* and began talking. By this time the operators were rested and restless for action. Like racehorses champing at the bit in their eagerness for the gates to open.

"As most of you realize," Smith said for openers, "there's a great deal of confusion in Washington about what is actually happening in Yugoslavia and even more confusion over the best way to handle the campaign against Serbia. The truth is, nobody *knows* the truth. Rather, no one wants to confront the truth. There's enough disinformation, propaganda, and counterintelligence being passed around Washington to confuse even wise old Solomon. CNN seems to be where Washington receives most of its information—and CNN is often plain wrong or so eager to make political points that it goes out of its way to feed politicians what they want to hear. The same is true of much of the media. That's unfortunate, but that's the way it seems to be."

He paused and looked around at the six SEALs sitting at the polished oval table. On the walls of the cramped room were framed photographs of the Aegis destroyer in various action phases—in convoy, in port, firing her missiles. Interspersed among them hung stern-looking portraits of previous commanders. The SEALs were not going to like what Smith had to say. They had already noticed how he neglected to bring to the briefing his customary maps, target folders, and supporting materials. There was not even a ballpoint pen on the table in front of him.

"Gentlemen, I realize that SEALs are trained to operate in teams, that you function best when there are six to twelve of you. I hate to have to break you up. However—"

Mad Dog Gavlik sprang to his feet with a roar. "Wait a minute!"

Even Dr. Death, who if truth were known preferred working alone, reacted to the news. "I assumed this was a team effort . . ."

Smith waited patiently until Lieutenant Hamilton restored order. Hamilton said, "Hear him out first." To Smith, he added, "This had better be necessary."

"It is. It will be temporary and you will reunite in country within a week or so. For reasons of security, each group will not be privy to the mission of the other until it becomes necessary. I'm going to ask all of you to leave at this time except for Lieutenant Hamilton."

Silence greeted the announcement for a few more heartbeats as the team waited for Smith to call further names. When none followed, impetuous Mad Dog demanded incredulously, "You're sending in Mr. Hamilton *alone?*"

"He won't be alone." Smith calmly replied. "He simply won't be with any of you."

"If he ain't with us, it's the same as being alone."

Hamilton took a deep breath. He was little enthused about developments himself. At the same time he was curious. He held up his hand to quiet the protests.

"I'm sure Mr. Smith has his reasons," he said.

"We're not sure about anything anymore—except for the six of us together." John Nighthorse said, eliciting a fresh wave of dissent.

It didn't last, however. Although human with all the faults, weaknesses, and passions common

to humans, SEALs were disciplined professionals honed into the most effective and dangerous
small combat unit the world had ever known. As
they filed reluctantly from the room, the lieutenant drew Chief Adcock aside.

"This puts you in charge," he said. It was
almost a question.

Chief Adcock knew what he was getting at.
"Skipper, my private life is in a separate compartment. I'll handle Marge when this is all
over."

Lieutenant Hamilton scrutinized the CPO for
a full thirty seconds, looking for chinks and
cracks. The chief gazed back at him, seemingly
as solid as ever. He stuck out his hand to shake
his commander's.

"Sir, we'll see you in Serbia in a few days."

The room seemed empty with so much of its
energy depleted. Hamilton reseated himself
across the table from Smith. He lifted both
hands in an exaggerated shrug that said, *Let's get
it on*. Smith obliged.

"I'll give you the brief answer," he said, hoist-
ing onto the table his briefcase and opening it.
"Then we'll get down to details. Mr. Hamilton,
you'll be inserted onto the coast of Montenegro
before dawn tomorrow by SDV. You'll be met
there by our contact driving a green Yugo with
PRESS signs on the doors. Once you're ashore,
the contact will provide you with documents

identifying you as a Canadian newspaper correspondent. Your destination is the Kosovo capital of Pristina. You'll go to the Grand Hotel, which is headquarters for the international news media."

The scowl on the lieutenant's face halted him. "Question?"

"Yes. Why me?"

"Our last agent in Pristina was exposed to the Russians, who naturally gave the intel to General Krleza. He was assassinated."

"How was he found out?"

"That we still don't know. We suspect, but can't confirm, that there's a link to his exposure and whoever it is that has been supplying Milosevic with NATO targets and other intelligence all along."

"Why won't the same thing happen to me?"

"Our agent wasn't posing as a newsman," Smith said. "We can't afford to take any more chances if we, and I mean the agency, have been compromised. That's why we're sending you in with a contact who has been reserved explicitly for No Man's Land. You and your SEALs, Lieutenant, along with our in-country staff working with you, are the deepest undercover we have at this point. There's no cause to think that you won't blend right in with all the other international reporters. Your background credentials have been thoroughly covered in case someone tries to snoop around."

The lieutenant nodded, noncommittal. "And the mission is?"

Undercover Investigation of the
Situation in Kosovo

"We've been talking the past few days about how unreliable the press has been in reporting what's going on inside Kosovo," he said, further confirming how Smith had been preparing him for this job. "There's no one in Kosovo at this time that Director Benefield can trust to provide objective truth about what is really occurring between the Serbs and the ethnic Albanians. I have a list of EEI, Essential Elements of Information, which you'll memorize to use as a guide."

He splayed one hand on the table and began closing a finger at a time as he ticked off some of the elements. "Is there really genocide or is it simply war fever propaganda designed to keep Americans pumped up for the war? Less than a year ago, the KLA was being branded as international terrorists and drug runners. Now, they're freedom fighters. What is the full story, notwithstanding the drug angle? What's the refugee status?

"In other words, the official version of the air campaign in Washington and the CNN version are the same. We have to know whether it's the truth from the point of a military analysis. You will document your report, which will be submitted by Director Benefield to both Congress and the White House. The national press corps will also receive copies to prevent politicians from spinning it to their own personal ends."

Cynicism these days, Hamilton thought, seemed to be the pervasive mood in America. Not necessarily without cause.

"There has to be a middle ground somewhere that we can use to solve this thing before it spirals past the point of no return," Smith concluded solemnly. "We are rapidly approaching that point now."

THE PREPARATION

The MARK VII SDV—SEAL Delivery Vehicle—provided no dry environment for either crew or passenger. The journey from the *Gonzalez* was dark, cold, wet, and lonely. Dressed in a wetsuit, alone in the rear compartment. Lieutenant Hamilton shifted around to get as comfortable as possible in the little underseas craft. He wore a dive mask and breathed through a regulator connected to the odd little boat's air tanks. He would not need tanks of his own.

Forward of him, two pilots at the instrument panel, also dressed in masks and wetsuits, guided the vessel toward the rocky shores of Montene-

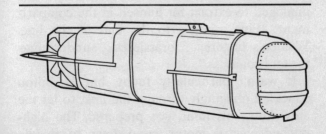

MARK VII SDV—SEAL Delivery Vehicle

gro. The water inside was tinged slightly red from the instruments, as though a fish were bleeding into the water. The forms of the pilots, whose backs were only visible to him, were shadowy and liquid. There were no portholes, not even for the operators. They "drove" using specialized sonar called a Doppler navigation system. Like airplane pilots flying on instruments. The electric motor filled the lieutenant's ear with a liquid monotonous humming. The water at depth was chilling. Hamilton hoped there was a sun in Montenegro when he came ashore.

He checked the luminous dial of his wrist-watch: 0400 hours. Occasional comments from the SDV crew through the intercom system were a welcome distraction as they navigated nearer the coast. They were taking no chances of being spotted by prowling patrol boats or coast watchers.

"There's no activity in the water," they said to Hamilton on the radio link.

A few minutes later, the same voice jarred the SEAL officer from whatever comfort he had managed to extract for himself in the compartment. "Five minutes to the end of the line. Women's lingerie . . . brassieres . . . underthings for fat broads . . ."

It wasn't particularly funny, but Hamilton chuckled obligingly through the link, to let the crew know his mind was prepared. The high-pitched electric motor eased down to an idle and the SDV lugged in the water. Hamilton opened the compartment door at his side even before he was instructed.

"Your course to shore is niner-one degrees, at a distance of four-hundred yards," the pilot's voice said.

Hamilton automatically repeated it. "Aye, aye. Niner-one at four-hundred."

"Good luck, whoever you are and whatever you're doing. I'm just as glad I'm in this thing as out there where you're going."

Hamilton adjusted the Glock 9mm in its holster around his waist. It was his only weapon. He slid out of the machine into the black surrounding waters and held on to it, still breathing through its tanks, while he slipped on his flippers and checked his depth gauge. Depth, thirty feet.

He took a last full breath, then let the mouthpiece float free. Arching his back, he extended his arms and with a flip of his fins rose gracefully to the surface.

There was no sun. He hadn't expected it yet. A widening golden strip separating the jagged eastern horizon from the sky told him it wouldn't be long. He was near enough shore to see the black outlines of trees and hills. He saw no lights anywhere. Satisfied of his isolation, he laid out on the water and propelled himself toward the golden sunrise, using a distance-grabbing crawl that soon brought him within sound of the surf rubbing against rock. For some reason, he felt vibrant and alive, like a kid setting forth on his first scouting adventure.

When his fins touched bottom, he took them off and waded the rest of the way in. He hid his fins and wetsuit in a fissure among a pile of boulders and looked around. He was now on a narrow gravel beach between the restless sea and a cliff 30 feet tall. The cliff eventually squeezed the gravel shoreline into the sea. He scouted around in the gradually expanding light until he found a trail where Smith said it should be during his briefing. He checked his watch. The Yugo with PRESS on its doors should be arriving within the half hour. Good timing.

Wearing only swim trunks and sneakers and carrying his holstered pistol, he cautiously climbed the trail leading up and off the beach, coming out above onto a grassy plateau with a scattering of trees growing around the edges of a meadow. A narrow road showing pale in the coming dawn edged out of some distant hills and curved toward the coastline to follow it as far as Hamilton could see in the opposite direction. He waited until he saw a vehicle appear on the road coming toward him, headlamps off in the gray dawn, before he found concealment among the trees.

When it was nearer, he recognized it as a green Yugo with PRESS on the door closest to him. It slowed and eventually stopped on the road. The engine continued running. He waited another minute before showing himself, checking first to make sure the car was not being followed.

Finally satisfied, he rose from hiding to show himself. The driver's door opened. Tori stepped out onto the road and smiled at him.

"When you make a date, you *make* a date," she said. "You really know how to show a girl a good time."

THE MISSION

Hamilton looked at the Yugo. "I expected another truck or maybe an ox cart," he joked.

"We're moving up in the world, going middle class."

She retrieved a bundle of clothing from the car which included a pair of used rough-out leather hiking boots. She came around the front of the car and thrust it into his arms. She grinned, teasing, "I don't often pick up a half-naked hitchhiker."

"What made me an exception?"

"Probably that forlorn look on your face. Get dressed quickly and let's go. I'll turn my back." She was still teasing.

She smelled of night air and open grassy meadows in mountains. Her nearness made him uncomfortable. She smiled again and turned her back to him. A cool breeze on damp skin made him shiver.

He looked up and down the road before slipping off his swim trunks and drawing on dry underwear and socks, a pair of faded khaki trousers, a loose tan sports shirt with long sleeves, and a woven leather belt. Tori was similarly dressed in jeans, form-fitting and attractive on her this time, and a dark blouse.

"I have more clothing for you in your bag," she said as he changed. "I figured you for a briefs man instead of boxers."

"The president and me."

"All your documents for journalist Keith Laub of the *Toronto Globe* are in the car. I'll call you Keith."

"And I'll call you . . . ?"

"Tori is still good enough."

He told himself the reason he was glad to see her was because she had proved herself to be a crack operator, a professional on whom he could depend.

"I like your name," he said. "I hope it's your real name."

"Tori Rogers, also of the *Toronto Globe*. There's a secret panel for your gun in the driver's door. We don't want to be caught armed at a roadblock. Papers or not, they'd march us to the side of the road and summarily put bullet holes in our skulls."

"A pleasant thought." He leaned against the

car to put on the hiking boots. "You can turn around now."

"Are you decent?"

"No, but you can still turn around."

It had been a long time since he had felt at ease enough around a woman to engage in innocent male-female sexual rapport. He had not dated since Judith died. He caught himself. Judith hadn't merely *died*. She was murdered.

"Why did they send you?" he asked her as she faced him and nodded her approval of his new look.

"Disappointed?" She smiled. "Get rid of your trunks and sneakers and let's get going before somebody chances along. We can exchange intimacies later."

"Promise?"

Hamilton drove since Tori thought it would look better it they ran into the KLA, who as Muslims were contemptuous of men who seemed to be subservient to their women. The road was the same rub board blacktop of every other "major" road in Yugoslavia.

"Okay, so why did they send you?" Hamilton said.

"Abbott had his Costello, Jerry Lewis his Dean Martin, and Lucy her Ricky."

"You like the old shows!"

"The world wasn't so insane back then. So why was I sent? Probably because I'm more unlikely to be known than anyone else in Europe." By "anyone else," she undoubtedly meant other CIA agents. "We also figured a man and a woman traveling together would be less conspicuous than two men or even a man alone. Besides, I speak the language and I know the country."

"How did that come about? I mean, your knowing the country?"

"My folks were born in Kosovo. So was I."

"You're Albanian?"

"Czech, actually, but I was still born here. I've already told you too much. Let's talk, but nothing personal. Okay?"

They chatted comfortably as they traveled, becoming more acquainted while at the same time avoiding details of each other's lives that could endanger them were one or the other captured and interrogated. When the sun came up, it came up blazing. The road soon turned into a gutted dirt lane filled with deep holes and ruts as it climbed into the mountains, a road out of the Middle Ages, allowed to degenerate with the seasons.

It was soon twisting precariously among hundreds of feet of sheer golden rock cliffs rising to one side while dropping off on the other into bottomless valleys choked with fires of green foliage, purple-and-white wildflowers growing on razor-honed chrome ridges, and altitude-stunted scrub pines jutting from limestone outcroppings. A steady clean wind riding through the canyons brought the mixed scents of water and pine forests.

Hamilton had always loved the mountains. Judith and he used to take off every winter to go skiing in the Colorado Rockies. Wolf Creek Pass and the little wonderful town of yellow pine buildings at its base. South Fork. Breakfasts at the Hungry Logger before driving up to the lifts.

He glanced at Tori, feeling slightly disloyal to Judith's memory for being with another woman. Enjoying it anyhow. He erased his memory, for the moment at least, and merely drove with the pretty woman at his side.

Once they crossed the mountains, the land swept downward toward the Kosovo basin to the east and even further to Asia Minor and the land of Ghengis Khan. Homesteads appeared infrequently, raked rooftops shingled in hand-carved pine so old it looked like slate. Some of the carts pulled by big-footed horses or oxen had wooden wheels. It was the Middle Ages all over again, and one of the loneliest lands Hamilton had ever visited. He was glad for Tori's company.

"A little daunting, isn't it?" Tori commented, reading his mind.

"The Serbs and the Kosovars are fighting over *this?*"

"For generations," Tori said. "Longer than the Catholics and Protestants have been brawling in Ireland."

" 'Blood ran knee deep in the glory of God,' " Hamilton said, quoting from a remark made by a Crusader during the siege of Hagia Sophia.

At Pec, they picked up the final highway to Kosovo's provincial capital at Pristina. They traveled through a barren scorched land only lightly touched by all the rain in the mountains north of here. It was sprinkled with villages all looking the same—red bricks, tile or pine-shingled roofs, and bad mortar work slopped around frames of thick timbers. Once they passed an abandoned burned hull of a car riddled with bullet holes, the only sign of war so far. A woman's bra stuck on a stick by the side of the road waved in the breeze like a battalion banner.

The most dangerous section of the road lay ahead, through embattled Serb military checkpoints and under brown hills that contained the snipers and guerrillas of the Kosovo Liberation Army. Their credentials were bound to be tested.

Around a curve and through a pass between two near hills, they came upon a plyboard shack by the side of the road and a rusted iron gate across the road. Two Serb cops wearing sky-blue uniforms and armed with icy stares and AK-47 rifles stood behind the gate.

"It's often less suspicious if we speak only English." Tori said.

They played the dumb journalist-tourist role and kept pointing down the road and saying,

"Pristina." The guards rifled through their duffel bags and camera bags, and attempted to question them about their credentials. It was obvious they couldn't read the papers. Hamilton pointed at his name and repeated it. "Keith Laub. Keith Laub. I'm a newsman." One of the guards circled the car, looking at it as though he were a used car dealer. Hamilton edged closer to the open driver's door and the pistol hidden in its panel.

The cop with hair erupting from his head like pig bristles went into a tirade. He gestured wildly at the car, at the strangers, at the surrounding hills and finished by brandishing his rifle.

"Doo hun-ret deutsche mark," he said, pointing at the car and then at the road beyond the iron gate.

"Two *hundred* marks! What for?" Hamilton demanded, playing the offended role. It made you look guilty if you gave in too easily.

"Doo hun-ret. Pristina," the cop repeated impatiently.

Grudgingly, Hamilton fished a pair of bills from the used wallet provided him by Tori. The iron gate swung open.

A mile further on, around another S curve, two more men stood in the middle of the road, aiming rifles at the Yugo's windshield. These wore camouflage vests over civilian clothing. Hamilton hit the brakes. He and Tori both thrust their hands above their heads. The riflemen gestured for them to get out. Cautiously, they opened their doors and stepped from the car, keeping their hands above their heads. Hamilton felt himself fuming inside; it was humiliating for a SEAL to be placed in these predicaments.

A red and black patch sewn onto one soldier's Yankee baseball cap and on the sleeve of the other identified them as KLA guerrillas. They wore crusty jeans and shirts and ratty sneakers and carried bayonet-fitted M1 rifles left over from Tito and World War II. Before the questioning and searching could begin, a yellow Land Rover with PRESS and BBC on its sides ripped around the curve and skidded to a startled halt. It was full of British reporters, all of whom thrust their hands into the air at the sight of the two guerrillas with rifles.

That made it easy for the guerrillas to decide what to do with the Yugo. One of them lowered his rifle and held out his hand.

"Doo hun-ret deutsche mark," he demanded and pointed in the direction of Pristina.

"Must be the going rate," Hamilton said to Tori as he fished out two more bills. "If the Serbs and Albanians can get together on price gouging, maybe they have more in common than they think."

Tori grew quiet as they crested a brown hill and saw Pristina spread out on the plains below like

a tumor. It was a filthy landfill shrouded in the
haze of rancid smog that stank of coal smoke
from a nearby power plant, roadside garbage,
and rotted meat. The buildings were made of
shattered concrete. Warped and teetering, they
reminded Hamilton of a comb missing teeth,
melted and twisted by heat and neglect. Albanian refugees from the countryside had gorged
the city's population into a gangrenous torso.
They shambled through the streets, going
through garbage looking for food while their
children hung out on street corners with wet
rags waiting for a red light so they could dash
out and scrub a windshield.

Trash blew like pollen through the gray
streets as the Yugo made its way toward the
Grand Hotel in downtown Pristina.

"Depressing," Tori murmured.

"The depressing thing is that so many people
are dying over it."

Hamilton pulled the Yugo up in front of the
eight-story Grand Hotel in the heart of the
downtown slums, the gutted, grimy headquarters
for the international media. Armored Land
Rovers, all distinctively marked with either TV or
PRESS, jammed the turnaround in front of the
outside staircase. Hamilton shrugged, drove the
little green car across the sidewalk, and parked it
between two planters turned into giant ash trays.

"When in Rome . . ." he apologized.

Carrying their duffel and camera bags, they

entered the hotel together across a worn carpet the color of weak chicken soup. At the desk, a fat greasy man with no hair on the top of his head looked at their papers. He smiled broadly.

"Welcome to beautiful Pristina," he effused in good English. "The *Toronto Globe* is welcome. We have been expecting you, Mr. Laub, Miss Rogers. I am certain you will be comfortable here."

Hamilton glanced, surprised at Tori.

"We try to take care of everything," she said, smiling.

After going to their separate rooms, showering and changing into fresh clothing, they met in the lobby to walk together to the government-run media center. It was a combination sports bar and spin-control center filled with cigarette smoke, booze fumes, and a polyglot of languages, all spoken loudly, the predominant of which seemed to be English.

Tori had changed into a simple print dress of a sheer material that snugged to her hips and legs when she walked. Added to that a touch of makeup to her wide mouth and enough to highlight eyes the color of green seawater and she was suddenly vivacious, provocative, and flirty. Hamilton found it hard to believe, looking at her now, that upon their first meeting he had judged her an unexceptional woman when it came to looks. She was immediately the center of attention in the male dominated room. It was like she was on stage performing a role. Hamilton felt a little jealous.

He was not much of a "party animal," as Judith would have put it. He was always more comfortable with rough men of action like Chief Adcock and Mad Dog Gavlik. He knew how to disassemble and assemble a machine gun in the dark, but could never be certain about which fork to use. Crowds made him uncomfortable. It was therefore mostly through Tori's efforts that the two of them established rapid contact and rapport with most of the news media present. Thanks to her, many of the newsmen were already advancing their assessments and evaluations of the situation, offering to share sources and proposing joint excursions into the countryside to pursue leads. They were accepted readily; since time for the mission was limited, they had to work quickly.

"Serbs won't allow reporters to go anywhere without an official escort," explained a *Washington Post* correspondent named Harry Golightly. He looked to be in his mid-thirties, but was already starting to bald on top and sag around the middle. He was obviously much taken with Tori and drinking too much. "But everything is so confused that the policy is not very strictly enforced. If you got the balls for it—excuse me. Tori—you can go about anywhere you want. Just make sure PRESS on your vehicle is big enough for snipers to see."

Shortly after NATO began bombing targets, Harry said, Serbia ordered the expulsion of all journalists belonging to NATO countries. That order was rescinded, however, because the Yugoslavian deputy prime minister said he wanted the world to know the truth.

"What *is* the truth?" Hamilton asked.

Harry shrugged from the philosophical depths of his near-empty glass. "Perhaps there is no truth, only spin and propaganda. You can't trust the Serbs to tell you anything except where the fighting is. Don't trust the Kosovars either. Most reports of the so-called atrocities and mass ethnic cleansing come from refugees who've stumbled across the mountains to Albania or Macedonia. To them, every police action is a massacre or an atrocity. Truth is, nobody is reporting the entire truth. Certainly you're not getting it in the United States, where the press *wants* there to be a noble cause as spun by the White House. Fact is, there are as many atrocities being committed on the one side as on the other."

He emptied his glass with a violent tip of the elbow. "Nobody wants to hear the truth," he lamented. "Neither will you after awhile. We had rather live with a lie if the lie supports what we want to believe."

NATO planes bombed Pristina that night. The first explosions nearly threw Hamilton out of bed, not so much because of their proximity as

to their mere occurrence. He was a light sleeper.
He padded to the window of the darkened room
in his bare feet and watched impassively as targets on the city's outskirts—a Serb barracks,
perhaps, or the radio station—went up in bright
strobe flashes. A few desultory anti-aircraft guns
crackled the night sky over the city with streaks
of fire ending in brief flaring blossoms. The guns
continued pom-poming even after the bombing
ended.

He turned toward a light tapping at his door.
Tori stood in the hallway. She still wore her
dress, or had put it back on when the bombing
started.

"It's hard for a girl to sleep with all the noise,"
she said. "I thought you might be up too."

"I'm watching the fireworks. It's the best show
in town. Want to join me?"

"I'd rather do that than loiter in the hallway
or lick a toad."

"It's 'kiss a frog,' not 'lick a toad.' "

She laughed softly. "I never believed frogs
turned into princes."

They stood at the window and watched the
anti-aircraft fire in the sky. Except for that, the
city looked abandoned under its blackout
orders. Hamilton felt uncomfortably aware of
the woman standing so near him their shoulders
touched.

"What do you know about No Man's Land?"
he asked her through the awkward silence,
speaking in a low tone. He had already checked

the room for bugs, finding only real ones in the form of cockroaches, but one could never be certain.

He shouldn't even be talking about it, but he had been thinking a lot lately. It occurred to him with increasing certainty that political struggles in Washington, D.C., mutual distrust, had prompted what might be considered a minor coup d'état by someone high enough in government to subvert channels of the American war machine toward goals countering stated national policy. He had this growing feeling that he and his SEALs were operating without the knowledge of, and approval of, the president and his staff. Might even, in fact, be working against the president.

"I'm provided one mission at a time," Tori responded, speaking in the same low tone and edging closer. "I know nothing beyond that."

She cast him a long, thoughtful look. "I've wondered the same thing," she confided, surprising him that she had read his mind. "We seem to be working outside all normal channels. My only contact is through Smith, same as you."

"You never know who to trust . . ." Hamilton caught himself and broke off. "Our society has gotten so weird, what with all this compassion and COOing in the military and sensitivity training and at the same time loss of standards and principles and honor—"

"You were too young for Vietnam," Tori said softly.

"Maybe Vietnam is what started it all." Then he said with sudden passion, turning to face her, "I'm an unabashed patriot, Tori. I believe in my country, but I no longer believe in it right or wrong. I'm beginning to doubt, Tori. I'm in the military, but I'm becoming afraid of what my own government can do. Sometimes I think politicians have usurped our government and turned it into a banana republic, subverted it to personal ends. Yet, at the same time, it worries me when our military begins to operate secretly outside civilian control."

"Do you believe that is happening with No Man's Land?"

"I . . . Yes. Maybe. I honestly don't know. I believe in my men. I believe the missions we've been tasked to accomplish are for the good of my country and the world. I believe that. Yet . . ."

He trailed off. So where did he go from here? There was nowhere to go. He had a job to do, an important job—preventing a possible third world war. He turned without further words and gazed out the window, frowning. The anti-aircraft fire had ceased and the city was dark and quiet again except for the distant wail of sirens running toward the bombing sites.

"Jeb . . ." Tori whispered, using his real name. "You are a good man. Your wife—"

He cut her off. "I'm a widower."

"I'm sorry, Jeb."

"It's all right. You couldn't know."

She let some moments hang between them. "Now I know where the sadness comes from. What happened to her?"

"Murdered by terrorists," he said. "Flight 187."

"The bombed plane that went down in Ireland?"

"She was a fashion designer coming back from Paris. I . . . She . . ."

Tori touched his arm. He flinched and withdrew from the contact. They were professionals. They had jobs to do. They could not be distracted by their personal lives. Wasn't that what he had said to Chief Adcock?

"The bombing is over," he said. "Maybe you should go back to your room. We have work to do tomorrow."

A man named Kavika, whose job with the KLA was to monitor highways with an unmounted rifle scope and a walkie-talkie from Radio Shack, escorted the three journalists—Harry Golightly, Keith Laub, and Tori Rogers—to an underground hangout for "Ooh-Chick-Ah," which was the phonetic Albanian pronunciation for KLA. They had all piled into the Yugo. Kavika said he was the owner of an Uzi submachine gun which was hidden in a safe place and which he said he had never fired. It and a sack of bullets were given to him the night his wife and children loaded into the back of a truck with other relatives and set out in the direction of Albania.

"So do you think you will kill Serbs?" Hamilton posing as reporter Keith Laub asked.

"When the time comes," Kavika replied.

"When will the time come?"

"Others have already killed Serbs."

"Where?"

"Here and about. An eye for an eye. It is in the Koran as it is in the Serbs' Bible. Ibraheim Rugova claims to be leader of the KLA, but he is like a weak woman. Always whimpering and begging for peace. It is not peace we want. We want independence. If it takes the whole world at war, so be it. It is Radovan Kradznic who speaks for the KLA military."

Kavika with Hamilton driving directed the way down a dark alleyway and into a parking lot filled with dusty Renaults and other Yugos. It was at a dead end on the outskirts of the city. On the right was a tumbled-down brick wall and on the left a field of brown hay. Pristina's local bars and pubs, especially those located like thieves' hideouts in the most unlikely places—in the basements of abandoned apartments buildings, at the ends of tunnels, in an old railway station, inside a closed-down factory—were where the guerrillas fueled their determination with strong *lovavacka*, an oily derivative of the grape, and even stronger talk.

"This is the place, a very good place," Kavika said.

Hamilton killed the engine. Harry, Tori, and he followed the guerrilla through an obscure doorway into a small room bare except for small tables and a wooden bar. A few naked bulbs overhead lit the smoke-filled air. The room was full of men. The younger ones wore Levi's and T-shirts, the older threadbare suit pants held up by safety pins tacked to their shirts.

The room fell into a hush when the strangers entered. Tori drew curious stares, being the only woman present. Tonight she wore loose jeans and an even looser shirt so as not to attract undue attention. This was a different environment than the Grand Hotel press center.

Everyone seemed to know Kavika. It wasn't long before the room settled down again to its normal din with everyone talking and wandering in and out, attempting to impress the journalists and particularly Tori. She smiled and interpreted for her companions. Harry spoke some Albanian, but not well.

Not all the Albanians were fleeing Kosovo, one of the "guerrillas" explained. Many women, children, and old people shuffling across the mountains passed rifles, pistols, and rockets back to the men who remained behind to fight by Kradznic's side.

"Further north and east we are better organized and have superior weapons," said one man. "We have Howitzers and I know of one unit that has a German tank. We had a major battle at a bridge the Serbs blew up in Kruse-vac. Soon I will join them. If the United States and NATO will not give us weapons to defeat the Serbs, we will acquire them from the Iranians and Iraqis or Chinese. Whoever will sell them to us."

"Even if it means using drug money?" Hamilton questioned through Tori.

The man stiffened. "What do I know or care about drugs? What is important is that we have the money to secure weapons for our survival and the ultimate independence of Kosovo."

So far, NATO's bombing had accomplished little toward changing the equation in Serbia. In Kosovo's capital, heavily armed Serb police were still on all the street corners and the majority Albanians considered it enemy-occupied territory.

"The KLA has not moved in force into Pristina because we do not want Pristina to become like Sarajevo," the guerrilla alibied. "We are strong enough to take it. We have taken other strategic sites."

Harry, in a wry aside, mentioned Belacevac, a few miles from Pristina. A band of guerrillas had walked into the Albanian town and declared "captured" the open-pit coal mine that fed the power plant in Kosovo that provided electricity to nearly one third of all Yugoslavia. They dug a few trenches and vowed to fight. When Serbs came and lobbed a few mortar rounds, however, most of the fighters stripped off their uniforms and fled into the woods.

At least one old man who had drunk far too much *lovavacka* was little impressed with either the KLA or Radovan Kradznic. "Bah!" he scoffed. "The KLA makes war on Serb women and children. Kradznic is more a bandit than a freedom fighter."

A young hothead wearing a baseball cap with the red-and-black KLA patch overheard. "Get out of here, old man!" he roared. "You are not Albanian. You are a lover of your masters, the Serbs."

The old man staggered out into the darkness.

"Do not listen to him," the hothead instructed, bending low and thrusting his face toward Tori's. "We are fighting the Serbs bravely. Pristina is as far as we will run. I kill Serbs because they are like animals who kill many of us. Maybe I will kill a Serb tomorrow. We in Kosovo and those in Bosnia have the common enemy—Milosevic."

He stood straight at the table. He had also drunk too much. His right hand jerked up in the closed-fist solidarity salute of the KLA.

"We will fight even harder," he vowed, "when the United States lands soldiers to fight the Serbs with us. We will fight the Serbs wherever they are and kill them. We will fight the Russians, for they have turned against Kosovo."

He let the salute drop. He hunkered both shoulders over his hands braced on the edge of the table. He leered at Tori. "Once I had a girlfriend who was Serb," he said. "It is something I am not proud of. If I see her today, I will set her on fire or shoot her."

Near Prekaz, a largely Albanian town, self-appointed undertakers in a field were complet-

ing the grim tasks of digging up about thirty relatively fresh graves and re-interring the bodies
properly. Radovan Kradznic himself sent secret
envoys to escort journalists to the site to record
Serb atrocities against Muslims. The unique
stench of rotting corpses clung to the field, to
clothing, and to the hairs inside nostrils. The
odor reminded Lieutenant Hamilton of a trench
full of executed Kuwaitis his team had come
upon during the Gulf War. Hardly anyone
spoke, they were so horrified.

Albanians buried inside the narrow holes had
been suspected of being "terrorist sympathiz-
ers." They were killed in a midnight shelling
blitzkrieg by the Serbs and then mopped up
house by house afterward by police and army
special forces. The dead, more than half of
whom were small children, had been tumbled
into crude wooden caskets. Serb police ordered
the Muslims to be buried immediately and to be
buried in a specific fashion—with their heads to
the west, away from Mecca. Now the corpses
were being identified and reburied.

"Is it an atrocity?" Harry Golightly asked
rhetorically. "Of course it is. Is it mass genocide?
No. But it will be genocide in the headlines
tomorrow."

Tori watched grimly as Hamilton shot photos
with the Nikon provided for the mission. He
peered down into a grave whose open-lidded
coffin underneath the blaze of the noonday sun
revealed the small charcoal stump of what

apparently once was a prepubescent girl. Both arms and legs were charred off at the joints and pointed like half-burned sticks of firewood. Fire hadn't killed her. A gunshot had taken off most of her face first, leaving only the hinge of her jaw looking like the bottom half of a Halloween jack-o'-lantern.

Hamilton took his pictures of the grotesque thing.

"Let's go," Harry said. "It's not good to keep looking at these things."

The main KLA stronghold was at Malisevo, about twenty miles from Pristina. Although there were many horror stories passed around the Grand Hotel about the roadblocks en route, reporters having been held at gunpoint by both sides, Hamilton thought it was something he should investigate. He and Tori accompanied by Harry, the *Washington Post* reporter, set out for the stronghold in the green Yugo. There were alternating Serb and KLA checkpoints along the route.

"T'ree hun-ret deutsche mark."

"The price of inflation," Hamilton commented.

Approaching Malisevo, they came to a sandbagged berm in the road outside town marked with a sign: MINA. A KLA sentry met them with a 30.06 Winchester rifle, which he pointed at them until they halted. He stepped cautiously from behind the sandbags, motioning the car forward. He grinned when he saw Tori. In a more friendly way, he ordered them to continue on into Malisevo. He didn't even ask for his "t'ree hun-ret mark."

"Proof again that a pretty face can open the gates of Troy," Hamilton cracked with a smile.

The town was a depressing little semifortress surrounded on three sides by Serb forces and artillery that NATO had been bombing for over two weeks with little outward effect. Purportedly home to the largest single group of KLA fighters in Kosovo, it was a tiny town whose main commerce appeared to center on black-market cigarettes. The Serbs had cut off electricity and water. Influxes of Albanian refuges from the countryside meant there were more people in town than there were houses.

Two main streets met at the market place, where stalls selling shriveled fruits and vegetables, drinking water, and black-market gasoline competed unsuccessfully with black-market cigarettes. Reuters News Service characterized Malisevo as a "rubble-strewn expanse where packs of hungry dogs, not guerrilla fighters, roam." Since the KLA had so far lost every single set-piece engagement with the Serbs, most of the guerrillas seemed to have carried the war into the hills from which they sniped at Serb roadblocks and ambushed small convoys.

"Where is the KLA base?" Tori asked an older kid in Albanian.

"Here—in Malisevo," he exclaimed.

"Where are the soldiers?"

"*I* am Ooo-Chick-Ah!"

"*You?*"

"Sure. I fight when the Serbs attack us."

The "news reporters" and gregarious Harry Golightly shared an outdoor table for lunch with a man wearing patched camouflage trousers. At the Grand Hotel, they had seen Euro News footage from satellite showing columns of camouflaged rebels marching near Malisevo. Where were these fighters now? Tori asked their lunchmate.

"They are not far," he replied vaguely.

"Why haven't the Serbs wiped out Malisevo?" Hamilton asked through Tori.

"They're scared."

"Scared of what?"

"Because the United States would then send in paratroopers of the 82d Airborne to kill them all. We in the KLA would fight shoulder to shoulder with the Americans. Radovan Kradznic is very smart in the head. Kradznic knows how to work the Americans. He will have them fighting the war for us. Are they not already bombing Milosevic back to the Stone Age? The Russians will send troops to Milosevic, but by then it will be too late. The Americans will already have landed."

Hamilton parked the Yugo halfway to the village among a dozen other press vehicles

because the road became too rough. He and
Tori slung camera bags over their shoulders and
pinned their press passes to their shirts so they
would be recognized, then hiked the remaining
mile through the forest with Harry Golightly,
who had become their ever-present and helpful
companion during their sojourns outside Pristina. This time, the media was being courted by
the Serbs, who wanted the international press
to record a KLA "atrocity." Reporters soon
stumbled on a scene being guarded by Serb
police.

In the front yard of a farmhouse lay nine bodies of a single Serb household. Three were children, the oldest of whom appeared about
twelve, a boy, and the youngest, a girl, about
three. Two were women. The grandmother was
naked except for baggy panties. The younger
woman's nightgown was pulled up above her
waist to reveal matted hair at her crotch. She
had apparently been raped.

All had been sleeping soundly, the press was
informed, when a guerrilla band stormed their
house and forced them outside in their underwear and pajamas. They were all shot, including
the toddler, and left where they fell. The corpses
lay flatter than living persons, with limbs bent in
grotesque positions. Harry counted ten bullet
holes in the chest of the patriarch. His wife had
her face shot off, her head exploding like a
melon to spill pink and blue matter onto the
dirt. The younger woman had been shot once in

the back of the head after her attackers finished with her. The bullet came out the front of her head, leaving an exit wound the size of a baseball into which the rest of her face seemed to have caved. Her mouth was wide open in a silent eternal scream. Swarms of black flies rose in clouds from the corpses when anyone walked near.

Tori paled. She thought she was going to be sick. She walked away by herself while Hamilton recorded everything with his camera.

Harry pointed out a Bible on a table inside the house, which they were allowed to enter, along with other evidence that this scene was exactly what it was purported to be.

"There is no doubt but what these dead are Serbs and Christians," he said. "Watch its metamorphosis in the world's headlines this week. This will become reversed so that instead of a KLA atrocity against the Serbs, it will be turned into further evidence of Serb ethnic cleansing against the Albanians. That will make major news. For the reporters who get it accurately, their copy will appear under a twelve-point head on about page fifty-seven or as a parting comment at the end of the CNN world report. I don't know how the Canadian press reports it, but that's the way it's being done in the U.S."

Cynicism. It was in the national mood.

"The civilized world has chosen sides through NATO and turned Milosevic into Satan," Harry continued grimly. "We don't want to believe that each side is equally guilty of outrage. The KLA are our noble 'freedom fighters'; Slobodan Milosevic is Hitler."

He stood looking down at the body of the young woman raped by her attackers.

"I've been in this country since before the bombing began," he went on. "I've seen these things from both sides. If you ask me, I'll tell you there *ain't* no good guys in this thing. Radovan Kradznic is biding his time until he can take power. If Milosevic is committing ethnic cleansing against the Albanian Muslims, wait until Kradznic has his opportunity to retaliate against the Serbs. We have a Hitler on each side. The U.S. merely picked one of the Hitlers to go to bed with."

"How will the *Washington Post* report this?" Hamilton asked him.

Harry's face set in bitter lines. "I'll go with the party line halfway. I'll say this was *reported* by the Serbs to be the work of the KLA, but I'll say it in such a way that it sounds like I don't believe it and neither should my readers. That's the only way I can make front page—and if I don't stay on the front page I'll be back in D.C. covering the crime beat or pol news conferences. In a way, the crime beat and the pols are the same thing, aren't they?"

THE REPORT

Tori used a dead letter drop arranged before-hand to get secret reports and film out of country. Everything reached Martin Smith in Italy through the hands of only two intermediaries, the first of whom whisked the package out of Pristina and passed it to the second, who crossed south into Macedonia. When CIA Director Louis Benefield received the materials at his Langley office, he summoned General Roger Norman, Chairman of JCS, and Assistant Director Mark Goodson to a meeting. The director seemed in high spirits.

"Gentlemen, this is dynamite stuff," he said, handing out copies along with color enlargements of dead bodies, combat sites, bomb damage scenes . . . "This proves conclusively that American interests lie neither in support of the KLA nor Milosevic; that the so-called 'ethnic cleansing' so decried by our government is as prevalent on one side as the other; that our government rushed with NATO into a campaign that, however it ends, will, at least, mire the United States in an ethnic conflict that has gone on for centuries, and, at the worst, into a global war. Gentlemen, we must continue to do what we can to end this as quickly as possible, return it to equilibrium, and withdraw U.S. support for either side."

The report was written clearly, concisely, and explosively, as direct and hard-hitting as a military operation order:

Fighting in Kosovo has gone beyond
conventional warfare back to medieval
times, spurred on by good intentions
and meddling from outside. We must
accept that there is a limit to what
outside military can accomplish. We
can't point guns and drop bombs and
order people to stop hating and killing their neighbors. We cannot con-
struct a free government out of thin
air. Even if the bombing succeeds, the
best we can expect is that the U.S.
will be mired here as policemen for at
least a generation, despised and
resisted by both sides. The U.S. will
eventually end up fighting both the
Serbs and the Albanians.

The situation with the spin of our
politicians has heavily distorted most
facts about what we are doing here.
Claims of mass genocide by the Serbs
against the Muslims seem unsupported
and certainly exaggerated in saying
that 20,000 Albanians have been killed
and placed in mass graves. The correct
number, while not insignificant, is
perhaps a tenth of that—2,000 or less.
Slobodan Milosevic and General Yevgeny
Krleza have the power now and it is
the Albanians who suffer and are fleeing.

Ibraheim Rugova, with whom the U.S.

secretary of state is negotiating for peace in Pristina, is merely a shadow head of the KLA. He has almost no influence over what the KLA will or will not do. The real power behind the KLA is Radovan Kradznic. Once he has power, it will be the Serbs' turn to flee or be killed.

The KLA is now a ragtag army, but it is growing rapidly and gaining power under the umbrella of NATO bombing. Once NATO has defeated Serbia, if that's in the scenario, Kradznic will emerge as the next villain to replace Milosevic and the tables will be turned.

Following this summary is a detailed analysis . . .

9: LOCKDOWN

PRE-MISSION

The wiry young man wearing glasses and a business suit rumpled from a red-eye flight from Italy shook hands with his boss and slumped wearily into the overstuffed chair in front of the desk. In appearance he resembled more a nosy Harvard professor of sociology than he did the chief of the ultrasecret No Man's Land operation in Yugoslavia.

"Coffee, Mr. Smith?" CIA Director Louis Benefield asked his visitor, tenting his hands beneath his chin the way he did when he had something on his mind.

"That I can use, sir. If it melts a spoon, it should be strong enough."

Director Benefield would never have called Smith in from the theater of operations for an idle chat. He buzzed his secretary in the outer office. Coffee and muffins were delivered on a silver tray a few minutes later. The two men waited until they were alone again before getting down to business.

"How are they holding up?" the Director asked.

"Our SEALs? They haven't missed yet."

"The operation isn't over."

"Don't worry about them, sir. Where do we continue to get such men in this age of self-indulgence?"

The director emitted a scornful sound. "Certainly we don't get them from Washington, D.C., Mr. Smith."

Director Benefield swiveled in his chair to look out his window over the CIA complex. He sat there lost in thought for a long minute.

"The White House is going to start sending Apache attack helicopters from Macedonia into Kosovo by next week," he announced slowly.

Martin Smith sat erect. "Apaches are *ground forces*. That's bound to draw a response from Russia."

"It already has. Russia is deploying more anti-aircraft SAMs to Belgrade. Two battalions of infantry will soon follow."

"Good God!" Smith exclaimed. "What can this administration be thinking?"

The director shook a cigarette from an open pack on his desk and lit it. "I gave up smoking," he said. "But . . . what the hell."

He gave a kick to swivel his chair back around and focus his entire attention on the inside of his office.

"Thanks to the Operation Underlord analysis, which I've passed on to certain members of the House Intelligence Committee and other key members of Congress, Washington may be waking up to the fact that choosing sides in Yugoslavia was not only ill-advised but even dangerous. Congress is starting to demand answers from the administration. It just adds to our problems that Congress and the White House are barely on speaking terms because of the president's pending impeachment trial. This whole thing is a lose-lose situation. It's eventually going to be another Somalia, only on a much greater scale."

Smith remained silent. He knew Director Benefield was working his way toward the reason why he had summoned the agent back to the United States.

"The UN is dragging its heels on indicting Milosevic and General Krleza for war crimes. We don't dare move on them until it does. This fellow Rugova may soon be forced to go into exile in Germany, which leaves Kradznic completely free to spread his hybrid ideology of Maoism, Swiss banks, Chinese guns, and heroin." He barked a bitter note of laughter. "What a tangled fuckin' web we're weaving, Mr. Smith."

He tented his hands again and looked directly at Smith through the thin haze of smoke drifting up from the cigarette still stuck between his fingers.

"Mr. Smith," he said, still using the agent's cover name. "I calculate we have one week, maybe a few days longer, before this whole thing starts to blow up in our faces. *One week* to act to stop an inevitable confrontation that will end up with all of Europe choosing sides. Your SEALs have to be ready to move. But first we have to prepare the way."

Now he was getting down to it. "Prepare the way, sir?" Smith asked, curiosity aroused.

"Operation Lockdown, Mr. Smith. *You* will handle this mission personally."

THE BRIEFING

The director began his briefing by saying, "The U.S. stealth F117A shot down over Yugoslavia *was not* a lucky shot. Reports of a spy in NATO have appeared in Britain's press and in *Jane's Defence Weekly*. They say a NATO staff officer informed GRU, Russian military intelligence, about the stealth's secret flight plans. The GRU told Belgrade, which used a Russian P-12 radar plane to track the stealth. A MiG-21 then fired two long-range missiles. One hit the port engine of the F117 Russian. GRU agents showed up to secure parts of the downed plane."

Smith nodded understanding, musing as he attempted to weave the pattern into a recognizable tapestry, "The Serbs showed up just as No Man's Land was rescuing the pilot . . . They found out where the suitcase nuke was hidden in Gracanica . . ."

"You didn't know this, but Serb soldiers came swarming onto the docks just before the Russian oil tanker *Lenin* blew up," Benefield added. "They went up with the ship."

"There's a common denominator here?"

"In each instance, Serbs showed up at the scene a minute late and a dollar short, to coin an old phrase. So far, the only information they've received in time to act on has been on target listings and flight plans. It's like the information gets there by following a convoluted route that takes time. They're getting better at it as the war goes on."

Smith frowned. "You think the mole may be on to No Man's Land?"

"It's all over the Hill that the Senate Armed Services Committee held hearings on the feasibility of political assassination. I think there is some suspicion that the idea has not gone away. Somebody may be starting to put two and two together. The results of No Man's Land haven't exactly been kept secret. Sooner or later, somebody has to figure out we have operators raising hell in Serbia, if it's not already figured out."

Smith's coffee, forgotten, sat cooling on the little table by his chair.

"There *is* a common denominator, Mr.

Smith," Director Benefield said. "I'm required by the president to deliver daily intelligence briefings to him or to his *designated staff.*" He laid heavy emphasis on the phrase. "In these briefings, I would face dereliction of duty if I failed to divulge intelligence about the downed pilot, for example, or the location of the suitcase nuke."

"And No Man's Land?"

"That's a for-eyes-only operation still underway. I think I can get by with keeping them under wraps for another week or so. I may be fired afterward, but it's worth it. Back to the common denominator . . .

"In each instance, after I had briefed the president or his *designated staff*, the information found its way to Belgrade. It's the same thing with NATO's daily target listings. They go to the president and his *designated staff* each morning for approval—"

Smith looked stunned. "The leak's not in NATO. It's from the White House!"

The director remained unruffled. He had already faced the possibility of a traitor inside the highest office in the land.

"It's not unheard of," he said. "President Franklin Roosevelt had a communist spy on his staff during all his meetings with Stalin. I think the intelligence always seems to be getting to Milosevic a little late because our bad guy here in Washington filters it through a NATO pro-

Russian contact. A Frenchman, we think. The Frenchman then passes it anonymously through some source in Belgrade before it reaches General Krleza. It's actually pretty amateurish, considering everything. If it hadn't been, No Man's Land may have already been compromised."

"Have you gone to the president?" Smith asked.

Benefield smiled. "I may as well hold a press conference."

Smith waited.

The director took a drag from his cigarette. "We have to get rid of the mole before we dare continue with No Man's Land. There is too much riding on those SEALs to have them compromised at a vital moment."

He snubbed out his cigarette, jabbing it viciously into his desk ashtray. "I've got to quit these damned things again." He looked up, his expression grave. "You do have contact with Solitary Elk inside Pristina?"

"Of course, sir. Through another contact by secure SATcom."

"Get word to Solitary Elk to observe and immediately report the results of what you and I are about to weave. The only way to root out the mole quickly is to provide him with false intelligence and then see how fast he works on it. This afternoon I'm giving another briefing to the president's staff—"

"And the staff will include—"

"Our suspect. I'm going to divulge that we've received a tip that the nuclear device whisked out of Gracanica was actually recovered by the KLA—and that this suitcase nuke is now hidden in Pristina at a precise location. If I'm right, Serb police will be swarming all over Kralja Petra I Oslobodioca Street within a few hours. It's a vacant building.

"Mr. Smith, it's generally assumed that cellular telephones cannot be traced. Because our guy is an amateur, I have no reason to believe he'll think differently. We suspect he simply calls his NATO man in Italy, who somehow relays the intel to his contact in Belgrade. We'll trace his call, then wait to see what else happens. We should know by early this evening if I'm right."

"And if you are, sir? The man's a traitor. We're talking about another White House scandal."

"Mr. Smith, that's where you come in. No arrests, no publicity to cause more disgrace on the office of the presidency. This nation cannot endure much more of this administration. This will have to be handled discreetly. With sensitivity."

Benefield winced. Damn! He was beginning to sound like a CYA politician.

"This will have to be handled," he finished brusquely.

Smith's eyes narrowed. It had to be done. The lives of his SEALs in the Balkans perhaps depended on it. On him. He had no doubt that

Hamilton and his rogue warriors would do the same for him if the circumstances were reversed.

THE PREPARATION

S-3 Systems, the acronym standing for Stealth, Security, and Surveillance, was the nation's largest corporation dedicated to black operations and Skunk Works projects. It was located on a five hundred–acre industrial complex on the outskirts of Dallas, Texas. The corporation had invented or developed all types of electronic or computer-based snooping devices— tiny mikes the size of a housefly; video cameras almost as small; secure radio communications; miniaturized silent drills used to insert bugs, software viruses that could hide in supercomputer networks to seek out passwords and code words. It had also developed a cell phone tracking system that allowed technicians to trace calls without knowing the number of the cell phone. The system had been sold to, among other agencies, the NSA, FBI, and CIA.

That afternoon after CIA Director Benefield's meeting with Mr. Smith, the director left the White House following his daily intelligence briefing and drove past a nondescript Ford Cherokee SUV parked on Pennsylvania Avenue at 17th Street. Its heavily tinted rear windows,

Benefield knew, concealed the cell phone tracking system acquired from S-3. His men were on the job. He drove past the SUV and kept driving.

Ned Cosic's e-mail early-warning system in Belgrade was up and running. The direct line to General Krleza's command headquarters both in Belgrade and to his *dacha* in the mountains was open. Cosic was beginning to relay target warnings when Cyber Phantom came up on-line.

Package missing from Gracanica now located Kralja Petra I Oslobodioca Street, Pristina. Suggest immediate action.

THE MISSION

Lieutenant Hamilton and Tori in Pristina did not have long to wait. Within two hours of beginning their stakeout, two vehicles loaded with police and military officers skidded up in front of the vacant building and rushed inside. The secure SATcom that reached Director Benefield contained a single word: *Bingo.*

THE REPORT

(AP)—A high ranking member of the president's cabinet was discovered dead this morning in what is being

termed an apparent suicide. The body
of Randall Palmer, 49, an underassis-
tant to secretary of state, was found
by a jogger in Fort Marcy Park in
downtown Washington, D.C., at 6:10 A.M.
Police say he had been dead for at
least three hours. He apparently died
of a gunshot wound. A revolver was
reportedly found at his side in the
park.

Police are releasing no further
details pending the outcome of the
investigation.

According to sources, Palmer was the
secretary of state's deputy to NATO in
its ongoing air campaign against Serbian President Slobodan Milosevic. His
position so close to the president's
cabinet had been highly criticized at
the time due to a book he published
three years ago, *Social Construction*,
which advocated socialism in the
United States. Palmer had been a professor of sociology at Yale Univer-
sity.

Palmer is the second staff member of
this administration to have committed
suicide, both of whose bodies were
found in Fort Marcy Park. In 1993, the
body of . . .

10: BISON HUMP

PRE-MISSION

Cooling their heels on the Adriatic Sea aboard the U.S.S. *Gonzalez* wore on the five SEALs left behind. Chief Adcock set up a schedule of physical workouts and training periods in which, among other tasks, they practiced firing their weapons off the destroyer's fantail, but there was still plenty of downtime. Too much downtime took the edge off a warrior, made him start to think or brood. Of the five, Mad Dog Gavlik was the most prone to restlessness. His normal cynicism took on a harder tone.

"I'm beginning to think Smith makes up these missions as we go along," he scoffed.

"It's the fog of war," Dr. Death said philosophically. "You have to change and adapt to it."

"How many men have you killed with that?"

Operation No Man's Land

Dog asked, pointing to the white-haired man's ever-present sniper rifle.

"Is the number important?" Dr. Death responded.

Dog shrugged. "It is if you're one of them."

A man like Dr. Death was easy to respect but difficult to like. Dog sometimes wondered what, if anything, inside the man made him human. He was so cold he almost made you shiver when he walked by. Dog teased that the man should be wearing a hooded black robe and carrying a scythe instead of his Haskins rifle. Harvesting souls for hell.

In spite of their differences, however, or perhaps even because of them, Dog and Dr. Death had formed a kind of strange bond, as had John Nighthorse and Preacher Hodges. It wasn't exactly friendship. Dr. Death always said he had no friends. Team members were his brothers, but that didn't make them friends. Still, if he ever felt a friendship for anyone, it was for the hulking mountaineer.

"That Haskins is one heavy piece of machinery," Dog said.

"It's the reason I'm included on the team—other than my sparkling personality."

Dog blinked. "That's a joke, ain't it? Hey, you made a joke. Hey, everybody. Dr. Death made a joke!"

To bleed off some of the big man's excess energy, Chief Adcock assigned him a rappelling rope to practice climbing techniques over the *Gonzalez*'s sides.

If Dog were the restless one, the Oklahoma Kiowa Indian was the most stoic. A true ascete, he sat for hours contemplating his inner space, even through the nightly barrages of Tomahawk cruise missiles sending their messages to Slobodan Milosevic.

Preacher was likewise quiet and introspective. He was seldom far away from his friend, his soulful dark face bent over his Bible as though searching for the answers to the mysteries of life and death. One of the ship's missilemen, an AO2, made the mistake of referring to him as an "African-American."

Preacher calmly looked at the sailor. His eyes blazed. "Do I look like an African to you?" he demanded.

"Well . . . I thought you was an African-American chaplain."

"I'm a black *American*," he said, and went back to reading his Bible.

The missileman continued to stand in front of him. "Who *are* you guys?" he asked. "What are you doing here?"

"If I told you, I'd have to kill you." Preacher said. "Now, go away. I'm trying to read my Bible."

Chief Adcock wrote a long letter to Marge. No matter how he assured Lieutenant Hamilton that his wife's threatened divorce did not affect his job, the truth was it had shook him to the core. The teams were hard on women, gone as the SEALs were for weeks and months at a time either on real-world missions, like now, or on training or MTTs. The chief thought he wouldn't know how to live without Marge. They had been together since they were sophomores in high school.

Mad Dog, divorced four times, often joked about a man not being Special Forces–qualified until he was divorced. If that was what it took to be a SEAL, losing his wife, then maybe it was time the chief turned in his trident. It was something he had to consider.

But not now. There was nothing he could do about his marriage until after the operation ended. He quit his letter home halfway through and forced himself to block Marge from his conscious thoughts. He hated this waiting as much as Mad Dog did.

It was a relief to all of them when word came to move out. Smith had left a couple of days earlier on some hush-hush thing, but promised to form up again with the team a little later. The team and its gear was plucked off the destroyer by Sea Stallion helicopter and flown to the flight deck of the carrier U.S.S. *Theodore Roosevelt*. A Chinook helicopter waited, already warmed up, blades turning, to transport them to the NATO base of operations in Skopje, Macedonia, near the Kosovo border.

"Isn't that where they've taken the Apache helicopters?" Dog wondered aloud.

"Looks like it's time for us to get back to work," Chief Adcock said.

THE BRIEFING

The base on flatlands outside Skopje resembled a migrants' tent city. The tents were in dress-right-dress lines, and everything looked dusty. While the north of Yugoslavia was being drenched in rains, the south was almost in drought. An airstrip was under construction; men and machines scurried about on it like ants. The Chinook with its cargo of SpecOps wearing BDUs circled in the clean morning air and flared in for a landing among a cluster of U.S. Apache helicopters. The Apaches were thin-fuselaged aircraft bristling with rocket pods and machine guns. They resembled dragon flies— *dangerous* dragon flies with stingers. They could even fly upside down. American GIs armed with M16s hustled about establishing security for the Apaches.

Smith met them on the landing pad. He also wore BDUs in order to blend with the normal motif. Other than the SEALs being more heavily armed than other soldiers and their carrying rucks to mark them as field soldiers rather than support ash and trash, there was little about their appearances to attract attention. Chief

Adcock looked around in amazement as he walked alongside Smith to a tent reserved for them.

"I thought we weren't supposed to have ground troops in Yugoslavia," he exclaimed disbelievingly.

"We don't—yet," Smith responded. "The border is that way a few more kilometers."

"Where's the lieutenant?" Mad Dog demanded.

"You'll see him later tonight."

Smith shoved open the flap of a tent guarded by an armed French soldier wearing a river turtle–shaped helmet. He motioned the SEALs inside, where there were a table and chairs. Smith carried a briefcase. He hefted it onto the table, opened it with a key he fished from his pocket, and in a businesslike manner distributed folders marked with the code name Bison Hump.

"Sit down," he invited. "What you're looking at," he said, displaying a photo from his own folder, "is one Radovan Kradznic."

"KLA general," John Nighthorse remarked. "Big ugly sucker. Reminds me of Mad Dog."

Dog made a smacking sound. "Kiss my nut," he said.

Smith waited for the SEALs to blow off their normal nervous energy before settling down to the briefing.

"Kradznic is your target," he said. "Your folders also include a description of him. He's a bear of a man all right, John. Six feet four, wide as an oak tree, and a beard like the ass of a grizzly. He likes being the center of attention. It's written that he's quite enjoyable to be around—except for one minor flaw: Don't turn your back on him. He's the same kind of character as Slobodan Milosevic. He's not too choosy who he kills. He's very good at playing both sides against the middle."

Dog looked at the photo and made a shrugging movement with his lips. "If he's our target, does this call for Dr. Death?" he asked.

Dr. Death gave him a rare icy smile.

"Not this time," Smith said. "We want him taken alive and brought out of country."

Chief Adcock shook his head questioningly. "If we need to get rid of him, why not pop him and get it over with?"

By way of answering the question, Smith asked one of his own. "Lieutenant Hamilton was in Bosnia. So were you, chief. What happened when accused war criminals were indicted by the UN?"

Chief Adcock let his disgust show on his face. The situation there had left him with a bad taste. The United States became the laughingstock of the world because, although Sarajevo was full of PIFWKs—people indicted for war crimes—orders came down from Washington that they would not be apprehended out of fear of a backlash that would disrupt the peace and because that violent backlash might jeopardize one of the administration's Holy Tenets—that it would make war but would not incur casualties. War criminals ran all over Sarajevo giving press conferences. American soldiers were told to look the other way, embarrassed at the same time by statements from Washington claiming the war criminals would be arrested if and when they could be found.

"This bunch of draft dodgers in Washington trying to make war is more screwed up than a monkey trying to fuck a basketball," Mad Dog opined.

"That's why we're going to move first this time, and we're going to move fast," Smith interjected. "The idea is for us to have war criminals under wraps and out of the way before the game of tag begins. If we put principals on both sides out of commission, we can shorten the war and maybe prevent its further escalation. We have to work fast."

"Do you really believe," Chief Adcock asked, "that the UN will indict anybody from the KLA after branding Milosevic as the Hitler of the Balkans? Let's get real."

"Kradznic probably has as much blood on his hands as General Krleza," Smith said patiently. "But politics is not our concern. What we are concerned with is getting Kradznic out of the way now so Ibraheim Rugova can try to resume leadership of the Albanians and work out some sort of compromise with Serbia. That's a step in the right direction. We have to make sure to take that step."

"I'm convinced," Chief Adcock acquiesced. "Go ahead with the briefing. What's the skinny on Kradznic? How do we do it?"

Smith nodded his approval. "I'm going to give you the overall view as usual, then you'll have six hours to study your target folders for times, locations, and synchronization of action. H-hour is at 2100. Chow'll be served right after the briefing. There's coffee over in the corner. Help yourselves."

He waited until the team had settled in again around the table.

"You'll be inserted by Soviet Mil-8 helicopter because the Hip is the same type flown by the Serbs," he began. "Your dropoff location as marked on your maps is mountainous terrain about twenty-five kilometers from the KLA-controlled town of Malisevo. Kradznic has a guerrilla command center and training camp fifteen klicks from where you're being inserted. Lieutenant Hamilton will meet you on the ground with transportation."

Dog groaned. Smith chuckled, understanding. "The lieutenant sent out word that he promises this time transportation will have nothing to do with pigs or cows."

"That leaves chickens, goats, or camels," Nighthorse said.

"Take that up with Mr. Hamilton when you see him. Okay. Your target, the camp, is a scattering of shacks in rugged terrain. Most of the Serb forces are further north near the Serbian border, although there are Serb policemen and support and infantry units around Pristina and infantry and artillery at Malisevo. The KLA is

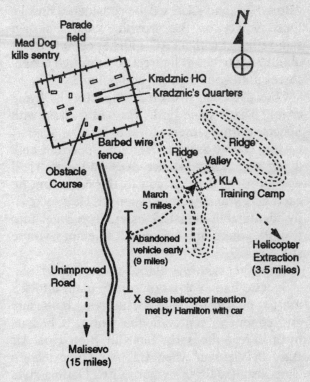

N

Parade field

Mad Dog kills sentry

Kradznic HQ

Kradznic's Quarters

Barbed wire fence

Obstacle Course

Ridge

Ridge

Valley

KLA Training Camp

March 5 miles

Abandoned vehicle early (9 miles)

Helicopter Extraction (3.5 miles)

Unimproved Road

X Seals helicopter insertion met by Hamilton with car

Malisevo (15 miles)

Snatching of KLA Leader Radovan Kradznic

sure to have patrols out around the camp. You are subject, therefore, to encountering either side on the march in."

" 'Let thine enemies be scattered,' " Preacher quoted, " 'and let them that hate thee flee before thee.' "

"Amen, Preach," Dog cheered.

Smith went on in his professorlike mode. "Both Serb and KLA will be considered hostile. Once you're on the ground, you'll maintain radio contact with an AC-130H Spectre flying at about 35,000 feet. It'll direct you through enemy forces until you reach the compound."

Chief Adcock whistled. "Spectre is flying cover? That's some bird." He had worked with Spectre during Desert Storm in Iraq.

"Not *cover*," Smith corrected. "Spectre is only flying your long-distance eyes and ears. He'll warn you, he'll guide you to the camp, but he can't give you air combat support. He's too easily identifiable as a U.S. asset. If you get into trouble, you're on your own. Remember, you're still black."

"Preacher is *always* black," Dog quipped.

Spectre had evolved out of Vietnam into the most sophisticated and fearful flying battleship and command center in the world. It had its birth during the early 1960s at Bien Hoa Air Base in Vietnam when U.S. Air Force technicians installed three six-barrel 7.62 Gatling-style miniguns in the door and port-side windows of a

World War II C-47 and added an *A* for "Attack" to its designation—AC-47. Dubbed "Spooky" because of its call sign, the plane saved the lives of many American soldiers by directing devastating fire against enemy troops.

The AC-47 proved so effective that the Air Force made a better Spooky from the much larger C-130 and called it the AC-130H Spectre. Its amazing armament, all arranged with its target-detection gear on the port side, consisted of two six-barrel 20mm Vulcan cannon mounted ahead of the wing for use against troops and light vehicles. A 40mm Bofors automatic cannon intended for trucks and light armor was aft of the main landing gear. Farthest aft was a 105mm Howitzer which could destroy tanks or buildings.

Its electronics were even more impressive, including a "snooper" described by one Spectre pilot as able to "whiff out a gnat if it so much as farted." Below the cockpit was an RDF, radio direction finder, that could hone in on a radio beacon or on the electronic noise produced by enemy vehicles' ignition systems. At a door aft of the nose wheel was a sensor mount that supported a low-light-level television camera, LLLTV, which used a photo multiplier to amplify even faint traces of starlight and expose the resulting image on a TV screen. Installed in a wheel well was an infrared system that displayed an image created by the emitted heat from a target.

Flying at altitudes well above sight and sound and out of range of anti-aircraft fire, Spectre could literally pick up and trace the movement of anything larger than a mouse that moved on the earth's crust.

"It can do anything for you except wash your laundry," Mad Dog said.

"Just don't dirty your laundry on this one," Smith said. "Spectre will guide you to the camp. On your photos and layout charts, you'll see the camp is in a kind of crater, a basin, surrounded by mountains. The shack where Kradznic stays when he's there is marked for you in the photos. It's near the center of the compound."

"How do we know Kradznic will be there tonight?" Chief Adcock asked.

"We have to trust our intelligence. You'll snatch Kradznic—*alive*, if possible—and spirit him out of camp."

"Spirit?" Dog chortled.

"Spirit, drag, carry, drive . . . Just get him out of camp. You then have about six kilometers to hump to this grid coordinate where the Hip will be waiting on the ground to extract both Kradznic and the team. You have the rest of the day to study the target folders. Take with you only your weapons and commo gear, plus Lieutenant Hamilton's gear. No rucks—travel light, freeze at night. But I doubt if you'll freeze. Things may get too hot. It's going to be balls to the wall. Or, in your case, Mad Dog, *ball* to the wall."

He sobered and looked around the tight ring of grim faces. "Good luck, SEALs," he said. Smith knew more than anyone, perhaps, just how important this mission was.

THE PREPARATION

As the Hip was a transport chopper built to carry up to thirty-two passengers, depending upon the seating arrangement, there was plenty of room aboard for five SEALs and their weapons. It had a range of nearly three hundred miles without refueling, but since it was traveling light it carried extra cans of fuel strapped forward in the cargo compartment. So far, Milosevic seemed content to let NATO control the night skies. The Hip therefore had little to fear from MiGs or other helicopters, and was relatively safe from anti-aircraft fire and SAMs as long as it avoided cities and built-up areas. The general consensus was that Milosevic was keeping his warplanes hid out so they could survive the bombing and be brought out when the inevitable ground war began.

The Hip took off from Skopje shortly after NATO began its night bombing runs over Serbia. It was noisy, like most Russian equipment, precluding conversation once the SEALs scrambled aboard with their gear. The doors closed, soft red light lit up the compartment to aid in night vision, and the chopper lifted into the air with a nose-down jerk. It would be a short flight, about an hour. Preacher took out his Bible, read a verse, then replaced it, his long, soulful face as expressionless as the surface of a pool.

Chief Adcock had already inspected the men and their gear—once in the tent before they jogged down to the helipad, then again prior to liftoff. He visually inspected them a third time as they rode silently in the web seating, looking as much for psychological preparation as for readiness of equipment. Jagged patterns of black, green, and loam camouflage makeup on their faces obscured all emotion, turned their faces into fierce unreadable masks. In Vietnam, SEALs had been known as "men with green faces." Chief Adcock had to be satisfied with a visual check of equipment, although there was nothing he could do now about it even if he had overlooked something.

Each man wore sterile cammies and an unmarked patrol cap. On their nylon web gear were attached combat knives, ammo pouches, PVS-5 night vision goggles, and grenades in varieties of frag, WP, and smoke. Every SEAL also carried a Claymore mine strapped to his belt, along with wire and a detonator clacker. Preacher distributed time fuses and det cord among them. As a team, they were armed with enough weapons to wage a miniwar. In addition to a primary weapon of choice, each fighter had a strapped-down holster on each thigh, one containing the Glock 9mm semiauto pistol, the other the short MP5K 9mm submachine gun.

Mad Dog leaned forward in his seat, elbows resting on his knees, the barrel of his light machine gun cradled between cupped hands. He seemed to be in deep thought, along with all the others. Feeling himself observed, he looked up into Chief Adcock's eyes. Adcock nodded at him. Dog nodded back. *Ready.*

The pilots flew NOE, nape of the earth, a roller-coaster ride underneath radar. They had the pedal to the metal too, skimming the crest of the earth through the night at full bore, changing courses frequently and suddenly to throw off

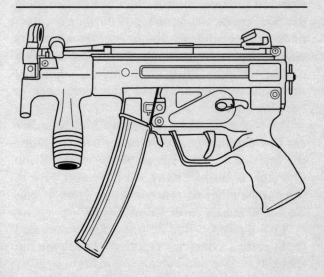

Heckler & Koch MP5K Submachine Gun

any radar or tracking plane that may have picked up the bird's signature.

Word came from up front: *Ten minutes*! Followed by a flurry of activity as the men unbuckled seat belts, gave each other a final check, and collected themselves mentally and physically. Chief Adcock punched in Spectre's proper frequency on the modified Motorola radio he wore strapped to his LBE harness. He then held up a questioning thumb, received answering thumbs. *Ready.*

The bird pulled collective, flared, and settled quickly to earth. The doors opened. The team exited in a rush, sailing out the door on either side and running into the clear before dropping to their knees, weapons ready. Within five seconds from touchdown, the helicopter was on its way again toward its holding area, its thudding engines quickly fading until only the silence of the night remained. The SEALs were back in No Man's Land.

The Motorola whispered into Chief Adcock's ear through thin headphones constructed along the lines of a jogger's portable headset: "Bison One, this is Bison Buddy. We have you. Five in the pot. Number six is approaching from a vehicle at 240 at fifty yards. Copy, Bison?"

"Five-by, Bison Buddy," the Chief responded to Spectre's contact. "Good to have you up there."

"Good to be up here, Bison. You're all clear

for a radius of two klicks. Will keep you advised. Out."

There was no moon yet, and it would be only a sliver when it rose later. Adcock may not have caught Lieutenant Hamilton's approach at all without prior warning from Spectre. He concentrated on the 240-degree azimuth until the lieutenant materialized not twenty feet away. There was no reaction from the SEALs, although they hadn't seen their leader in nearly two weeks. They maintained a 360-degree defense perimeter, eyes scanning outward, while Hamilton quickly changed into cammies and strapped on his weapons. He swiped a cammie stick at his face and made sure his AKMS was fully loaded.

"Did you get the full skinny on Bison Hump?" Chief Adcock asked him, whispering toward the ground so his voice would not carry.

"Basics," Hamilton answered. "You can fill in the details on the way. I'm ready. Let's get out of here. I have a car."

"No pigs, cows, camels, or goats?"

THE MISSION

Fitting six hefty warriors and their equipment into a Yugo was equivalent to Volkswagen stuffing by college football jocks when Hamilton was at Notre Dame. In the end, Dog and Dr. Death rode outside clinging to the car's short hood as

Hamilton maneuvered the vehicle without lights along a dusty pot-holed goat path. Chief Adcock provided him with a second Motorola. Hamilton clipped it to his harness and inserted an earplug into one ear while leaving the other ear open. Bison Buddy gave them clearance for a kilometer along the road.

"Bison, there's a farmhouse to the right with a trail leading off to it. Three cows and two dogs are in the yard. No lights on, no people visible, no vehicles. Over."

"Roger that, Buddy."

As Hamilton drove, Chief Adcock gave him the *Cliff Notes* version of the briefing provided by Smith at Skopje. Hamilton committed essential details to memory. Kidnap Kradznic? A shrewd maneuver if it worked and if they followed up by eliminating Kradznic's counterpart among the Serbs—either Milosevic himself or General Krleza, perhaps both. Get rid of bad guys in both camps, keep the two sides at bay and apart, bring them together more susceptible to talking a deal once their leaders were gone, prevent World War III. Simple equation when put like that.

Nothing was ever as simple as it sounded.

"Where did you get the car, Skipper?" Adcock asked.

"From a lady."

"Oh? Anybody we know?"

"Maybe."

"The redhead? Are we going to see her again?"

Hamilton leaned forward over the wheel, peering intently between Dog and Dr. Death on either fender as he attempted to miss pot holes in the dark.

"One day," Adcock teased, "you'll have to tell us about what you've been doing with a beautiful redhead for the past two weeks while the rest of us were stuck at sea. She's not going to show up at the camp, is she?"

"It doesn't surprise me anymore where she appears. But I doubt any of us will see her again."

There was something in the tone of his voice, the old sadness. Chief Adcock threw him a sharp look. He could tell nothing of Hamilton's expression in the darkness.

The Motorola hissed in the lieutenant's ear: "Bison, danger! Vehicle on the road. Appears to be an armored car."

Ahead a hundred yards a grove of trees loomed alongside the road. Hamilton gassed the Yugo to reach it.

"Bison, vehicle is closing the gap, heading your way . . ."

The Yugo darted deep into the shadows of the trees, out of sight. Hamilton cut the engine. They waited, listening in the abrupt silence.

The guttering thrum of the armored car's

approach quickly drowned out the spring cho-
rusing of tree frogs. It halted on the road next to
the trees, its deep engine rumbling in idle gear.
It sat there for long minutes, like a predator
sniffing the wind for prey. None of the SEALs
dared move.

Gears clanked, the engine revved.

"It's moving on," Chief Adcock breathed.

"It's coming into the trees!" John Nighthorse
said.

"Out!" Hamilton hissed.

The team dismounted. The Yugo had served
faithfully, but it was time to abandon it. Press
signs had been removed from the doors and
nothing remained inside to indicate who owned
it or who might have used it. They were less than
two klicks from their intended kickoff point
anyhow.

Hamilton gave a signal and the team, moving
as a single organism in the diamond formation,
scuttled down a tree-choked draw that seemed
to narrow toward the base of some hills in the
distance. The armored vehicle, likely Serbian but
possibly KLA, nosed through the trees behind
them, apparently looking for a safe place to
bivouac for the rest of the night. They didn't
wait to determine if the Yugo were discovered.

The team marched hard for the next two hours,
depending as much on Spectre for a heading as
on compass readings. High above, both out of

sight and earshot, Spectre technicians watched the six men on infrared TV screens and suggested best paths toward the KLA camp in the mountains. A mother hen constantly circling her chicks, alert for any danger that might blip up on her sensors.

"Bison, there's a canyon ahead. Veer off to the left and follow that row of trees at the foot of that bald hill. There's a house on the other side. You need to avoid it by cutting up the mountain and crossing that way. So far, no other movement in sight. Copy, Bison?"

They crossed a series of barbed wire–enclosed fields unploughed and overgrown with weeds due to neglect caused by the nation's troubles. A ridgeline loomed out of a narrow plain ahead. Spectre informed them that the cantonment area lay in the basin on the other side of the ridge, snugged up hard against it in a forest of stunted cedar and strewn boulders. There were no roads in or out, only foot paths.

The men nursed their strength and maintained less than a forced-march pace. Energy was needed for the raid on the camp and the getaway afterward. Tension mounted as they climbed and neared the crest of the ridge. Hamilton reduced the pace even more to give the Kiowa on point time to sniff out any danger that may have escaped Spectre's scrutiny.

Spectre kept up a running commentary into the ears of both team leaders, Hamilton and

Adcock. A roving patrol of three soldiers crossed the downhill end of the camp. There was movement from various points among the buildings, probably sentries. A single barbed-wire fence surrounded a total of eighteen small buildings, shacks really, and a parade field that included what appeared to be an obstacle course. It was obvious the cantonment was never meant to be a defensive position, although there were a few sandbagged fighting positions scattered about.

Shortly after midnight, the team, moving together like coordinated shadows, topped the low ridge overlooking the stronghold and paused to gather its bearings and don night-vision goggles. The tricky point was coming up—infiltrating the camp itself without tripping an alarm. Wearing the goggles, the SEALs were able to make out the buildings scattered across the large clearing. They were unpainted and weathered, rather like an abandoned mining camp. There were no lights anywhere. Preacher's hand fell lightly on Lieutenant Hamilton's shoulder.

"I see him," the lieutenant murmured. "Send Dog up."

Chief Adcock keyed his Motorola. "Buddy, we got it from here on," he radioed. Coordination between Spectre and the team inside the camp would be too distracting; the SEALs needed to concentrate totally upon the job.

"Roger that, Bison. We'll be waiting for you

when you come out the other side. Can you see that draw to your right?"

"Affirmative. Thanks, Buddy."

The draw was their escape route.

Dog dropped down next to the lieutenant. Hamilton was always amazed at how silently and quickly the big man moved about on his thick, stubby legs. He not only resembled an ape, he was also as agile and strong as one. The skipper pointed out the lone sentry standing against a hut, smoking a cigarette. His M-1 carbine leaned against the wall next to him. The tip of his cigarette arced in Dog's night vision goggles, leaving an amazingly bright signature. Goggles would have to be removed if a firefight resulted, as during the pilot's rescue, to prevent the magnified light of explosions and muzzle flashes from burning retinas and leaving the team members blind.

The sentry was no more than one hundred feet ahead. The only thing between him and the intruders was the barbed-wire fence. He had to be taken out in order for the SEALs to reach Kradznic. No bad guy could be left alive in their wake to raise the alarm.

During his military career, over a dozen years of which had been in SpecOps, Mad Dog Gavlik had discovered there were different degrees in the methods of killing a man. You could mortar his position from a distance of two miles away and never even see him, although he still died; you could shoot him with a rifle at two hundred yards, which was a higher degree because you actually saw the target when you pulled the trigger, and you saw him fall; the highest degree of killing was in hand-to-hand combat, and the peak of that was in slitting a man's throat, butchering him before he hardly knew of your presence. You felt the man's blood, and you smelled it. Men who might kill with a mortar or an airplane or a ship's missile could not always kill with a rifle, and a rifleman could not always kill with a knife.

Dog eased his equipment-laden battle harness to the ground without question or comment, his narrowed eyes glued on the sentry. In his mind, the man was already dead. His rubber-soled hiking boots issued not a whisper of sound as he eased forward to the barbed wire fence. He wore his goggles for vision and carried his razor-sharp K-bar in one fist. Dr. Death covered with his Winchester 1200 in case the guy heard something and had to be taken out with a load of double-aught buck. That was a last resort only to save Dog's life. If that occurred, the sentry would be raising hell anyhow, destroying the need for further stealth.

Dog slid on his back underneath the bottom strand of wire. Then he was on his feet again, as smooth and noiseless as oil spreading on water. In a single crouching jog he reached the corner of the building, the opposite corner of which the sentry was holding up while he smoked.

He watched the guard for a few seconds through his goggles before deciding the guy was half-asleep from boredom. Death, he thought wryly, didn't always arrive with bands playing and shells bursting. Death, to quote Preacher, came like a thief in the night.

Dog placed his goggles on the ground at his feet to get them out of his way. He was near enough his target now that they were more hindrance than asset. He worked his way along the wall toward the guy, nearly invisible to all save his teammates watching him through their own goggles.

The sentry scuffed his feet on the ground and shifted his position slightly. Dog froze.

The cigarette glowed a bright prick in the dark as the man sucked air through it. He stood now looking out toward the fence, but still leaning against the building wall. The cigarette butt arched through the darkness as he flipped it away.

Bending slightly at the knees, Dog groped on the ground at his feet. Finding what he sought, a small stone, he tossed it over the sentry's head. The guard stiffened at the noise when the stone hit. His head ratcheted toward the sound, away from Dog's direction. It was an old trick, but it always seemed to work. Bad guys never seemed to watch the same movies good guys did.

During that moment of the guard's confusion, Dog sprang with the K-bar gripped in his right hand. The takedown occurred in a single violent movement. His left hand caught the lower half of the man's face, stifling an outcry, while his right knee slammed up into the small of the guy's back. Using this leverage, he wrenched back the man's head to expose his throat and its life-pulsing jugular.

He swiped the knife blade swiftly across the tender flesh, sinking it deep, slitting. He felt sharp steel grating on bone disc. Sudden warmth gushed over his knife hand.

He dropped to the ground with the guy, holding him almost tenderly while he waited for his death throes to subside. It took a surprisingly long time for a man to die, even with his head sliced half off. His heels drummed spasmodically against the earth while Mad Dog hunched over him, fastening his body to the earth.

Blood poured out onto the ground, filling the night with a nauseating slaughterhouse stench. It was curious, Dog thought, how different diets from different nations determined blood's odor.

The heel drumming weakened. Then the guy was still and the night was still and the man had smoked his last cigarette.

"The Surgeon General warned you those things were hazardous to your health," Dog murmured.

With the sentry eliminated, the team stole its way among the buildings in a world turned greenish through their night-vision devices, moving like a machine tuned and humming along, a well-orchestrated drama with Lieutenant Hamilton leading and directing. His senses were sharp and focused, working overtime and at double pace.

Chief Adcock and Dr. Death with his shotgun, his ever-present Haskins disassembled and attached in a small butt pack to his harness, crept ahead on point from building to building. Dr. Death wore his patrol cap pulled low to hide his white hair and had camouflaged the short sides and back with cammie paint. Nighthorse slipped along on the left flank, Preacher on the right. Hamilton pulled drag security with Dog, where he could maintain overall control.

He thought it curious that there was so little activity in camp, considering the KLA leader himself was supposed to be present. You would think the guerrillas would be up all night— unless Kradznic wasn't here after all.

Now was no time to play with doubts. After all, it was late and even guerrillas had to sleep.

Chief Adcock signaled and pointed. They had reached the parade ground and obstacle course, on the far side of which lay their target building. There was a ropes course and a wall with a sand pit. The chief knelt in the moon shadow of a tree. Around him five other SEALs went still in place for a long, five-minute listening and watching halt. Nothing stirred. There weren't even any dogs in camp. If there were, they weren't barking.

The SEALs crossed the open ground, hugging the edges. They approached the target, where Hamilton called another listening halt. Except for the troop barracks, which were themselves nothing more than bloated shacks, Kradznic's headquarters appeared to be the largest and best in camp. There were no lights in its windows. No sentries either; the team watched and waited for a good ten minutes to make sure.

Lieutenant Hamilton was about to give the order for action when from the corner of his eye he detected light in a building ten yards to the left of KLA headquarters. It was only a fleeting flash, as though someone inside had adjusted a blackout blanket over a window and inadvertently released a flicker. At least *that* structure was occupied.

Perhaps *all* were occupied behind their blackout curtains.

Hamilton hesitated. It occurred to him that *both* these buildings, set so near each other, might be part of the guerrilla leader's headquarters. Maybe he lived and slept in one when he was in residence while he worked out of the other.

But which was which?

He decided to stick with the original plan, but modify it a bit to take into account the possibility posed by the second cabin. He jabbed a finger first at Preacher, then at Dog, and finally at the structure from which light had escaped. The two SEALs understood. They shifted positions to cover it from a small copse of trees.

The lieutenant then gave the signal for the assault. Chief Adcock faced outward, away from the targets to keep rear guard. Nighthorse and Dr. Death with his building-clearing shotgun rose with the skipper and sprinted in low profile toward the door of the larger, nearest building. They flatted themselves against the wall to either side of the door and listened. It was still dark, and still quiet.

Hamilton tried the door knob. It gave easily. The door was unlocked.

Ready?

Hamilton took a small bottle of ether from a cargo pocket and soaked a wad of gauze. He replaced the cap and stuck the bottle back into his pocket for easy access in case more was required. Kradznic was supposed to be a huge man. Rendering him unconscious meant they had to carry his two hundred–pound plus dead weight, but they were prepared for it. It was better than trying to gag him, tie him, and then fight him all the way free of the compound.

Now . . . *Ready?*

Hamilton pushed the door wide in a single movement. The three SEALs burst into the shack for the building search. One large room. It contained a cookstove, a table, a desk in one corner, a tall shelf of books, and a bed. The goggles let them determine almost immediately that the house was unoccupied. Kradznic was not in residence.

They wasted no time inside. They rushed back out and Hamilton issued the "dry hole" signal. Dog pointed at the second cabin, a question.

"Cover me," Hamilton said to Dr. Death and the Kiowa.

He crabbed across the small gap that separated the two buildings. Nighthorse and Dr. Death remained flattened against the side wall while the lieutenant slipped entirely around the house, checking the windows in hopes of catching a glimpse inside. No chance.

He returned with Nighthorse and Dr. Death to where the others pulled security in the trees.

"The bird has flown?" Chief Adcock asked.

"Maybe not." Hamilton's glance shifted to the second hut. "There are lights inside. It's two A.M. I'll bet there's some kind of meeting."

"Or a poker game," Dr. Death said, dry-voiced as always.

"It's a gamble," Hamilton admitted.

"I say we draw in and try to fill our hand," Nighthorse recommended.

Hamilton thought about it. "Things could heat up."

"We go back dragging our tails? Poker game or meeting, chances are that's where Kradznic is if he's in town."

Hamilton thought it over quickly. It was a risk, but a risk that had to be taken considering everything that depended on Kradznic's being removed from the Yugoslav equation.

"Okay," he said. "Here's the plan. John, knock on the door and tell them you've seen a helicopter. As soon as the door opens, we bust in. Let's try to avoid gunplay. But if it happens . . ." He shrugged "We'll have to try to get Kradznic out in all the confusion."

There was still no activity in the general area. Sentries appeared to be posted on the camp's perimeter, but not inside. That was a plus.

Once more, the lieutenant led the three-man assault on the cabin. They removed their goggles to prevent blindness from the lights inside when the door opened. Nighthorse quieted his breathing and knocked lightly on the door.

They heard chair legs scraping on wood, footsteps approaching the door.

"Da? . . . Da?" a voice queried.

Nighthorse delivered his message in Albanian. There was a moment's hesitation. Whoever was on the other side seemed suspicious.

Then the door eased open, letting out a crack of dim light, as from a kerosene lantern. Of course there would be no electricity in camp. Immediately, the SEALs exploded into action.

Hamilton rammed his shoulder into the door as though he were busting through the defensive line at Army or Navy. Momentum carried him inside. The Albanian spiraled back into the room ahead of him. Dr. Death literally leaped halfway into the cabin, shotgun at the ready and

sweeping back and forth to cover the four startled men still attempting to rise from a table littered with maps and papers. A kerosene lamp
burning on the table cast fleeting grotesque
shadows across their faces and failed to dispel
even more shadows from the corners.

Nighthorse shouted in Albanian, ordering the
guerrillas not to move.

The first man who had been knocked away
from the door was so pumped up he dived for a
rifle propped against a file cabinet. Hamilton
took a sidestep to intercept and delivered a
vicious front kick to the man's chin and throat.
It cracked like a rifle shot. The guy's cap went
one direction, he the other. He ended up in a
half-unconscious heap, gagging and gurgling and
clawing weakly at his throat, trying to get air.

The others made their move during the
momentary diversion.

The bearded giant at the head of the table,
Kradznic no doubt, roared like a cannon as he
sprang to his feet, heaving the table at the
intruders. Lamp and papers crashed to the floor.
The lamp exploded, fuel splashing and flames
licking out to ignite the papers with a gaseous
discharge of illumination. Within the circle of
this strange fluttering light, shadows and silhou-
ettes darted and flitted violently as the fight was
engaged at close quarters.

Dr. Death dodged the flying table and butt-
stroked the nearest enemy, knocking the guy

crashing down on top of the fire. He went up in instant flames from the spilled fuel. He crawled screaming toward the door, a human torch on all fours. He rolled out the doorway, where Chief Adcock ran up and silenced him with a kick to the throat, followed by a butt stroke that crushed his skull. Flames continued to flutter from his clothing.

Kradznic made his move. A formidable mountain man of power and fury, he caught Nighthorse a blow to the chin that crumpled the Indian to his knees. That opened the path for escape. He cleared the flames and disappeared into the night all in the same leap.

That left two guerrillas still standing. One of them reached his rifle and was turning with it, pointing it in Hamilton's direction. Hamilton had already turned his back in pursuit of Kradznic.

"Watch out!" Dr. Death shouted.

At the same time he squeezed the trigger of his Winchester. The boom of the shotgun filled the single room with flame, smoke, and noise. The rifleman caught the full load in his chest. It picked him off the floor and slammed him against the far wall. He crashed to the floor, leaving the wall smeared with blood.

Dr. Death racked the pump on his weapon and in the same motion shotgunned his second foe. Few men survived taking a full load of buckshot in the bread basket at short range.

The double blasts from the shotgun reverberated through the camp and seemed to echo inside Hamilton's skull as he sailed out the door in pursuit of Kradznic. He landed on his feet outside in a cat crouch, almost on top of Chief Adcock and Mad Dog. There was almost as much activity outside the cabin as inside.

Chief Adcock, no small man himself with his towering height and broad shoulders, was finishing off the human torch when Kradznic attempted to bail out of the fracas. Kradznic hesitated an instant in surprise at the intruder who seemed to be waiting for him. That instant was all the chief needed. He swung viciously with his machine gun, up from way in the outfield and drove the muzzle deep into the bearded man's solar plexus.

The guerrilla chief doubled over with an agonizing expulsion of breath and fell to his knees. Adcock followed up with a knife hand chop to the base of the man's skull that flattened him face down. That still didn't end the fight. Kradznic was a bull. Roaring with pain and anger, he was halfway to regaining his feet when Mad Dog appeared with a roar of his own.

The combined weight of the two SEALs overpowered Kradznic, weakened and stunned. Dog chopped him again at the base of his skull. While he was temporarily unconscious, Chief Adcock flex-cuffed his ankles and then cuffed his hands behind him.

"That's Kradznic!" Hamilton shouted. "Don't kill him."

"Don't worry, Skipper. We recognized him," Chief Adcock assured him.

Kradznic was coming to, beginning to struggle against his bonds. Firelight sheened across his contorted features. The tinderbox cabin was almost fully engulfed in flames. They were licking out the door, their sound like desert wind howling through high pinnacles. Hamilton was peripherally aware of the stutter of Preacher's M16 as he raked bullets into the front of a building out of which several half-dressed guerrillas attempted to exit. The rebels ducked back inside.

"Skipper, we've agitated 'em," Nighthorse said, escaping the inferno with Dr. Death.

"Agitated, my left nut!" Dog retorted. "We've pissed 'em off."

Hamilton knelt beside the feebly struggling guerrilla commander and anesthetized him with ether. He went limp. At the same time, Chief Adcock unfolded a nylon poncho and spread it on the ground. They rolled Kradznic onto it. Rope harnesses had been previously attached to either end of the poncho with carrying their captive in mind. Dog and Chief Adcock, per the prior arrangement, slipped the harnesses over their shoulders and hefted Kradznic's weight between them, like he were asleep in a hammock.

Receiving Nighthorse's assurances that he had only been stunned when Kradznic made his explosive escape attempt, that he was all right now, Lieutenant Hamilton ordered the withdrawal—and none too soon.

Bullets from a hidden AK-47 stitched geysers across the front of the cabin, coming so near they kicked dirt against the SEALs' trouser legs. They were perfect targets outlined against the firelight.

"Go! Go!" Hamilton shouted.

Chief Adcock and Dog with Kradznic cocooned between them jogged out of the light and back into darkness. Hamilton and Dr. Death pulled in behind them as security. Nighthorse dropped back to assist Preacher; it sounded like the Holy Man had engaged half the camp in a firefight. A lot of shooting was coming from his sector, both from Preacher's tinny-sounding M16 and the deeper-throated chatter of Chicom AKs. There were explosions too and strobe flashes as Preacher unlimbered his grenade launcher.

The camp erupted in pandemonium. Fortunately, in the confusion of having been awakened in the middle of the night, plus seeing one of their cabins afire, none of the guerrillas had any idea of what was going on. Most of them didn't even bother to dress. They grabbed whatever weapons were at hand and charged toward the blaze, hoping to discover there the source of the gunfire and be told what to do. Guerrillas were seldom well-disciplined.

It was in this charged atmosphere of turmoil and bedlam that the kidnappers made their way unopposed to the far edge of the camp and the draw that concealed their escape. Hamilton called a halt to wait for Preacher and Nighthorse. He still heard AK fire rattling and banging supercharged at various locations around the compound as rebels engaged shadow foes and phantom attackers, but the distinctive noise of American weapons had ceased. It sounded like the guerrillas were fighting each other while the Oklahoma Kiowa and Preacher slipped away.

"This big sonofabitch is trying to wake up again," Mad Dog said.

Hamilton tossed him the ether. "Give him another dose."

Afterward, they rigged trip wires and attached them to Claymore mines as a booby trap. Pursuers wouldn't be so anxious to continue the chase once they stumbled into *this*. By the time they finished, two figures materialized out of the backdrop of shouting, zigzagging tracers and shooting that had transformed the guerrilla compound into an anarchists' playground.

"Preacher is hit." Nighthorse announced, sweating and breathing heavily.

Hamilton started toward him, calling for Chief Adcock. Adcock was cross-trained as a medic.

"I can make it," Preacher said, but there was a catch in his voice and an underlying wheeze.

"They'll . . . start to sort things out. Let's go."

"You sure, Preacher? We can rig a stretcher—"

"*Let's go!* Sir."

POST-MISSION

Once free of the camp, Hamilton contacted Bison Buddy in the sky to guide them to the waiting Hip helicopter. They hurried downdraw through terrain of continuing scrubby cedar and rock that gradually flattened into grasslands as the draw widened into a valley. There was a moon now, a sliver of it that made the entire sky glow like a planetarium. The night was dry and cool and would have been pleasant under other circumstances.

The Claymore booby trap remained un-tripped. Bison Buddy reported no pursuit. It looked like the guerrillas had no idea of what had happened. They were fighting fire that had now spread to the adjacent shack, a glow that lit up the back horizon.

Preacher, wheezing and stumbling, fell behind. Hamilton took his weapons and web-gear to carry for him, over his protests, but it soon became obvious Preacher couldn't make it to the extraction helicopter under his own power. He refused to delay the team for treatment.

"Wait till we're in the chopper," he insisted. "God walks with me."

He finally collapsed, slumping to the ground. The team gathered around him as Chief Adcock tore open the wiry man's blood-soaked blouse. The entrance wound was a puckered blood-crusted hole in the right upper chest, surrounded by severe bruising and edema. Adcock gently turned him over to reveal the exit wound. It was the size of a man's fist out of which bubbled foamy aerated blood and lung tissue.

Chief Adcock looked up at Hamilton, his face grim and pale in the moonlight. All had seen sucking chest wounds before. The chief stood up.

"I don't see how he made it this far," he said in a low voice.

Hamilton looked at the black man. "Guts," he said. "Sheer guts. Can you patch him up?"

Adcock took plastic bandage wrappers, cut them into two squares and used them to seal off the wounds front and back to prevent further collapse of the lungs. He applied pressure bandages over those, wrapped the chest tightly to keep everything in place.

Bloody foam issued from Preacher's lips and he coughed up chunks of tissue every time he attempted to speak. He was weak now from loss of blood. John Nighthorse knelt over him and gripped his hand hard.

"Hang on, Preacher. We'll get you out of here."

It was like a plea that it would be true. Hamilton placed his ear next to Preacher's lips.

"Lateisha . . . my wife," Preacher murmured.

"Yes?"

"Tell . . . Lateisha . . . Tell my daughters . . . I love them. I will see Jesus . . ."

"Not yet you won't, Preacher. Save your strength—"

"Bible . . ." Preacher managed, growing visibly weaker. "Read to me. It's marked."

He attempted to extract the little scripture from his cargo pocket. Nighthorse did it for him.

"Read it . . ."

Mad Dog knelt on the other side of the wounded SEAL. "For God's sake," he said. "Read the damned thing. That's the least we can do."

Using the red glow from Lieutenant Hamilton's pen light for illumination, the Kiowa found the underlined passage. He started to read: " 'Man that is born of a woman is of a few days—' "

He choked up and could not continue. He cleared his throat, then began over. " 'Man that is born of a woman is of a few days, and full of trouble. He cometh forth like a flower . . . ' Preacher . . . ?"

"Please . . . John . . . ?"

" 'He cometh forth like a flower, and is cut down: he fleeth also like a shadow . . . and continueth not . . . ' "

His voice trailed off across the dry plains beneath the high wide sky. As the last note was absorbed, the Claymores at the near end of the guerrilla camp detonated with a thudding boom and a flash of lightning. The clap of thunder reverberated down the valley, clapping in diminishing overlaps. Dog sprang to his feet.

"They're trying to come!"

"Bison, this is Buddy?" Spectre urged into Hamilton's ear.

"That's okay, Buddy. We set them off."

"What's your delay, Bison?"

Hamilton took a deep breath. "No delay. Buddy, we're on our way again."

Preacher's hand rose slowly, grasping for leverage. It collapsed under its own weight. "Leave . . . me . . ." he pleaded.

"Like hell we will." Dog bent and scooped up Preacher as though he were a child. "I'm ready," he announced.

Nighthorse took Dog's place helping Chief Adcock carry the Kradznic stretcher. An hour later, they came upon the helicopter.

"How's Preacher?" Lieutenant Hamilton asked.

Dog got on the Hip with the smaller man limp in his arms. "He's dead," Dog said.

THE REPORT

At tent city in Skopje, Macedonia, Lieutenant Hamilton sat at a table laboring over the mission's After Action Report. It was brief and tersely worded: so many guerrillas estimated KIA; one captive brought back; one friendly KIA: Ordnanceman Second Class Albert Leon Hodges, U.S. Navy SEAL Team Two, Little Creek, Virginia. Survived by a wife and three daughters.

Hamilton laid down his pen and wearily rubbed his eyes with both hands. The rest of the team had gone to chow, although the weight of the operation's first loss had robbed them of appetite. The lieutenant sat alone. He was thinking how he would have to go see Lateisha after this was all over, try to tell her what happened. What it boiled down to was: Your husband's dead. Nothing he could say beyond would have much impact. Not now. Not yet.

The tent flap opened. Martin Smith walked in. He looked at the worn SEAL commander slumped at the table, face in hands. He walked over and sat down across from the lieutenant. Hamilton shoved the report across to him. Smith glanced at it.

"Preacher's death will have to be listed as a training accident," he said.

Hamilton said nothing. He expected it.

"This is a black operation." It was like he was apologizing. "We can't admit to having troops on the ground."

Hamilton remained silent.

"One day," Smith said softly, "one day, maybe we can tell the real story."

The lieutenant slowly lifted his face from his hands and looked across the table at the spook. "Yeah," was all he said.

11: HUSH PUPPY

PRE-MISSION

Adolf Hitler had his "Wolf's Lair" retreat in the mountains, Saddam Hussein his palaces scattered all over Iraq, Stalin his Winter Palace. In the mind of General Yevgeny Krleza, President Milosevic's minister of state, admirer of the USSR before it fell and still a Russian fan, the great heads of state should have retreats to which they could retire to replenish their mental and physical resources. As testimony to the position General Krleza occupied in President Milosevic's government, he had been awarded his own *dacha* in the mountains southeast of Belgrade.

A black four-door sedan traveled at high speed along a well-repaired macadam road that twisted through mountain passes of breathtaking beauty. General Krleza, who rode in the back seat with his aide and a bleached-blond mistress, insisted that it be black. Stalin and

Lenin had used black, as President Yeltsin did to this day. Black was a sign of power.

General Krleza needed some time to think. NATO bombings had continued now into the month of April, night after night, day after day. Although they had had relatively little impact upon his military, physically, they were beginning to wear on the nation when it came to morale. Even President Milosevic, the fool, had spoken of the possibility that they might have to negotiate. Negotiate now, he said, as a delaying maneuver, something Machiavelli would have recommended. Later, they could continue their endeavors to wipe out opposition in Kosovo and reunite the nation's provinces under a stronger Yugoslavia. The United States and NATO would never have the resolve to reintroduce their campaign of aggression once they ceased bombing the first time.

General Krleza disagreed. Continue now while they had the momentum. The separatist Albanians were on the run, scattering out of Kosovo and into neighboring countries where their power was neutralized. Russia offered to sign a mutual aggression pact that provided Serbia the steel umbrella of Russian might against NATO invasion. Use what they had now, General Krleza argued. Use Russian aid and defeat the Kosovo rebels once and for all. Once Serbs established control and order in Kosovo, even the United States with its unceasing "human rights" mantra would back off.

The black Mercedes came out of the mountains and onto a short-grass plain. General Krleza's eyes swept across the plain. He already felt the tension departing. He smiled and licked thick lips as his small eyes, punched into a face that seemed made of old dough, shifted to the blonde snuggled next to him. He looked down the front of her dress, cut so low that he could see the tops of her areolas. He grinned wolfishly at his aide, on the other end of the seat, who made a studious project of staring out the window at the sunset and avoiding being caught casting glances at the blonde's bodice and bare legs.

The road cut across the plain for nearly four kilometers before it ended in a circular drive in front of the *dacha*. General Krleza leaned forward eagerly in the seat to catch a first glimpse of it. Although he was not completely free of his duties, what with the war, he still enjoyed his weekends here immensely.

Conifers concealed much of the house from this distance, but the general knew its every line and cornice and high window by heart. It was a mansion, fit to be a palace, and fit for a king or a general. Two stories tall with huge porch pillars, built much along the lines of a plantation house of the antebellum South in nineteenth-century America. Only so much more luxurious, with a Russian outline added to the roof in the form of spires.

"Driver?" the General said. "Can you go faster?"

The nearer he came to the retreat, the quicker and more completely his anxieties fled. There had indeed been some setbacks in his and President Milosevic's plans to reunite Yugoslavia and rid the nation of the noisy Albanians, starting with NATO's bombing campaign. That could be weathered, of course. The U.S. president didn't have the balls or the political support to turn the air campaign into a ground war.

The other setbacks were minor. Some commando actions in Kosovo, a nuisance that seemed, curiously, to strike at the KLA as often as at Serbian forces. There had also been the matter of that idiot freelancer Ned Cosic, whose Cyber Phantom had been providing valuable intelligence on U.S. and NATO plans until recently. Cyber Phantom still lived, but had reported one last time to Cosic that he was going dormant out of fear for his life. His contact in the U.S., he passed on in his last message, had committed suicide. Cyber Phantom did not believe it was suicide.

All such troubles disappeared from General Krleza's mind as the black sedan circled in to the *dacha* and stopped. The driver jumped out and opened the door for him and the blonde. Krleza labored his corpulent body out into the fresh air turning purple as the last rays of the sun winked out. The house backed up against the edge of a great shadowed valley. The general sucked in hungry lungfuls of the clean-tasting air as two uniformed soldiers clacked their heels in front of him and gave rifle salutes. He ignored them and helped the blonde dismount.

There was a whitewashed barracks set off at a distance from the house, in front of which two soldiers manned a sandbagged machine gun emplacement. A platoon of soldiers in formation rendered the rifle salute to the arriving dignitary and master. General Krleza ignored them too.

His eyes swept past the two helicopters—one American-made Huey and an aging Russian Hind—to the stables, where he made out his horses waiting for him. It was going to be a good working holiday.

As he turned to walk into the house, something flashed across his peripheral vision. He turned to look. A small indistinct form was just disappearing in the dusk of gathering darkness. It was very fast and its wings made no sound. It swooped past the back of the car and skimmed at window level past the side of the house. It vanished into the darkening valley as swiftly as it appeared.

"It's that owl again!" General Krleza exclaimed, startled.

At the bomber base in Aviano, Italy, No Man's Land was allowed to drift for three days to recover from the loss of one of its members. On the fourth morning, Martin Smith called a meeting of the remaining five SEALs.

"Do you need more time?" he asked.

"We've already had too much time," Lieutenant Hamilton said.

"We could stand down the operation," Smith offered.

Mad Dog cleared his throat noisily. "Smith, we might not have the exact required number of balls among us—but we got *big* balls. This war ain't over yet."

Smith nodded his approval.

"Let's get on with the job," Chief Adcock said. "Preacher wouldn't have had it any other way. Neither would any of us."

THE BRIEFING

"I'm going to be honest with you," Martin Smith said, falling into his Harvard style of briefing. He looked directly at Dr. Death, meeting those lidless cold eyes, as unnerving as it was for him to do so. "Hush Puppy is extremely hazardous for all of you—for you, Dr. Death, the odds of your survival are slim to none. But if anyone can do this mission, you can. You're the best shooter there is."

Dr. Death's expression remained unchanged. His cropped hair glowed like silver in the overhead lights of the same briefing room the SEALs had used at Aviano when they received their very first briefing of No Man's Land, the rescue of the downed pilot. All that was missing was the general and his two eager majors. And, of course, Preacher.

Behind his mask, Dr. Death was intrigued. Smith knew how to get to him. "What is the mission?" he asked.

"It's so top secret I couldn't tell you until now when you're ready to be inserted. It's vital, and it's extremely dangerous."

"What've the others been—cake walks?" Dog sneered.

"Compared to this one," Smith said into the hush. "It's so dangerous, you have the option of declining it. You'll have to volunteer or decline knowing no more than that. If you decline, we'll have to get somebody else whose chances of success and survival are a lot less than yours."

Lieutenant Hamilton looked at Dr. Death. "It's a shooting?" he asked.

Smith nodded.

Hamilton studied the set faces of his men and felt a sudden rush of admiration and affection for them, his family. Although their expressions may have been unreadable to an outsider, even to Smith, their decision was written in bold type for their skipper. They couldn't let someone else take a risk like this, not when it was virtually suicide. At least they had a *chance*. Besides, it was a part of their nature not to pass up a challenge.

"Tell us about Hush Puppy," Lieutenant Hamilton invited.

Smith rushed into the briefing as though he had expected no other answer.

"Since the beginning we've had a Franco-American intelligence operation designed to closely track the movements of President Milosevic and General Krleza," he said solemnly. "Your mission is to sneak into a satellite Serb command post, get within rifle range of the target—and eliminate him."

"Assassination?" Lieutenant Hamilton asked bluntly. "Have they been indicted?"

"The UN has indicted General Krleza for war crimes," Smith acknowledged. "They're still dragging their feet on Milosevic. I think every country is leery—including the U.S.—that if Milosevic is indicted it could set a precedence for indicting heads of state. You can imagine how politicians are squirming over that one."

Lieutenant Hamilton drew in a deep breath and let it out slowly. "Political assassination is against U.S. law," he reminded the spook.

Of course Smith would know that. "We accepted that option when we signed on to this operation," he said.

The two men looked deep into each other's eyes, each weighing the other's character. Lieutenant Hamilton didn't want his men left out to take the heat if something went wrong. Could he trust Smith to buffer them? Could Smith trust the CIA director or whoever above him was responsible for issuing No Man's Land missions?

Smith let the silence ride on, permitting the SEAL officer time to make up his mind.

Hamilton finally came to a conclusion. "Milosevic?"

The impact was the same as if he had mentioned assassinating the president of the United States. Had it been like this during the plot to kill John Kennedy?

"Krleza," Smith said.

Oh. Not the president, the *vice* president.

"Milosevic is beginning to waver on negotiating a settlement," Smith explained. "We think General Krleza's death will serve two purposes: First, it'll push Milosevic into negotiations; second, it'll let him know that he can be assassinated just as readily. General Krleza is the architect of the Serb campaign to put down the Kosovo rebellion, and he also has the stronger ties to Russia. Eliminating him—"

"Killing his ass," Mad Dog corrected. "Let's not pussyfoot."

"*Killing* him," Smith conceded. "Getting General Krleza out of the way will serve the same purpose as getting Kradznic out of the KLA. With Kradznic in jail in Italy, Ibraheim Rugova has recovered some of his power over the KLA. The KLA wants to start talking now. We think the same thing will happen to the Serbs when Milosevic realizes General Krleza, his right hand, has been chopped off. We think it's a chance worth taking to bring peace to Yugoslavia."

"If you know where he is, which you apparently do, why not use an air strike?" Nighthorse asked. "*That* wouldn't be called an assassination, would it?"

"He might survive an air strike," Smith explained. "Even if he didn't, it wouldn't have the same impact on Milosevic as a surgical amputation. The message we want Milosevic to receive is that the same thing is going to happen to *him* as soon as he's indicted—if he doesn't come to the table."

"And end the war before it becomes a *real* war," Chief Adcock finished for him.

"Yes. And end the war before it becomes a *real* war."

THE TARGET FOLDER

A satellite recon photo showed a grove of pines and beech trees clogging the lip of a forested valley on the south. The enemy headquarters/retreat sat among the trees, protected from the rear by the valley. The other three approaches were open, grassy fields at least two miles in width. The photo showed an outbuilding, barracks for a reinforced platoon of infantry, Smith said; a sandbagged emplacement for a .51-caliber machine gun; and two helicopters, one a Russian Hind and the other a Huey, parked on a landing apron made of steel mesh. Smith said the area was heavily patrolled by infantry, dogs and helicopters.

"Milosevic has been like Saddam," Smith said.

"He never sleeps in the same bed two nights in a row. Sometimes he gets up in the middle of the night and goes somewhere else. General Krleza, on the other hand, likes to take his retreats to the countryside, where he has established a command post of sorts. Krleza has habits—and habits will be his downfall."

"What matters to us," Dr. Death said, making

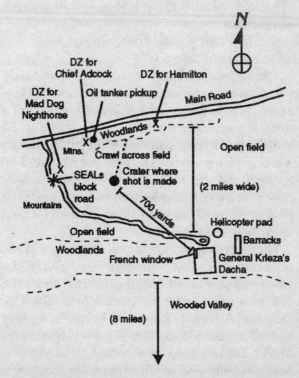

Sniping assassination of General Krleza

a gesture that included the other SEALs, "is that the target is where he's supposed to be when we get there."

"He's there now." Smith produced more photos, amazing closeups that all but showed the color of the general's eyes and the dark roots of the scantily clad blonde woman getting out of a black Mercedes with him.

"Wow!" Dog wheezed. "Look at them tits! What did you do? Have a photographer standing there?"

"An owl," Smith said mysteriously.

Dog blinked. "An owl?"

The spook produced more photos obviously taken on different days. Each one showed General Krleza sitting at a desk directly in front of a wide French-style window. In one of these he was dressed in blue pajamas, while in another he wore a yellow robe. He was bare-chested in another and was staring pensively out the window with a coffee cup hooked on one finger. The photos were all snapped from outside, focused in through the window.

They were taken, Smith explained, by a MAV, or sensor-equipped Miniature Air Vehicle, the latest of a new breed of flying cameras about the size of a large insect or a small bird. The U.S. Defense Advance Research Projects Agency had allocated $35 million for development of MAVs. The one used on general Krleza had artificial feathers and artificial muscles that let it flap its wings in flight—and a miniature camera inserted to peer out the owl's open beak and snap pictures at more than thirty frames per second.

"I was pretty skeptical myself," Smith admitted, "until I saw it fly. You can judge the results for yourself. We've used it to observe General Krleza at different times when he's been at his retreat. What the photos reveal is that he's up early every morning to have a coffee at his desk. The window overlooks the open fields. He's a

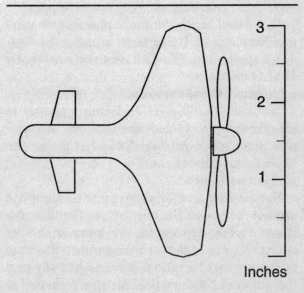

Approx. size of the MAV
(Miniature Air Vehicle)

perfect target if you can get close enough. That's what I mean by habits being his downfall."

The SEALs carefully studied the lay of the terrain surrounding the general's *dacha*. Only one road, a blacktop, led in or out. It was about five miles long, winding through mountains, before it junctioned with a two-laned east-west road.

"We can have a vehicle waiting off the main road to pick you up after the mission," Smith said.

"I'm not getting shit on by any more cows or pigs," Mad Dog balked. "Why not a chopper?"

"It's out of helicopter range now that we can't use Romania or Bulgaria as a base," the CIA agent apologized. "You'll have to be inserted by HALO parachute."

"When?" Hamilton asked.

"Tonight. That'll give Dr. Death a chance to observe the target tomorrow, then get into position tomorrow night." He looked at the sniper. "You'll only get one shot."

"That's all I need."

Not a single tree or shrub grew on the plain around the house. The only cover offered across it was a slight depression, like a dry wash, that cut its way out of the forest and ended in a kind of shallow bowl a little more than halfway past the center of the open field. Yet, the plain had to be it. Attempting to approach by the wooded valley was too long a distance from an acceptable DZ and offered no escape route afterward.

Dr. Death decided if he could reach the bowl, he would make it his final firing point. He would approach the bowl across the field, then use the dry wash for his escape route. He never entered and exited a hide by the same route.

The general's habits decided for him that the best time to hit him was in the morning when he entered his office for his cup of coffee. Shooting the general, if it were noticed, which surely it would be, was going to stir up that place like a nest of angry wasps poked with a stick.

Lieutenant Hamilton pointed to the macadam road into the *dacha*. "If we can block this road out," he said, "it'll slow down their pursuit . . ."

"What about the helicopters?" Dog pointed out.

"We'll have to take them out at the same time," Dr. Death said. "Providing they're not in the air."

"We need a major diversion to cover your escape," Lieutenant Hamilton proposed thoughtfully.

Thus the planning got underway. Once inhibitions against assassination, the technical breaking of the law, were overcome, the mission became simply another job easily justifiable by men who put country and duty ahead of all other considerations, even their own lives.

THE PREPARATION

Even after hundreds of parachute jumps, Lieutenant Hamilton experienced that familiar rush of adrenalin as he stood in the C-141 Star-lifter's open door. His black-helmeted head stuck out into the wind, eyes protected by goggles, he studied the earth far below. At an altitude of 15,000 feet, he made out the curvature of the earth all around, a black ball in the night, with no pinpricks of light to mar its symmetry. The moon had yet to rise, but starlight bathed the night in a soft glow.

He stepped back from the door and sucked a last breath of oxygen from the mask hung from the airplane's bulkhead. He had spotted the road. The green light would come on momentarily to announce their calculated release point for the HALO—High Altitude, Low Opening. Dr. Death stood next in the stick, second man out the door behind the lieutenant. He took his last breath from the hung oxygen bottles; they wouldn't need oxygen on the trip straight down, not during the few seconds it required them to "fly" to below 10,000 feet. The SEALs behind Dr. Death also oxygenated their lungs—and they were ready for the green light.

None wore night-vision goggles on this trip. The eerie liquid vision they provided could be disorienting during freefall. Other than his weapons, each man carried only a small butt pack containing food and water. The packs of

Dr. Death and Lieutenant Hamilton each included an additional item—a Ghillie suit for camouflage. The two of them would make the stalk on the general; Dr. Death had argued that he should go alone, but Hamilton overruled him.

Each of the other men had his assigned duties to ensure the mission's success. Nighthorse would split off to the west once they were in the air, to land near the blacktop leading out of the general's retreat. He would either blow the road or set up an ambush on it, whichever seemed appropriate, in order to delay vehicular pursuit. Mad Dog and Chief Adcock would land with the sniper team, but then split off to the east on foot, using the forest as cover in order to approach the Serb barracks from behind. Dog kept his machine gun, but Chief Adcock switched to Preacher's M16 with its attached M203 grenade launcher. He was nearly as deadly with the 40mm chunker as Preacher had been. With luck, he would blast the Serb .51-caliber machine gun and both helicopters out of commission before they could be used.

Hamilton looked at Dr. Death and lifted a questioning thumb. *Ready? Ready,* the sniper thumbed back, the sign replicated by the three jumpers behind him.

For some odd reason, looking at Dr. Death, Hamilton recalled quotes he had read in a book titled *One Shot-One Kill*, required reading at the Marine Corps Sniper School.

"There survives one lone wolf of the battle-field"—Dr. Death was certainly that lone wolf. "He hunts not with the pack. Single-handed, or accompanied by one companion, he seeks cover near the fighting. His game is not to send a hail of rapid fire into a squad or company; it is to pick off with one well-directed, rapidly delivered shot a single enemy. He must harass the foe. He must hammer relentlessly upon the nerves of the rank and file of the opposing forces, until his rifle crack becomes a menace more to be feared than the shrieking shells from cannon, or the explosive hail from the mortars. His bullets must come from *nowhere . . .*"

The green light erupted at the door.

Hamilton launched himself out the doorway into the stream of air. It hurtled him away from the aircraft. He maintained a closed body position for a count of three before he spread his arms and legs to slow his fall and regain control. Behind him, the four other SEALs had piled out of the Starlifter literally on top of the shoulders of the man ahead. For the first 10,000 feet of the freefall, the men would stay as close together as safety permitted.

Their BDUs flapped violently, dragging on equipment harnesses. Each man kept an eye on the glow face of his altimeter, careful to control his rate of descent. They quickly flew into an echelon formation, each jumper a little higher than the jumper in front of him and offset to the right. Starlight provided sufficient illumination to make out hills and forests and clearings, allowing them to mark their respective landing zones.

John Nighthorse broke away at 5,000 feet altitude. He dropped one hand, lifted the other and soared away.

At six hundred feet above ground, Lieutenant Hamilton pulled his ripcord. As his pilot 'chute, then the main parafoil, a black sports square, opened, jerking him upward, the other three SEALs seemed to fall past him. Then their 'chutes popped and clawed air. They were so near their clearing, a perfect shot, that their feet hit grass almost immediately.

THE MISSION

Dr. Death and Hamilton gave Dog and Chief Adcock an hour's head start since they had the greater distance to travel to reach the Serb barracks. Then they made their way under cover of darkness through the forest for five klicks until, low-crawling the last short distance, they reached the large clearing depicted on their briefing maps and SAT photos. While it was still dark, they donned their Ghillie suits—long straps of brown and green burlap dangling everywhere from their field uniforms and headgear, making them look like huge clumps of dried weeds. Anything but attractive, Ghillie suits broke up the human outline and blended with the terrain, an idea in camouflage the Marines picked up from the British Royal Marines, who borrowed it originally from old Scottish gamekeepers.

When the sun rose, it bathed the plain in that special soft light of morning. The two SEALs hid in the treeline and carefully studied the lay of the terrain, comparing it to the map, while Dr. Death made a final decision on a route across the open.

Grass and reeds about three feet tall in places covered the plain. Its brownish-green sweep disappeared, curving both to the right and left as it protectively encircled the grove of trees in which General Krleza's *dacha* resided. The distance to the mansion, Dr. Death calculated, was approximately four klicks. The house was white and tall with even taller spires extending above the surrounding cedar and pine. Behind it and to the left was the outbuilding barracks housing the platoon of infantry guards. Two helicopters remained on their landing pads; that was a good sign, providing they remained in that same position tomorrow morning. In front of the barracks was a twin .51-caliber machine gun capable of laying fire across the entire plain.

By now, Chief Adcock and Dog must be hiding deep in the forest behind the barracks, prepared to move up after nightfall.

Peering through his scope, Dr. Death saw camouflage-clad Serbs doing soldierly things among the trees, while a patrol of six guards was

just returning from sweeping the plain to his
left. From the briefing, the SEALs knew General Krleza's office occupied the room behind
the broad French windows to the right of the
front door. Hamilton glassed the window with
binoculars, picking out a shadowy form inside.
Another good sign for tomorrow morning.

The place appeared impregnable, what with
the helicopters, machine guns, patrols, and at
least a platoon of regular infantry bivouacked in
the barracks. There was no cover across the
plain except the grass, which grew sparse in
places, and the dry wash that led to the bowl
depression near the center of the field, Dr.
Death's final firing point.

On the positive side, however, security
seemed lax. The general must feel safe. Guards
among the trees often sat down or gathered in
little clumps to talk. The plain was too large for
the patrols to cover it with any thoroughness.
During the day, while the two SEALs maintained observation on target in shifts, one
watching while the other napped in the trees or
ate, patrols often went single-file across the
plain, out and back with their weapons thrown
across their shoulders like garden hoes.

None of the patrols ventured in their direction.

It could be done. Dr. Death had both the
training and the experience.

Students of the Marine Sniper School at
Quantico had to conduct nine successful stalks,

the toughest phase of the toughest course in the Corps, in order to graduate. During the stalk, students in Ghillie suits had to crawl, slither, or otherwise traverse about 800 yards across a field covered with low brush, then set up and fire two blank rounds at a target—without being detected. The target the students faced were two trained snipers, school instructors. The most dangerous thing a sniper could confront in the field was another sniper, because a sniper knew just what to look for.

Students headed toward the observer targets across a channeled area, from a known distance, during broad daylight, with a four-hour time limit. They had to approach to within two hundred yards of the observers, set up, and fire, then wait. The observers were equipped with high-powered spotting scopes. If the observers failed to see where the first shot came from, the student fired again. If his position still wasn't spotted, the student had made a "possible" kill on that stalk. It was believed that if prospective snipers could successfully stalk and set up on the trained snipers, with the deck really stacked against them, they could set up on anyone.

Dr. Death had proved that hypothesis during fifty-three kills in Africa and Haiti, Iraq, Iran, and Bosnia. General Krleza was going to be his fifty-fourth kill.

They were ready to go by the time the sun went down blood-red and quick purple darkness settled gently over the field. There was no moon, no wind. Lieutenant Hamilton took a deep breath to get rid of the ice trying to clog his veins. Dr. Death dropped onto his side with the scoped Haskins tucked against his chest. He led the way crawling from the relative security of the forest. Hamilton followed, committing himself totally to the mission, armed with his AKMS assault rifle. Other than the rifles, they took only a canteen each of water, caching their butt packs.

The next hours were the most important of their lives, because they might be their last.

They soon established a rhythm of propelling themselves along an inch at a time with one leg and their free hand. As the Serbs possibly had night-vision devices, the SEALs dared not let them see the unnatural motion of even one blade of grass. After each painstaking movement ahead, they stopped and used the toes of their boots to slowly prop up the grass their bodies had flattened.

Progress was measured in feet per hour.

They had traveled no more than two hundred feet from the treeline before they heard the whispering of grasses as something passed through them. They held their breath for an agonizing length of time, afraid the Serbs would hear it.

They were afraid the Serbs would *smell* them. Afraid they would *step* on them. Hamilton thought they might hear his heart thudding against the damp earth.

The shadow of a moving man loomed above the grass. Dr. Death spotted another to its left. They were thirty feet apart. They passed in the tall grass on either side of the cowering SEALs, their forms backlighted by starlight.

Others followed, a file of them on either side of where the invaders lay flattened and helpless in the grass. They went by laughing and talking among themselves, like none-too-successful squirrel hunters in their own backyards. Hamilton was thankful Dr. Death had had the foresight to cover their backtrail. The precaution may have saved their lives.

They inched on, like slow, giant worms. Hamilton traveled on his right side, not daring to switch to his left for fear of creating unnecessary grass movement. They kept on creeping across the meadow, inch by inch, foot by foot. It was like getting down on your belly and taking half the night to crawl across your front lawn. They had to be in their hide, the crater, before daybreak.

Sometimes they paused for a sip from their canteens. They continued at a snail's pace for hours, depending on their memorization of maps and SAT photos and upon their innate sense of direction to keep them on course. They dared not lift their heads above the grass to check their progress.

The night dragged on, so weary from effort and tension that sleep threatened to overcome them. It might be a sleep from which they would never awaken. Or if they did awake, it would be in enemy hands headed for interrogation and ultimately death.

When they came to the thicker grass, Dr. Death stopped to let them doze for a few minutes. They held their heads off the ground a couple of inches and closed their eyes. Chins striking the ground awoke them and prevented their falling into a deep sleep.

The only thing that kept them going was knowing they were drawing near Dr. Death's final firing point and should reach it in time to prepare for a morning shot. The nearer they came to the time and place for General Krleza's reckoning, the more critical things became. In a few more hours, if they weren't stopped, the general would be a fat old *dead* man.

Inch by inch. Hour after hour. It was a rhythm. Their faces were so near the earth as they crawled that it restricted their view to a foot or two ahead.

Their luck held. They crawled through the night. Dr. Death in the lead worked himself forward until his leading hand found the edge of the depression from which he would deliver General Krleza's fatal bullet. They eased into the crater. It was only about six inches deep, but it was wide enough for both men to lie in side by side.

So far, so good. Now, if only some patrol didn't stumble upon them before daybreak, which was still a good two hours away. And if only the general kept to his schedule.

After landing alone on his DZ, John Nighthorse made his way carefully to the only road, the blacktop, leading from General Krleza's *dacha*. He laid up most of the following day in a thicket, waiting for that night and the following morning's action, when Dr. Death would nail the coffin on the general. Before dark, he worked down to the road and scouted it before finding a rock ledge jutting up on the lee side of a curve. Opposite it, the terrain plunged off steeply away from the road.

He packed C-4 explosives into the lower side of the ledge, using far more than was required to drop it over the road and block it. Preacher would have known exactly how much to use and where to place it for optimum effect. But Preacher was dead. Nighthorse missed the black man, not only because of his talents with things that went *boom* but also because he was a good, honest man. Preacher had been looking forward to leaving the SEALs and pastoring his own church.

Nighthorse disguised his work from all but the most careful observation. He pressed electrical caps into the soft plastic and ran det cord from them back into the woods. Night was falling. So far, he had seen no patrols on the road and expected none this far from the *dacha*. He wallowed a trough in the ground, filled it with a

mattress of green leaves, then settled down to
nap and wait for dawn. His signal to blow the
ledge and block off ingress or egress would
come from Chief Adcock and Dog when they
attacked the machine gun and helicopters.
Everything had to be coordinated immediately
after Dr. Death's shot in order to create diversion and provide an escape window for the
sniper and Lieutenant Hamilton.

In the meantime, Chief Adcock and Mad Dog
were also laying up for the day in a small cave
they located in the bank of a stream bed no
more than two hundred yards behind the Serb
barracks. Once twilight oozed over the land-
scape, Dog slipped to within twenty yards of the
barracks. There was no back door, an omission
he found both puzzling and comforting. He
crawled on his belly to a better vantage point at
an angle off the corner of the barracks. He lay
there in thick underbrush and calculated the
range across the open plain to where the two
helicopters were parked on their pads. Thirty
yards max—well within range of the chief's
M203 grenade launcher.

To the right of the choppers, where the
machine gun could cover the entire plain, a Serb
manning the .51-cal removed his black helmet
and wiped his forehead with the sleeve of his
uniform tunic. He tossed the helmet to his
buddy. Then he stretched out on top of the sand
bags and seemed to fall asleep.

Using binoculars with glareproof lenses, Dog glassed the plain stretched before him. He studied the distant treeline out of which Dr. Death and the skipper should be crawling as soon as night fell in order to make their way to Dr. Death's FFP. A patrol of five Serbs in uniform crossed the plain at an angle, returning to the barracks.

Movement at the house then caught his attention. He swung the binoculars and watched as the heavyset man depicted in the photos from their target folder came out onto the porch. He wore baggy riding breeches and an open, baggier shirt designed to cover up some of his ample belly. The young blonde with him wore calfskin breeches much snugger and presented a more appealing picture. Mad Dog grinned to himself and adjusted the binoculars, focusing on her ass. *Wonder what her legs would feel like wrapped around my head.*

With that thought playing pleasantly in his head, he eased out of his hide and returned to the cave where Chief Adcock awaited him. A close-in recon was too risky for both men to go.

"The general is *in*," Dog whispered, his lips close to Adcock's ear. "I've found a hidey hole. We can move up in the dark. I saw the general location where the good Doctor will make his shot. As soon as we hear it, we can chunk grenades on both choppers and the machine gun position. The troops in the barracks will never see us or know what happened as long as we don't fire rifles and give away our position. That place is going to go crazy at sunrise."

"Did you ever hear of Murphy's Law?" Chief Adcock asked after a pause.

"I never had much use for the law," Dog admitted.

"It says that anything that can go wrong, will."

"You're thinking of what happened to Preacher. Don't do that to yourself, Chief."

The chief wasn't thinking of Preacher. He was thinking of Margie. And of the skipper and Dr. Death, who should, right about now, be starting their interminable journey across the field.

It was the longest night of Lieutenant Hamilton's life. He had insisted on accompanying Dr. Death to give him cover, as the sniper carried only the single-shot Haskins. Now he had nothing to do but lie waiting for the good shooting light of morning. He tried to rest, sleeping in that awkward way with his chin off the ground. He thought of Judith, whose face, irritatingly, blended into Tori's. He thought of Preacher and what he would say to Preacher's wife.

Once, they heard a patrol, but it passed and they did not see the soldiers. It was not until the eastern sky behind them began to pale that Hamilton felt they might actually carry this thing off after all.

As more light brought objects into view, Dr. Death unfolded an OD-green handkerchief-sized cloth and laid it down so his weapon's muzzle would not kick up dust when he fired and give them away. He checked the Haskins for clogged dirt or grass. Then, satisfied that the Elite scope was correctly adjusted, he removed the bolt and chambered a round. Hamilton saw it was the same type of tungsten-carbide explosive round he had used on the drug runners' helicopter. There indeed would not be enough left of the target to sing in Preacher's heavenly choir.

The eastern sky oranged and reddened and yellowed. Presently, enough light existed for them to see the general's *dacha*. Dr. Death watched through his scope and Hamilton through binoculars as the household began to stir. Patrols drifted in and others went out. One followed the blacktop that led toward the mountains, the main highway and the position where Mad Dog and Nighthorse should be prepared to block the road. Another patrol left the trees and headed directly for the crater.

Grass in the depression was shorter than in the rest of the field. If the Serbs kept coming, they couldn't help seeing the Americans. Alternative plans raced through Dr. Death's mind.

He swung the scope and settled it on the general's windows. He caught glimpses of him inside while aides and couriers were coming and going off the front porch. He considered nailing a vital part of the guy's ample torso, then letting the lieutenant kick over a couple of the Serbs in the patrol with his AKMS before making a break for safety during the confusion.

He knew it was a foolhardy plan. The advancing patrol would pinpoint them with the first shot he fired. The Serbs had vehicles. The SEALs stood no chance of escaping if the enemy knew where the shot came from.

It came down to which was the most important—saving their own lives or killing the general? Killing the general, as Smith stressed, could mean saving the world from total war.

Dr. Death was looking for the general to show enough of himself that he could make the sacrifice worthwhile when the oncoming patrol unexpectedly veered away. It slogged off across the plain east of them, soon disappearing. It took him another minute or two to believe it. He eased loose on the trigger.

He barely had time to congratulate himself on their continuing luck before activity picked up at headquarters. Someone drove the black Mercedes up in front of the mansion and parked it. The general must be getting ready to go somewhere. At the chopper pads, a crew chief looked over the Hind, then prepared the Huey for take-off. Two pilots in black flight suits came out and climbed into the cockpit. The rotor blades jerk-started and quickly became a humming blur. The crew chief jumped into the chopper's cargo area, behind a mounted machine gun, and the bird lifted tail-high off the ground.

Hamilton thought his heart would stop beating. Dr. Death's normally inscrutable features turned pale. Even in their Ghillie suits, their chances of escaping observation by the chopper were slim if it flew in their direction.

The Huey hovered, its nose facing toward them. It picked up speed, rapidly gaining altitude. The SEALs buried their faces in the dirt, attempting by sheer willpower to become a part of the earth itself.

Suddenly, the chopper banked off to port, rising and swooping above the general's house. When the sound of its engine diminished, the SEALs looked up to watch it flying away from them, out over the valley beyond. Dr. Death and Hamilton exchanged looks of relief, both hoping the same thing—that it would keep going. It wouldn't do for the Serbs to have air after Dr. Death's shot. All they needed for Preacher to have SEAL company in the afterworld was a helicopter mucking up escape plans.

From their own hide off the corner of the Serb barracks, Chief Adcock and Dog were hoping the same thing—that the chopper kept going. Adcock lay out several HE grenade rounds on the ground next to him, and he was ready.

The morning was cool with a very light, variable wind. Range to target was only about seven hundred yards. The light couldn't have been better. There was no morning fog or mist to create distortions.

Dr. Death mentally pulled himself into his "bubble" where nothing could distract his concentration. Inside the bubble he felt neither hunger, thirst, weariness, nor fear. Even the chill he had felt earlier from tension disappeared. He knew he would get only one chance; he wanted to make it count.

He watched the window through his rifle scope, biding his time for exactly the right moment. The general wore the blue pajamas again. He yawned mightily and rose from his desk to stretch his muscles. He bent toward the window and opened it to let in the morning breeze. He stood there framed in the window, looking out and breathing deeply, unknowingly presenting himself as the perfect target.

Dr. Death lowered the crosshairs to General Krleza's heart. He had previously computed the exact range, using the map and recon photos during mission briefing. He took a full breath, let half of it out, held the rest, and was squeezing the trigger, caressing it, when the General stepped back into the room away from the window.

Damn!

He eased off the trigger.

A moment later, Krleza appeared back in the window. Dr. Death's scope picture again filled with the general's broad pajama top. This time he didn't hesitate. The rifle jarred against his shoulder. He brought it out of recoil. The general had disappeared from the window, but the windowpane and the wall outside the pane were painted dripping red from blood left by the explosion of the one-ounce .50-cal tungsten-carbide bullet. There seemed to be chunks of flesh left on the windowsill.

Officers and aides hanging around the porch and the Mercedes scrambled for cover. It was obvious they didn't know where the shot came from, nor as of yet exactly what had happened.

They had actually done it—killed General Krleza, President Slobodan Milosevic's minister of state.

POST-MISSION

No time for celebration. From their distant vantage point, Chief Adcock and Mad Dog heard the hollow muffled boom of Dr. Death's Haskins. They could never have pinpointed it had they not known the sniper's location beforehand. General Krleza's window was out of their field of view; they only assumed the Doctor had not missed in his surgical excision. Whichever, their task was to create a diversion and eliminate immediate threats to the sniper team's withdrawal.

Immediately, Adcock aimed his presighted M203 and chunked a grenade. Dog was impressed as hell. The first round arced high in the sky and landed directly on the .51-cal machine gun. It bounced into the air and exploded in a bright brief blossom. The sandbagged circle around the weapon filled with smoke. The SEALs were not near enough to hear the screams of the gunners, if in fact they had time to scream before shrapnel ripped into their flesh.

Adcock's next grenade exploded to the left of the parked Hind. Nearby troops, already confused and racing about like blind chickens with a fox in their henhouse, hit the dirt. Chief Adcock calmly jammed in a fresh round. That one thunked directly through the chopper's open door. Sparks, smoke, and burning hydraulic fluids streaked flames in all directions. Adcock reloaded his weapon.

"*Now,* let's get the hell out of here," he said.

The two SEALs melted back into the forest, unnoticed in all the confusion. They raced around the edge of the plain, keeping in the cover of the trees. They would fall in behind Dr. Death and Lieutenant Hamilton and act as a rear guard. After two nights and one day of careful and calculated movement, time was now of the essence. Transportation was waiting for them off the main highway.

Unless Murphy's Law raised its unexpected head.

While it took Dr. Death and Lieutenant Hamilton most of the night to crawl into position, it took them less than five minutes to scramble along the dry wash for the treeline. They heard a tremendous explosion that came from along the blacktop where it entered the mountains after winding away from the general's house. It sent tremors through the ground. In blockading the road, Nighthorse must have used enough demo to throw a mountain down on top of it. He should now be on his way to securing their escape vehicle and making sure it was not compromised.

Hamilton looked back, saw that the pine grove remained in a state of confusion, not only from the assassination but also from the attack on the helicopter and machine-gun position. The Hind burned with a fierce blue-red blaze, throwing a column of black oil-and-hydraulics smoke into the morning air. Soldiers were running all over the place and shouting at each other. One knelt with a submachine gun and sprayed bullets at shadows in the forest behind the mansion. Two or three others opened up with their weapons, imagining enemies everywhere, actually seeing them nowhere.

No one was actually pursuing the SEALs.

Hamilton led the way, ducking toward the nearby treeline. Something caught his eye—a large black speck in the morning sky. Coming fast toward them.

"It's the Huey!" he shouted at the Doctor. "It's coming back!"

The helicopter from its higher vantage point had spotted them, no doubt. Its door gunner opened up, sparking his weapon, even as the bird soared above the *dacha*'s rooftop.

Geysers of dirt erupted all around the running SEALs as machine-gun fire chewed the earth out from underneath them. Looking back over his shoulder, running as hard as he could, Hamilton realized the raging chopper would be on top of them before they reached cover and concealment.

It loomed, seeming to fill the entire sky. He saw the pilot's faces, the contour of the earth reflected in their sun visors. The machine gun spat flame and death from its open door. Supersonic insects filled the dangerous air.

Desperate and at bay, he wheeled and opened up on the attacking bird with his assault rifle. The craft came at him like through a zoom lens until it appeared to fill his entire life. The green belly passed so low overhead he could have counted the rivets. A tornado of air tore at his clothing and whipped his patrol bush hat off his head.

He saw the door gunner leaning out on his tether line over him, the awful snout of his machine gun spitting directly into his face. He twisted to follow the bird with his rifle, continuing to fire.

A bullet snatched his left leg out from underneath him and lifted him off the ground. A second bullet impacted him low in the ribs while he was still in midair. It slammed him back to the ground. He felt all three impacts, the two bullets and the fall, only as dull blows. He glimpsed Dr.

Death kneeling on one knee ahead of him, unflappable as always, coiled like a viper prepared to strike.

He fought against the black swirl of approaching unconsciousness, trying to lift his head off the ground. Even as he plummeted into total darkness, he heard the .50-cal rifle boom.

The Huey soared by and banked for another pass, skidding across the air just above treetop level. It shuddered in the air. Mist sprayed from the cowling area as Dr. Death's big cartridge slammed into it.

It was not a fatal hit. Apparently, the bullet had only cut a fuel line or something as it pierced through the aircraft.

The door gunner kept banging away at the SEALs. Only the instability of his airborne platform prevented his zoning in on his two targets, one of whom was already down. The other remained kneeling and dangerous, fumbling with his weapon. The Huey corrected for its overshoot and came out of its air skid. It seemed to hesitate, as though getting ready to pounce. Then it poured on the coal and came roaring back at its cornered prey. Machine-gun fire sprayed the ground around Dr. Death like widely scattered hail, only far more deadly.

The Haskins was not made for speed. Dr. Death had the bolt out and another heavy round in the chamber. He was not going to make it in time. He looked up to meet his fate, to face and accept it head on, the way he and all SEALs lived.

Mad Dog Gavlik appeared out of nowhere, amazingly light and fast on his short, thick legs, a strong man who, in a single movement, scooped the lieutenant off the ground and tossed him over his shoulder.

"Run!" he yelled at Dr. Death, who himself was willing to die rather than abandon his skipper. "Run like hell!"

Dog, with Hamilton over his shoulder, was already sprinting through the bullet geysers toward the forest. Dr. Death heard the tinny rattle of an M16. The toy-looking weapon looked absurdly small in the big hands of Chief Adcock as the CPO opened up on the attacking helicopter. Dr. Death heard the loud ticking of bullets penetrating the aircraft's thin skin.

The unexpected appearance of the two additional SEALs and Adcock's accurate hail of fire chewing at the bird, shattering plexiglass, caused the door gunner to cease fire and fall back out of the doorway. The helicopter roared overhead once more, skidding through the air as the pilots attempted to pull cyclic into a hover. The moment of confusion offered a momentary reprieve. Dr. Death and Chief Adcock darted toward the timber and reached its cover an instant before a storm of 7.62 bullets cut a swath into the trees behind them, exploding bark and branches and leaves.

Dog's breath blew hoarse and rasping from his lungs. Even a man with his incredible strength could not maintain such a pace while carrying two hundred pounds over his shoulder.

The three men still on their feet ran for their lives, ducking and dodging as the chopper criss-crossed overhead, back and forth, the gunner firing indiscriminately whenever he picked up movement in the trees. From the distance, above the passing roar of the Huey, the SEALs heard shouting and a vehicle engine racing across the open plain, converging upon them.

Time was running out. They had poked a stick into an active nest of hornets. And, boy, had it pissed them off.

Adcock called a halt underneath the concealing branches of a particularly large and leafy live oak—a Robin Hood sort of tree. The helicopter scooted over above, sniffing for them.

"It'll follow us to our transportation," Adcock pointed out, panting and sweating from exertion. "If it finds our truck, we're all goners. They've also got troops on the way. Hear them?"

"What'll we do—a last stand?" Dog demanded.

"I'm not ready for that yet," Adcock retorted. "Did you notice something about that Huey?"

"Yeah. It don't like us."

"No. The gunner's door is open, but the opposite door is closed."

"Chief, this is no time for riddles," Dr. Death snapped, closing the bolt on his Haskins and readying it for another shot.

"No riddle," Adcock said hurriedly. The Huey

was coming back. "If I can shoot a grenade through the open door, it'll stay inside."

"It's moving too fast above the trees," Dog said, bracing his legs wide against the unconscious Hamilton's weight.

"But if we can decoy it into a hover . . ."

There was no time to mull it over. Dog was already lowering the skipper gently to the ground. Dr. Death grabbed his arm.

"You keep the lieutenant," he said. "I'll do it."

In front of them the forest thinned into a semiclearing of smaller, shorter trees that offered little concealment.

"Ready?" Dr. Death asked. They heard the helicopter's approach.

"I have to have the left door toward me," Adcock insisted.

"You'll get it, Chief."

Hatless—he had lost his bush cap—and with white hair silver in the morning light, Dr. Death darted out from hiding. He ran across the clearing, as though panicked. The Huey surged into the chase after the decoy, machine gun chattering.

Halfway across the opening, Dr. Death fishhooked back toward the big live oak. The Huey banked hard left above him—and for a brief instant its open door with the gunner leaning out on his tether line, banging away at the fugitive below, was exposed to Chief Adcock and his deadly M203.

A launched grenade arced across the sky.

Almost instantly the Huey disintegrated in the air, a ball of flames. Pieces of it flew in all directions. The gunner's body sailed out and landed in top of the live oak and hung there. What was left of the helicopter collapsed in the air like a duck killed in flight and crashed in a blazing inferno.

"Skipper, we have to get you on your feet."

He must have passed out. The nearby fire and secondary explosions of fuel and armaments from the helicopter seared his face. He attempted to struggle to his feet, but his left leg refused to hold him. It was numb, dead. Pain in waves of agony washed through the right side of his torso. He smelled blood, his own blood, and the world swirled around him. Down on both hands and the one good knee, the other stretched out behind, he retched and felt better. Then he was surprised to discover Chief Adcock and Mad Dog leaning over him with Dr. Death.

"Save yourselves," he urged them.

"We're going out of here together," Dr. Death vowed.

Regretfully, he tossed the Haskins aside and slung Hamilton's AKMS across his back; it was the more practical weapon now. Dog knelt next to the SEAL officer and lifted him to his feet with an arm around the man's waist for support. Hamilton placed his left arm around Dog's shoulders and hung on, assisting as much as he could with one leg, dragging the other.

"How bad . . . am I bleeding?" he managed.

"There don't seem to be any arteries hit. Lean on me, sir. We're going fast. I might hurt you . . ."

In that manner, melded together as a single entity, both covered with blood, they worked downhill through the forest toward the main highway. Only half-conscious, consumed with pain, Hamilton was barely aware of his surroundings. Trees swirled around him. Sometimes he saw feet, but he couldn't tell which feet were his. He saw Judith—or was it Tori?—and reached for her, mumbling.

Somewhere during the flight, he became aware of another explosion on their backtrail. Minutes later, John Nighthorse caught up with them.

"I set a little surprise to delay our bloodhounds," he explained to Adcock.

After what seemed hours, but could have been minutes or perhaps even days for all Hamilton knew, they came upon an oil tanker parked concealed in trees on a side road off the highway.

"How bad is it?" It sounded like Nighthorse.

"We've stopped the bleeding. That's all we can do for now." That was Mad Dog. Hamilton was sure of it.

"Dog, you and Nighthorse help get him inside the truck," Adcock ordered.

Hamilton became vaguely aware of being lifted and stuffed through a hidden door into the bottom of the huge oil truck. The other SEALs crowded into the stuffy darkness around him, and the door was sealed with them inside.

"Everybody . . . ?" He tried to clear his head, but he was afraid he was going to be sick again.

"We're all here, Skipper," Nighthorse assured him.

THE REPORT

Lieutenant Hamilton opened his eyes. His mind was clear. He saw he was in a tent and that the sun shone through the OD fabric. He couldn't move his left leg and his torso felt compressed. He looked down and saw clean sterile bandages encasing most of his body from the chest down. Martin Smith by his bedside stood up and smiled down at him.

"How did you . . . ?" Hamilton began. "Where am I?"

"Skopje, Macedonia. At the NATO base, U.S. section."

The SEAL commander had lost so much time from when he was shot that he struggled now to fill in the pieces. "How did I get here?"

"Do you want the *Cliff Notes* version?"

"That'll do for now."

"You and your team were stuffed into the false bottom of a Serbian oil tanker truck and driven south into Kosovo. Once you were within range of the Hip, we picked you up and airlifted you here."

"Am I crippled?"

"Only temporarily."

"And the others?"

"They're waiting nearby to make sure you're all right."

Martin Smith pulled his chair closer to the bed and sat down. He was beaming. "You did it, Mr. Hamilton! We had the wires tapped, and the lines were buzzing. We knew it almost as soon as the hit occurred. All hell is breaking loose. Your mission is accomplished. All sides are more willing to negotiate. NATO is talking about ordering a temporary cessation of bombing if Russia and Serbia will meet us at the table. It looks like No Man's Land will be standing down."

He laughed and squeezed the lieutenant's shoulder. "Mr. Hamilton, the world will probably never know how much it owes to six men with five and a half pairs of the biggest balls on this planet."

EPILOGUE

Kosovo was no longer news two months after the bombing ended. It couldn't even be called history. It was more like paleontology—buried underneath news strata of JFK Jr.'s plane crash or soccer star Brandi Chastain's bra. President Slobodan Milosevic had finally capitulated and agreed to remove his forces from Kosovo, although he remained both indicted for war crimes by the UN *and* still in power. Kosovo was not granted independence, only provided more autonomy underneath continued Yugoslavian leadership. The international peacekeeping force called K-For had moved into the beleaguered little province, but a convincing case could be made that Kosovo fallout for the West was far from over. U.S. troopers were still stationed in neighboring Bosnia three years after the one-year deadline the president had set for their withdrawal. It was likely the United States would be mired in the Balkans as far in the future as anyone could see.

CIA Director Louis Benefield sat at his desk in Langley, hands tented beneath his chin, a cigarette smoking itself in the ashtray next to his elbow. Across from him in the overstuffed chair slouched young "Martin Smith."

"We calculate the final figure of dead in Kosovo will be five thousand at most," said Smith, whom Director Benefield had put in charge of assessing the aftermath of the war that was still not being called a war. "That includes a lot of strange deaths that cannot be blamed on anyone. The death toll is going to go higher now that the UN has released Radovan Kradznic to return to Kosovo to take charge of the KLA as a 'police force.' Fourteen Serbs were murdered today by KLA terrorists. NATO has just handed control of Kosovo to a bunch no more or less ethical and humane than the Serbs under the command of Milosevic and General Krleza, God rest his black soul. I still can't believe NATO released Kradznic instead of indicting him after our SEALs risked their lives and lost one man in capturing him."

"Believe it. Milosevic has been indicted, but do you think he'll ever be arrested? Hah!" said the CIA director, looking at his agent with his hard-sad cop's eyes. "It's back to politics as usual. The White House is declaring its strategy a victory even though it damned near ended in a world war—and would have except for you and your people and six brave U.S. Navy SEALs."

"Sir, when you consider that fifteen hundred

civilians or more were killed during NATO bombing, you have to ask yourself whether intervention was justified."

"The casualty rate could have been much, much higher if it hadn't been for No Man's Land. Removing leadership from both sides, sowing confusion, preventing the war's escalation . . . *That* was what brought this war to an end before politicians plummeted us into hell."

Director Benefield swiveled in his chair to face the window. He realized he had acted extralegal, outside his powers, especially in the matter of General Krleza's assassination—but

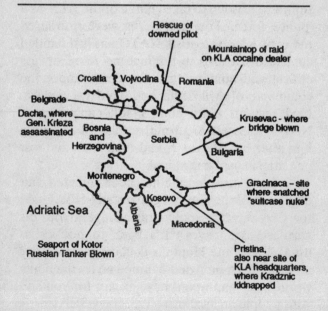

Serbia and area

what else could he as a loyal, patriotic American have done considering the disaster he saw looming ahead for his country? He had done what he had done and was willing to accept the consequences of his behavior were he found out. He had been willing to risk everything. Well, *he* hadn't risked everything. The SEALs of No Man's Land were the ones who risked everything, including their own lives.

"How is Lieutenant Jeb Hamilton recovering?" he asked Smith.

"He's *Lieutenant Commander* Jeb Hamilton now, sir. Thanks to your intervention. Limping, but he's up and about."

Benefield prayed it never became necessary again to operate outside U.S. law and without the sanction of Congress and the president of the United States. It opened too many doors for the abuse of power. The U.S. Constitution was already under assault from all sides.

He turned toward Smith. "Are the SEALs here yet?"

Smith smiled. "I think they've just arrived."

He got up, opened the door, and motioned to someone in the outer office. The five SEALs, in dress blue uniforms, entered, Lieutenant Commander Hamilton in the lead, limping slightly. Behind him, his shoulders filling the opening, came Chief Gene Adcock, followed by the hulking, cynical mountaineer George "Mad Dog" Gavlik. John Nighthorse the Kiowa ranged to one flank of the tiny band, silent and watchful, while white-haired Ram "Dr. Death" Keithline stood staring from his cold, emotionless eyes.

Director Benefield jumped up and warmly shook the hand of each SEAL.

"You all deserve more than a handshake," he said. "Unfortunately, the world can't know what actually happened in Yugoslavia to end World War III before it began. But *you* will always know what you did. One of you gave the ultimate sacrifice for the betterment of humanity, and all of you risked it. Someday, I hope, history will record what actually happened and the contributions made by six of the bravest men I've ever known."

Before the SEALs left the director's office, after nearly an hour inside, Smith detained them for one moment longer.

"Someone asked to see you before you left," he said to Lieutenant Commander Hamilton, smiling. He went to the door and beckoned into the outer office.

Tori appeared, stunning in the slinky dress from Pristina, her copper hair highlighted and falling long down her slender back. Speechless from surprise, Hamilton approached her slowly, staring, standing in front of her.

"Tori," she said. "It's my real name. Tori Javanovic."

"Jeb Hamilton," he finally managed. "We're going to have to stop meeting like this."